UP NORTH

ALLISON TEMPLE

This is a work of fiction. Names, characters, places, and incidents are a product
of the author's imagination or are used fictitiously. Any resemblance to actual
events, places, or persons, living or dead, is entirely coincidental.

Cover Design: Samantha Santana, AMAI Designs
Development Editing: Susie Selva, LesCourt Author Services
Copy Editing: Adam Mongaya, Tessera Editorial
Proofreading: Kiki Clark

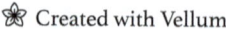 Created with Vellum

For Jenni

For news on future releases, join the A-List, my monthly newsletter. (http://allisontemplebooks.com/newsletter)

1

DAMIAN

EXTRAtainment UPDATE!
> DAMIAN MARSHALL IN EXPLETIVE-LADEN RANT AT CANNES

The Cannes Film Festival is known for its glamour and elegance, but that atmosphere took a turn to the profane this weekend when superstar Damian Marshall went off on a seemingly unprovoked tirade against director Anderson Lind while walking the red carpet with his co-stars for the premiere of Shadow League: Through Darkness. While the cast posed for photographers, Marshall broke away from the group suddenly and began to berate his director.

The rant, which lasted over two and a half minutes, was captured by fans and reporters alike. It has already been seen over 20 million times online since it was posted yesterday and includes Marshall referring to Lind as a "f*cking sadist" and a manipulative liar before storming off. He did not return for the film's premiere or subsequent Q&A session with the film's cast and director.

Asked after the fact, Lind could only express sympathy for the star. "Damian and I have worked together on three Shadow League films and our relationship has always been a great one. I have to assume it was only the stress of our promotional tour that caused him to say things he didn't mean."

Lind, who won the Academy Award for Best Director last year for *his work on* 100 Miles Home, *would not answer questions on whether this was the first time there had been conflict between him and his star, currently the highest-paid actor in Hollywood. But this rift, coupled with the lukewarm reviews from critics for the latest* Shadow League *offering, does reignite questions as to the future of the series. The release date for* Shadow League: Through Darkness *was pushed back twice last year, reportedly because Lind and representatives from New Film Cinema studios couldn't agree on a final cut. Both Lind and Marshall are slated to work on the fifth* Shadow League *installment, set to begin shooting this fall.*

Neither Marshall nor any of his representatives could be reached for comment, either regarding the incident at Cannes or about his future in the world's most profitable film franchise.

———

NO ONE TELLS you that the entire world watching your every move can be lonely as hell.

It's been ten days since I called my director a festering dog's anus in public. Nine days since the studio sent me home from the promotional tour. Eight days since my agent said to lie low until she told me it was safe to leave the house. Seven days since a photographer tried to climb the bougainvillea in front of my pool house to get a picture of me. Six days since I've spoken to another human being face-to-face.

Safe to say, my cabin fever is reaching epic proportions.

"Put on your dancing shoes," I say when Vin walks through my front door.

"What?" He pulls off his sunglasses, even though the sun's been down for close to an hour. My best friend is a slave to fashion. "No, come on. Roberta says we need to lie low."

"Since when did you do everything Roberta says?"

"Since she said my name's on the list for junior agent?"

The statement makes me pause. Vin and I met close to a

decade ago. I was so new to LA I wasn't even a struggling actor yet. He'd been grinding it out in the audition trenches and background ranks for a year already and said he'd show me the ropes. In the end, his teachings worked so well, I landed roles I could only dream of, and Vin realized he was better suited to the business side of the industry. He's been one part fixer, one part assistant for my agent, Roberta, for the last three years.

"Then we need to go out and celebrate. Come on. I'm already dressed." After I cycled through the same clickbait headlines for the seventh time in an hour this afternoon, I gave up and squeezed into the skintight jeans and Balenciaga jacket I was gifted at a photo shoot last fall. Time for a jailbreak.

Vin sighs heavily. "But Roberta said—"

I'm done listening to Roberta. It's been almost a week since Cannes, and I've barely been allowed to leave my house. The rant has gone viral about twenty times over. I'm a talking point, a meme, and a catchphrase. I tried to go for a run yesterday and got a block from my house before a car went by and someone hollered "you fucking sadist!" from the passenger window.

But I can't let them win.

"I already called Jamari. He's going to bring us in the back door. I'll sit in the corner and drink. No one will even know we're there." Jamari is a bouncer at a dive bar we discovered not long after I first met Vin. He was also the object of Vin's hopeless crush for a year after, so we spent a lot of time drinking there before it got too hard for me to go out and mingle with the general public.

"No." Vin slumps on the stairs that lead up to the second floor. "Please, you don't want to piss off Roberta more than you already have."

"What Roberta doesn't know won't hurt her. How will she find out? Now, do you want to change or what?"

He's never one to be left out of a party, even a party he doesn't want to go to, so by eleven we're making our way to

Highland Park. Vin, who always has a few clothes at my house, has found a mesh top and a pair of orange pleather pants that have been a staple in his wardrobe for as long as I've known him. Despite all his protests, he has no idea how to fly under the radar.

The driver, who is used to the weird requests people like me make, has no problem pulling us around to the back of the bar, and Jamari opens the door to guide us through the narrow hall that stinks of piss and spilled beer.

Inside, the drinks pour fast and freely. Everyone here is a regular, and no one cares who I am. Turns out it's karaoke night anyway, so their attention is toward the front. Vin sings "Baby Got Back" to everyone's horror and amusement. I sing nothing and keep myself out of trouble, focusing on enjoying the bar rail brown liquor that's the staple at a place like this. See? Nothing to worry about.

Until Vin's hand lands on my thigh like a vise.

"What?" I ask. I'm feeling warm and mellow and really glad we came out here tonight.

"Look." He points toward the bar.

When I glance across the crowded space, Anderson Lind's white-blond hair is unmistakable, as is the self-satisfied smirk on his face.

"Are you fucking kidding me?" Rage and annoyance immediately boil beneath my skin. I throw the rest of my drink back, enjoying the way its warmth spreads inside me, firing me up further. I was doing a good job keeping my head down. This asshole doesn't get to ruin that.

"Okay." Vin wraps a hand around my arm and pulls, even though he's nearly a foot shorter than I am, so he doesn't have much leverage. "Time to go."

"What? No. I'm not going anywhere."

"Damian." He tugs again, nearly tumbling out of his chair. "Please. Roberta said—"

"No." Maybe it's whisky fuelling my determination, maybe frustration. Either way, I am a rock. A glacier. Moving me takes a force of nature, not Vin. "We were here first. He can go drink somewhere else."

"Shit." Vin ducks down. "I think he saw us."

He did. He locks eyes with me, and even beneath the haze of alcohol, my brain goes on alert. Because in fact, Anderson is the last person I need to see right now. He's been the director of the last three *Shadow League* movies, the franchise that has made my career.

He's also my ex. Ex-what is not totally clear. We were never serious enough to be boyfriends. But while we were in Cairo and Vietnam on the shoot for *Shadow League 4*, we certainly fucked enough that we'd been something. I broke things off with him once filming wrapped, but I guess Anderson was more into our arrangement than I was, because let's just say he did not take it well. I've got the text messages to prove it. And the emails. The voicemails. The notes that basically said he'd end my career.

What I don't have is a recording of him leaning in to whisper to me while we were standing on the red carpet at Cannes, saying I'd never land another blockbuster if the studios knew I was gay.

And then the world's entertainment press corps got an all-access pass when I finally lost my shit right there in front of the Théâtre Lumière and the entire planet and called him, along with a sadist and a liar, such highlights as "a predatory fuck goblin."

Needless to say, the comment ruffled some feathers and got a fair bit of coverage. The rumor mills have been going ever since. Speculation has run from the truth—that it was a lover's tiff—to me having an undiagnosed mental illness or substance abuse problem. It's ugly and largely unfounded, and despite all my best efforts to pretend nothing happened, it won't go away. So Roberta ordered me to lie low to see if the story drops if I'm out of the spotlight for a few days. Of course, it doesn't help that Anderson has been happy to talk to anyone, saying he values what I've brought to the franchise and hopes I get the help I need without ever specifying what that might be.

But he's holding all the cards because a voice in the back of my head is still whispering that he might be right. That if I admit we had a relationship—that all the relationships I've ever had were with men—I'll be quietly excluded from consideration for the next slate of big projects, and my career will slowly evaporate until I'm stuck doing medical procedurals on network TV.

And now that asshole is here, and he's walking toward me.

I stand, and Vin mutters, tugging on my sleeve and still begging me to leave.

I can't let Anderson win.

But he's not even close enough to speak to when another voice echoes over the space.

"Oh my God, it's Damian Marshall!"

The karaoke dies, and a bar full of heads all turn in my direction. I can practically hear the collective gasp.

Then someone says, "I think that's Anderson Lind."

I should probably be pleased that I'm instantly recognizable whereas Anderson is a guess at best, but instead, all I can feel is the panic finally breaking through the booze as people press toward us and a sea of cellphones is raised in the air, all hoping to capture whatever happens next.

"Damian. So good to see you. How have you been?" Anderson's voice is soft and lightly accented, a remnant from a childhood spent in Stockholm before his parents got divorced and his mother moved him to the States.

Maybe we *were* in a relationship. I know more about his history than an average fuck buddy would. But it's weird when you're away from home for months at a time and see the same handful of people over and over. Things happen. We never promised each other anything.

He holds out his hand for me to shake, and too late I realize I'm already screwed. Because either I shake it and we can say we buried the hatchet, in which case Anderson wins, or else I tell him to fuck off and continue to look like the asshole.

I go to step around him, and he puts a palm on my arm. On reflex, I grab his wrist. "Don't you touch me," I say, then fling his hand away. He stumbles back maybe more than justified and crashes into a table behind us, looking surprised.

"I was just trying to say hi," he says.

The rapid-fire repeat of a camera shutter pulls my inebriated attention off Anderson's smug face, and a man with a ridiculously huge camera lens smiles as he tries to get a better angle.

"Parasites," I mutter.

"Got anything to say, Damian?" he calls. "Want to double down on your comments from Cannes?"

"Okay." Vin puts his hands on my chest and shoves for all he's worth. "Time to go."

"Don't go on my account." Anderson smirks.

"Are you so much of a hack that the only way you know to get some attention is to ride my coattails?" I ask. The shutter repeats again, and what feels like a million phones bob in the corner of my vision. I hold my arms out. "See that? They're here for me. Without me, no one would even know who you are."

"Damian," Vin says urgently, "this is the exact opposite of keeping a low profile."

"Damian," the guy with the camera says. "What set you off in France? Was it drugs? Stress?"

"Yes, Damian." The light in Anderson's eyes says he's only too happy to play this game. "What was that about? I still haven't received an apology."

"You asshole." I lunge for him, but Vin gets in front of me. He's not tall, but he's big enough and I'm drunk, and I bang into a table instead.

"Okay." Vin puts an arm around my waist. "Time to call it a

night." He leads me toward the kitchen door as the shutter goes again.

"He's such an asshole," I say, shouting the last word over my shoulder.

"Yeah, yeah, I know. I've already called the car. Let's go."

But someone's tipped off the press that I'm here, because even as we push open the back door of the bar, shouted questions volley toward us.

"Damian! What's your relationship with Anderson Lind?"

"Damian! Is it true you've been kicked off *Shadow League 5*?"

"Damian!"

I put a hand out so the flashes don't blind me and barrel through the scrum. Paparazzi are like leeches, practically clinging to me. Vin scrambles to keep up. The car is waiting at the end of the alley, and we dive through the door as reporters continue to shout questions.

"Roberta's going to murder us." Vin sighs as the driver pulls away from the curb. "We should have stayed home."

"She doesn't need to know," I say, head spinning.

"Are you kidding? She knows everything. She'll have called me before we get back to the house, just watch."

"Let her call," I say, watching a darkened LA roll by.

She can't murder us if my career is already dead.

———

"I'm sending you to Alaska."

The next morning, Roberta glares at me from behind her desk. The expression is one hundred percent do-not-fuck-with-me, and I resent it to the core of my being. If anyone's been fucked with, it's me.

"Alaska?"

"You're lucky it's not somewhere farther," she says. "After your outburst last night, the studio is very unhappy. A bar fight with your director is not the kind of publicity they want right now."

"It wasn't a bar fight. He was being a drama queen. And I'm not exactly tap dancing with joy either." In fact, I'm pacing on the rug. Sitting still is impossible. My whole body feels electric with anxiety.

"Yes, but you don't stand to lose three hundred million dollars when this film flops. The premiere weekend box office numbers aren't good."

"That's not my fault. If they hired someone who knew how to write dialogue better than a middle schooler, we'd be in much better shape."

"That may be." She knows as well as I do the script for *Shadow League 4* was written and rewritten by no less than nine people over the last two years. Over the course of a bloated nearly three-hour final cut, my character, supposedly a mafia son out for revenge, had done everything from drive a tank through the jungle to perform open-heart surgery on his assassin girlfriend while they were hiding out from the bad guys on a glacier. It was nonsensical. "But you calling your director a" —she glances down at a legal pad on her desk—"'talentless prick jockey' in front of the entire world means it's easy enough to pin the failure on you. And then you decide to pick a fight with him at a dive bar."

"How many times do I have to tell you it wasn't a fight? He made it—"

She cuts me off. "And that, in turn, will make it very difficult for you to work on any future franchises at this level again. How badly do you want to keep your job, Damian?"

She's right. It's already starting. The headlines this morning when I checked them still included recaps from the Cannes incident, but also featured new eye-catching titles like "Damian Marshall in Barroom Brawl" and "Is it Time to Cancel Damian Marshall?"

I sink into a chair. "Hawaii is farther. I could go to Hawaii."

Unfortunately though, Roberta is bulletproof. She's been around the block too many times to be swayed by my appeal. Instead of melting and booking me a jet to Honolulu, she arches a perfectly plucked eyebrow—quite the feat considering her face hasn't moved in at least the last thirty years—and says, "Would you rather it be North Dakota?"

I cross my arms over my chest. "No need to say hurtful things like that. I thought we were friends."

"I'm never friendly with the talent. Wouldn't want you to get the wrong idea about how this relationship works."

"I don't understand." I'm trying not to whine, but I'm not succeeding. Roberta is the kind of woman who makes men revert to their childhood selves. Her lipstick is a slash of red across her mouth, and the rock on her left ring finger is enough to give most people arthritis. I've never heard of or seen any trace of the man who might have given it to her. She probably bought it for herself a long, long time ago.

"Of course you understand." She smiles softly through her lipstick. Despite her she-wolf reputation, she's actually one of the kindest people I know. "You were to keep your head down and you didn't. Desperate times. It's Alaska or you find another way to divert their attention."

Another way. She isn't talking about adopting a rescue puppy or letting the paparazzi take pictures of me in my sweats on the way to the grocery store. She means something big. An official announcement. A *60 Minutes* confessional. A man on my arm on the next red carpet like I have nothing to hide.

I shudder.

"I know." Roberta smiles again. Things must be pretty rough if she's willing to crack her paint twice in one day for me. "And that's why I'm not pushing it. Even with all this commotion, you don't owe them that if you don't want to."

My agent is the grande dame of La-La Land gatekeepers, but

the thing that has kept us together for the last eight years is her heart of gold. Roberta always has my back. She knows I'm gay. She flat-out asked me the first time we had lunch together and then, as I stammered through an answer, told me she'd never ask again, as long as my penis didn't show up anywhere public that she hadn't pre-approved. It's an agreement that's worked for us. Roberta's got a foolproof formula for my career, and she's never steered me wrong.

"It's only two weeks," she says. "And then we'll see."

"Sure." Dread spreads down my sternum. The uncertainty is the worst part. Hollywood is fickle, and what barely makes the news with some people is a career killer for others. The video of my outburst might be buried within a week, or it might bury me for life.

Roberta taps a pointed nail on her desk like a judge with a gavel. "Good. Go home. Don't talk to anyone. Pack your parka, and we'll see you in fourteen days. Enjoy your vacation."

I groan involuntarily. I haven't had a proper vacation in . . . God, I can't even remember. Before the most recent *Shadow League* press tour, there'd been the junket for *The Iron Machine*. Before that, filming for both. That takes me back almost two years. There was the two months in Malaysia filming *God of Simple Pleasures*, even though we still haven't heard anything about a release date on that. And before that, I was doing another *Shadow League*.

So yeah, maybe this wouldn't be so bad after all.

"Don't get that look." In another era, Roberta would have taken a drag from a cigarette in a long holder to punctuate her scowl.

"What look?"

"The one where you're planning the kinds of shenanigans you and Vin get up to without me to hold your leashes. He has his marching orders. I'm sending him to keep an eye on you, not to party with you."

"Vin's coming?"

"If I sent you alone, you'd hitch a ride with the first burly dogsledder you found and be back in my office by the end of the week."

She's not wrong on one front anyway. The rugged look is awfully appealing. I wouldn't say no to a ride. But with the man-of-the-land image often comes the "you can take my gun from my cold dead hands" attitude and a conviction that the gay agenda is slowly disintegrating the fabric of society. I know because I grew up with those people. The ones who told me to be ashamed of who I was. When I left, I said I was going to be famous, and they laughed and said no one would ever want to see someone like me on the screen.

So yeah, the exterior may be nice to look at, but the inside is rotten.

Just like Hollywood when I think about it, which I try not to most of the time. No sense peeling back the covers on the cesspool that gave me a career and a name known around the world. Because if I look too deeply at the celebrity machine, what will I find about myself?

I laugh quietly.

"Something funny?" Roberta says.

"Nothing. Sorry. I must be tired."

"Then this will be perfect for you. You rest. Commune with nature. Go fishing."

"Fishing?"

"You'll love it." Roberta stands from her desk and walks around to her office door. That's the signal, the international sign that this conversation is over. When Roberta Feuerstein opens her office door, you are dismissed. Many hearts have been broken this way, and today I'm left defeated.

Yet as I pass her, she reaches out to pat my cheek affectionately.

"I'm sorry it's come to this, David."

I flinch at the sound of my real name. Very few people use it anymore. To the public, my fans, even my friends—except Vin —and colleagues, I am Damian Marshall, the world's highest-paid actor and current reigning Sexiest Man on the Planet. David got left behind in North Dakota, and I don't miss him even a little bit.

I give Roberta a tired smile because she didn't call me David to be cruel, only sincere.

"You better have booked us somewhere nice," I say, throwing an accusatory finger her way.

She purses her lips, and not a single wrinkle appears. "The Regal Beaver Inn or something like that. Ivy did the booking. She said it was the best she could find. Oh, and it's a floating hotel, so it'll be nice and quiet, away from everyone and everything." She opens the door wider.

Normally, Roberta walks her best clients across the lobby and ends their meetings with a kiss on each cheek. It's a pageant, meant to impress whatever bigwig or wannabe is sitting in her lobby. There's always someone. Sometimes I see people I know. Often, precious newbies with dreams in their eyes and hope on their lips watch me, speechless as I make my way through the space like I own the place. I don't. Roberta does. But her commission on my work has paid for a lot of the upgrades to the office since we teamed up.

And we have been that. A team.

Today though, I walk alone.

2

JACK

My bed at the Wild Eagle Lodge is more comfortable than my bed at home, and it annoys me. The food is better too, though that's hardly surprising since I'm not much of a cook. Still, the fluffy waffles and perfectly crisp bacon taunt me as I load up my plate.

"Okay, everyone!"

I nearly drop my meal as Harper, the lodge's general manager, strides into the staff kitchen. She's blonde and perfectly pressed, from her collared shirt to her brown deck boots that don't have a single scuff on them. "Today is the day. Our guest will be here at three this afternoon, and I want everyone on the dock to greet him."

"And you still won't tell us who it is?" Marci, who works at the front desk, asks.

"Now," Harper says, like Marci was only joking, "we've talked about this. You are to call our guest 'Mr. Morgan.' Nothing else. He is paying for our discretion and—"

I tune her out and stuff a chunk of waffle into my mouth. She's given us this speech at least three times since announcing yesterday we would be moving up the lodge's opening to accommodate a request from a very important VIP guest who wanted the place to himself. That's how she always says it too. "A very important VIP." Like he's so important we need to be reminded twice. She also likes to remind us that we signed nondisclosure agreements when we applied to work here. She never says what will happen if we violate the terms of the NDA, though I'm pretty sure it involves giving up at least one kidney and any future offspring.

"So let's put on our best Wild Eagle faces and make sure he feels welcome!" Harper finishes, and a cheer goes up around the room.

I hate working here, and it hasn't even been a month. I should have known it was a mistake when they told me I had to come up before the lodge opened for training. I've been fishing my entire life. What could they possibly teach me that I don't already know? And sure, the first aid and CPR training were nice refreshers, but the seminars on something called the "Wild Eagle Way" were unbelievably boring and the title still feels suspiciously like cultural appropriation. Actually, this whole place does, designed and built as it was by a firm from New York City who think they know what the "real" Alaska is supposed to be. Hardly any of the people I've met on staff so far are even from here. Apparently, this kind of resort attracts people who move from one seasonal property to the next. Marci's done whale watching cruises in Mexico and worked at some kind of adult summer camp in the Catskills. I've heard other people talking about dogsledding in Wisconsin, or spending the off-season snowboarding in New Zealand. They're like eco-tourism robots. Why they need to invade my corner of the world when I've never crashed their party is beyond me.

I head back to my room, mostly to avoid any more pep talks or team building. I have to be on the dock at three. The rest of the day is mine.

I start by calling Stef. The lodge has spotty cell service. They advertise it as a perk, a chance to get away from the outside world, but they also know that being completely cut off would be a fate worse than death for many of their very important VIPs, so the entire building is equipped with flawless satellite internet.

I hadn't expected that to matter to me too much, but it means I can video call Stef and Robbie without the usual crackle and lag.

My sister's smiling face greets me when the call connects.

"Hi!" Her grin makes my chest ache. I haven't seen it enough since she came home.

"Hi there. Hi, Robbie." My ten-year-old nephew is standing just behind Stef, eyes focused on something beyond the webcam, before he wanders out of view. He doesn't reply to my greeting, but that's typical Robbie. I'm glad to see them.

"How's it going?" Stef asks.

I nod. "Yeah, fine."

"Got your first guest yet?"

"Today, yeah." I carefully step around any details that might tip her off as to who our VI-VIP might be, even though I have none. "Any word from Graham?"

Her smile slips like I knew it would. I hate to upset her, but I need a reminder about why I signed up for Harper's hype squad.

"He's still in Guatemala."

My jaw tightens. "They don't have phones in Guatemala? Fax machines? Mail?"

"Jack." Stef sighs.

"No. Isn't this the point? That he's never around? That his career is more important than his family?"

"It's not that simple. He's still Robbie's father. I can't push too hard. I'm not . . ." Now she looks miserable.

"Sorry. I know. I know. I'm just . . ." I echo her sigh. We've been trying to get Stef's almost ex-husband to sign the divorce papers for more than six months, but he works with a charity medical group that sends him all over the world. In fact, he spends more time abroad than at home with Stef and Robbie, and eventually Stef realized that wasn't really much of a marriage. Without the divorce finalized though, she's still his wife and technically has access to his money, even though—despite his outwardly benevolent lifestyle—Graham isn't the kind to share. And that leaves Stef with bills to pay with money she doesn't have.

Which is why I'm here, itching in a designer polo shirt. I am so not a polo shirt kind of guy.

"Hey, I was thinking," Stef says, drawing me out of my head.

"Yeah?"

"When you get home—"

"In four months?"

"Yes, in four months, at the end of the summer. I was thinking, if it goes well where you are, maybe you could get a job at one of the winter resorts? There's a bunch near Anchorage."

"I don't know anything about skiing."

"Not just skiing. You can take people out on snow machines or—"

"I'm a fisherman."

She purses her lips. She looks so much like our mom when she does that. I wait for her to say something, because I'm not going down that rabbit hole with her again. She's always trying to find me a job. Suggesting I try something new. Stef may be younger than me, but sometimes it feels like she's done a lot more living than I have. She left Alaska as soon as she finished high school. She met Graham in college, backpacked through parts of South America, then got married when she had Robbie and Graham was done with med school. Her life has been so much bigger than mine, and it's almost like she feels guilty about that, so she tries to make amends by keeping me employed. But I can handle myself, thank you.

"Robbie made something for you," she says.

"Oh yeah?"

"Yeah." She glances offscreen. "Robbie. Come show Uncle Jack what you drew." Soon, Robbie reappears. This time, he holds a sheet of paper. He lifts it to the screen, and the drawing on it is spectacular, even through a hundred miles of digital signals.

"Is that a fish?" I say, voice full of astonishment even though all Robbie ever draws is fish.

"It's a king salmon," he says.

"It's amazing, buddy!"

Robbie is on the autism spectrum. He isn't great with people, particularly strangers, but he loves Stef to death and has learned to tolerate me in the months since they left Massachusetts. But what he loves most in the world is fish. He'll be a marine biologist someday. Or a fisheries scientist. He knows things I didn't know after a lifetime in and near the industry. And his drawings are always perfect.

"He worked hard on it," Stef says.

"I can tell."

Robbie pulls on her hand, attention already elsewhere again now that show-and-tell is over.

"We should probably go. Time to get ready for school."

By school, she means homeschooling. We tried sending Robbie to the local public school in our small fishing town, but they weren't equipped to accommodate his needs, no matter how many times Stef went in for meetings. The teachers did their best, but after the third time he up and walked off school property during recess without any warning, they asked if he could be educated elsewhere. Stef argued that he found outdoor recess overwhelming with all the other kids running around and shouting. She suggested he stay inside, but there didn't seem to be any flexibility on the school's part.

Much like Graham. He seemed to think his job was to find Robbie referrals to specialists and to send Stef research articles to read, and then leave her to do all the day-to-day work of teacher meetings and therapy appointment while he was off in other countries helping other people's children. And even when he was home, things weren't great because his comings and goings would set Robbie off. Robbie likes it best when everything is on a predictable schedule, and Graham never seemed to know more than a week in advance when he was leaving again, or he would come home with very little warning. Stef tried her best, but Graham wouldn't bend or cut back on his work schedule, and finally she gave up and came back here.

There's a great school in Anchorage. With a little help from Graham, Stef could move there, and Robbie could go to school with teachers and therapists who could help him succeed and become a marine biologist or anything else he wants to do. Or, if the divorce was final, Stef could apply for financial aid and get him in.

But Graham won't sign, and the school won't change their position until Stef is officially a single mom. So she's stuck at my house trying to do the best she can for Robbie, and now I've left them alone for the next four months. One thing I will say for the Wild Eagle Lodge: they pay well. And money is something we need right now.

"You okay?" I ask.

Stef gives me a brave smile, the kind she used to give me when we'd go cliff jumping as kids. "I'm fine. You?"

I still hate it here. But I have to stay. "Yeah."

"Call me when you know what famous person you're carting around this week."

She knows I can't. She likes to needle me.

"Love you," I say.

"You too."

And so I stay.

———

AT TEN PAST THREE, I'm standing on the Wild Eagle Lodge's main dock, trying not to itch. I'm at the end of a long line of staff, all dressed in matching polo shirts and down vests. At least I was allowed to wear my own boots. It was the only thing that had passed muster when I arrived.

This is not a fishing lodge. Fishing lodges smell of mice, mold, and stale beer. They sleep ten if you didn't mind sharing the floor with someone else or sleeping in the top bunk of a rickety bed that's older than you are. In comparison, this place is a plastic Alaskan theme park catering to the rich, famous, and bored.

"Who do you think it is?" Marci whispers. She bounces on her toes, making the mirrored sunglasses perched on her forehead wink in the sunlight. The sunglasses are also part of our official uniform. Oakleys. I looked them up online. A new pair costs more than a month's worth of groceries.

"No idea."

In the distance, a single prop plane hums, and like she'd been waiting for it, Harper appears in the lodge door.

"Showtime!" She claps her hands and we snap to attention. "I don't need to remind you that this first impression will set the tone for the rest of our very important VIP's stay. And that you've all signed NDAs, so not a word about anything for the duration of his time with us."

As if we could forget the NDAs.

"I feel like we're at Downton Abbey," Marci says.

"Is that another hotel?" I ask.

She glances at me like I've grown another head. "You don't know *Downton Abbey*?"

Whatever. I slide my sunglasses into place so she can't see me roll my eyes. Humiliating. People who stay somewhere like this don't need a fishing guide. They want someone to do the fishing for them while they take photos and ask if it really is dark all the time in the winter. And do I own a dogsled? And is it true that the polar bears are all homeless now thanks to global warming?

The floatplane appears over the west side of the cove, circles once, and lands smoothly.

Marci practically vibrates next to me. "Maybe it's a movie star. I heard Diego Pascal came up to the Royal Alaskan Resort last summer. My girlfriend is a housekeeper there. She said someone was on call to bring him fresh pillows twenty-four hours a day."

I grunt in reply. First off, I have no idea who Diego Pascal is. Secondly, what a life. Imagine a pillow valet just for him. It's ridiculous.

The plane's engine cuts as it lines up with the dock. Everything falls quiet like the whole world is waiting for what comes next. Even the gulls and crows hold their breaths.

A dark head wearing darker sunglasses appears first. His hair is shaved on the sides, longer on the top and squashed at a weird angle, like the body underneath it was asleep until very recently . . . or maybe it had been squished against the top of the plane's cabin, because as the rest of the man attached to it emerges, it isn't that he climbs down the ladder so much as he extends one endlessly long leg down to the pontoon below, then finishes unfolding his frame as he steps onto the dock. A few staff members offer him a hand across, but he ignores them, stuffing his hands into the pockets of his heavy parka, which is too warm for this time of year. He doesn't take his glasses off or acknowledge the people in front of him at all.

A bodyguard? I've never actually seen a bodyguard in the flesh, but this guy has that don't-fuck-with-me look that I would expect. He also has a jawline that could be used as an anchor in a pinch.

Not that I'm paying attention to that kind of thing. It's not the Wild Eagle Way. We are here to serve and make every experience exceptional. We don't get to have an opinion about our guests' appearances.

"Oh my God." Marci has her hands to her mouth, and her eyes are wide.

Even before the next person exits the plane, their voice is audible. "And you wouldn't even believe me if I told you where we were. The plane? It was like a toy! So tiny! And noisy, which is why I couldn't call sooner."

"It's him!" Marci squeals.

A flurry of color erupts through the door like a tropical bird crash-landing somewhere it has no business being. This new man is small, thin, and clad in a screamingly pink shirt. His conversation cuts off midsentence with a shriek, and he flails wildly, missing the first step of the ladder. Harper and her guest services staff are on it though and manage to get him onto the dock before he or the phone in his hand can hit the water.

"I'm fine. Fine. But everything is wobbly." He bounces his knees up and down, making the dock sway under him. He giggles. "Or else it's the mimosas they served on the way to Anchorage. But Ivy!" He steps away from the plane, and the tall, silent man falls in behind him. "You should see this place. It's like Hannah Montana without the Hannah." His pink shirt is printed with beach balls, and his pressed baby blue pants don't quite reach his ankles. Did he not pack a jacket?

He keeps talking into his phone, the rubber soles of his green deck shoes smacking against the boards as he goes. "And did I tell you about the guy on the plane? Lord, that flight attendant had the best ass when he pushed that drink cart by me. Those uniform pants are usually a disgrace, but that boy knew how to work it!"

His giant bodyguard shadow follows silently, and they disappear inside the hulking shape of the lodge with Harper trailing after.

"Can you believe it?" Marci nudges me. "He's even better-looking in person."

"Sure." Honestly, I don't see what the fuss is about. Mr. Cellphone isn't my type at least. He obviously takes care of his appearance, but with the money someone like that has, he could afford to do it. He definitely doesn't look like the kind of guy who would have any interest in fishing though. So I get two weeks to lie around and earn some money on the off chance our guest feels like a boat ride.

As jobs go, this one is humiliating, but at least it'll be easy.

3

DAMIAN

E XTRAtainment Update!
DAMIAN MARSHALL RUNS FROM HOLLYWOOD

Damian Marshall is on the run. After his recent meltdown in Cannes got a sequel at a Highland Park bar, Marshall was seen this morning boarding a private jet. Destination: unknown. The actor, usually not one to shy away from the spotlight, has been surprisingly closemouthed about his recent behavior. His most recent encounter with director Anderson Lind could hardly be called friendly, though Lind did his best to appear cordial. Marshall, on the other hand, referred to Lind as a "hack" who was riding Marshall's coattails to fame.

Once again, Marshall and his representation refused to comment on recent incidents or where the star might be headed. It's rumored the rift between actor and director was sparked by a disagreement over the script for Shadow League: Deep Shadows. *Apparently, Lind felt Marshall's time at the head of the franchise was coming to a natural end and had campaigned hard for his character, Dex Russo, to be killed off at the end of the upcoming film, which won't begin shooting until early this fall. Marshall, who stands to make $25 million in each of the next two* Shadow League *installments, was understandably* *disappointed with the move and fought back, both behind-the-scenes and, apparently, in public.*

———

As we enter my hotel room, I unzip my puffy down parka with a gasp. "Why the hell did you dress me like a yeti?"

Vin coos. "You know you get chilly."

I unpeel myself from the layers of feathers and Gore-Tex. "Then why do you look like you just rolled in from a weekend in Santa Barbara?"

"Duh." He rolls his eyes. "Because I didn't exactly have time to pack. Not after I spent all night listening to Roberta lecture me about what will happen if you step so much as a hair out of line over the next two weeks. You don't even know how pissed she is about the Anderson thing. I told you it was a bad idea."

"That wasn't my fault." I collapse onto the bed. The thing is giant, with what looks like small trees holding up the corners and thick planks running along the head and footboard. For my six-foot-four frame, it is the perfect height to flop down on, but Vin has to climb the mattress like Jack climbing the beanstalk, grunting and squeaking until he spreads out in the space next to me.

I pull my phone out of my pocket and flinch at the latest headlines.

"No." Vin snatches the phone out of my hand. "None of that."

"What?"

"You aren't here to torture yourself for the next two weeks."

"Then what am I supposed to do?" I fling an arm over my face.

"Did you see the view as we flew in?"

"No." Just like now, my eyes were closed. After my meeting with Roberta, I may have drowned my sorrows at home for the rest of the day. The effort has left me with a raging hangover pulsing angrily just inside my skull. Vin's insistence on a mimosa breakfast on the private jet from LA to Anchorage hadn't helped the situation.

"It was so pretty. Like they painted it for us."

If he's going to get all poetic and shit, I don't know if I want him here after all. I want to sulk, not monologue about the particular shade of peach that coats the sky as the sun sets.

I wrinkle my nose on an inhale. The room is lavish, but a chemical smell hangs in the air, like someone only recently finished painting. It isn't doing anything for my headache.

"Did Ivy say how long this place has been open?"

"No. She only said it was the best of the best." Vin hops off the bed, nearly disappearing over the side before popping up again. His new Tom Ford sunglasses with the olive green lenses he swears will be on trend within the next three months are perched on top of his immaculately coiffed hair. He couldn't find time to pack, but he'll always find time to do his hair.

While I continue to wallow, he strolls across the suite. It's a decent size; far from the largest I've ever been given, but respectable and obviously decorated on theme. It glows in warm gold and green with Indigenous art on the walls and a leather sofa set arranged around a rough-hewn coffee table in the center. Champagne chills in a bucket, and Vin picks up a small note card propped up against it.

"A selection of local Alaskan delicacies is available in our dining room courtesy of Marc-André Philippe, executive chef at the Wild Eagle Lodge." He flips it over and reads a moment longer before he snorts. "Authentic Alaskan smoked salmon chowder. He wouldn't know good chowder if it bit him in his executive ass." Despite his California beachboy persona, Vin grew up in Boston. He hides it well . . . Most of the time.

"Are you going to open that bottle?" I ask, pointing at the champagne.

"Two hours ago, you said you were never drinking again."

"Two hours ago, we were paddling out to a plane that looked more like a tin can with a propeller. I wasn't ready to die that way."

Vin pops the cork. It flies out of his hand, bouncing off the silvery taxidermy fish mounted to the wall. "Oh, shit!"

I sigh. "So hard to find good help these days." I take the bottle from Vin and pour the champagne so fast it overflows and splatters on the rug.

"To exile," I say as I hand a flute to Vin, who takes it with a smirk.

"Oh, please. If one of us is going to get all dramatic about this, it is not you. You screwed up, and they reward you with a vacation on the set of a nature documentary."

"And what do you get?"

"Two weeks of watching you mope."

The champagne is drier than I usually like, and the bubbles scald my throat when I swallow too quickly. I hide my grimace by walking out to the balcony that extends the length of the suite. My fingers itch for my phone because I want to know what's going on. What's being said about me? Has anyone else called their director an arrogant shit weasel this week or accidentally posted a dick pic on Instagram so maybe we can move on from my gaffe?

"I'm sorry," I say when Vin joins me. And I truly am. He has responsibilities. Plans. He'll be the youngest agent at Roberta's agency, and he can't do that if he's doing damage control and babysitting me while we wait to see what's left in the rubble of my career.

Vin says, "Honey. You done fucked up. You know it. I know it. It'll go away, and we'll be back on the West Coast in no time!"

"Pretty sure this is still the West Coast."

"Nuh-uh! This is the North Coast at least."

"No one calls it 'the North Coast.'"

"Well, they should."

"This resort has to have a fitness center, right?"

"No!" Vin droops over the railing. "You can't spend the next fourteen days running away from your problems on a treadmill. You know where that'll get you."

I'm not in the mood for his philosophizing any more than I was in the mood for his poetry. I go to pour myself another glass, but Vin grabs my wrist.

"Come on, babe. You can pout all you want tonight, but tomorrow we are taking in some local culture."

I spin, laughing so loudly birds take flight in the trees. "Local culture. Do you know where we are? The only person who knows how to get here is the old guy with the seaplane who flew us in, and I'm pretty sure he only had one eye. We are in the middle of fucking nowhere. There is no culture. There is nothing! Not a single goddamned thing but you and me and . . ." I fling an arm out toward the wide blue ocean beyond the bay. "That."

Vin tilts his head to down the rest of his champagne, then makes kissy noises as he squishes my cheeks between his palms. "Yes, baby. Just you and me and the army of man candy downstairs. Did you not see them?"

"Who?" I remember passing by what looked like the entire resort staff. I don't remember any other guests.

"The squad of Alaskan Ken dolls waiting to greet us? I mean, sure, there was some lady candy too, but since neither of us swing that way, let's focus on what's on the buffet that matches our dietary restrictions."

Vin always was classy.

"What are you talking about?"

"Do you remember that magazine spread you did for Polo last year?"

I hate doing those things. Roberta's always pushing them as a way of making a quick million here and there. It's all part of her grand scheme for my career. When we first met, I said I wanted to be famous, and she said she could make that happen if I followed her formula. Blockbusters with lots of special effects, bad guys the audience wants to hate, and a love story in every plot. Be charming in interviews and circumspect in my personal life. Select occasional luxury brand photo shoots that enhance my profile and reinforce the idea that I'm untouchable. It's a formula that works, but as my filming and publicity schedule has gotten busier and busier, the photo shoots have all blurred together. "Was Polo the one with the dogs?"

"No, doofus. The dogs were at the Burberry shoot. That was three years ago. You remember. Polo. You and a bunch of platinum blonde clones on a boat?"

Oh. That one. The designer had brought in what looked like a troop of Scandinavian replicas. He said they would help my darker features stand out even more. We'd been bundled up on a yacht with no shade in hundred-degree Miami heat while we modeled the following year's fall and winter collections. Two of the models were whisked away for heatstroke, and by the end of the day, my clothes stuck to my body so badly that they had to Photoshop a whole new wardrobe onto me.

"And?"

"It's like that downstairs. But with beards!" Vin claps his hands before his smile dims. "Which is not so much my thing. But any port in a storm. I will survive. And I know you dig it."

To say I have a type is generous. My life is so chaotic I never stay in one place long enough to be with anyone seriously. A few on-set hookups. A couple of friends who were willing to help scratch a mutual itch. And Anderson, but clearly that was a mistake. Usually, I go alone to premieres. And to bed. So yeah, not even the paparazzi can claim I have a preference in the men I'm with, but if push comes to shove, I do like a bear.

But that doesn't make what Vin is suggesting a good idea. "Places like this get fussy when the staff sleeps with the guests."

In my younger—hornier and dumber—years, I tried. Hotel employees at this level must sign over the souls of their mothers and their firstborn, to be forfeited if they screw around with the clientele. I have never managed to get one to crack.

"But you're Damian fucking Marshall!" Vin says, jazz hands spread wide.

Unless I'm not anymore. Who knows who I'll be if the dust doesn't settle? Time for Vin to go before I get too maudlin. I scoop up the champagne bottle and pull a Roberta.

"Where are you staying?" I ask as I open the door.

Vin blows me a kiss as he walks by. "Same place, one floor down. You have three hours to sulk, then I'm dragging your skinny ass downstairs to view the merchandise—I mean, have dinner."

I can't help my smile. This is why Roberta sent Vin along. I can't stay sad when he's around. I nudge him as he walks through the door.

"We'll try some of those local Alaskan delicacies?"

Vin's smile is radiant against his pink shirt. "There's my boy."

4

JACK

The nice thing about spring in Alaska is that the sun comes up early. The downside is that spring fever comes with it, and the staff at the Wild Eagle Lodge has it bad. Although I have a room to myself in the staff quarters, many others are not sleeping alone. Harper, along with her NDAs and drill sergeant attitude, undoubtedly has rules about employee fraternization, but she's either turning a blind eye, or her official general manager's residence is far enough away that she can't hear the night-long chorus of squeaks and moans as my colleagues get to know each other better.

I, unfortunately, have a front row seat. When the couple in the room next to mine starts up for round six shortly after four o'clock in the morning, I give up on sleep and head out to the docks. It's dark, and the boards are slick with rain that has fallen overnight. I nearly brain myself on a piling when I slip on a wet spot. No doubt I'm supposed to report the health and safety issue, but since no one's up but me, it can wait for now.

Eventually, I come to where the *Winter Hawk* is tied up. Everything about this place is wrong, brand-new and plastic against the ancient forests and mountains behind it, but at least whoever was in charge of buying boats knew their shit. The

Hawk must be custom-made, with a black-painted hull, sparkling aluminum decks, a flybridge, and a fish locker that has never seen a drop of saltwater, much less the inside of a fish's guts.

I will be fixing that. My VI-VIPs want the authentic northern experience after all.

I step aboard, rolling with the boat as she rocks gently under my weight. Not only does the *Hawk* have everything I need to pull in a whale if I feel like it, but the galley is fully stocked too, including coffee. I tried some of the coffee that's available twenty-four seven at the lodge and nearly spat it out on the spotlessly polished silver carafe. It had a weird nutty flavor to it. Almost sweet. My tastes lean more toward mud in a mug.

Despite the lodge's best efforts to shape the whole wilderness experience to its vision, at least the sunrises are real. Pink and orange while a tern screams and the water laps softly at the *Hawk*'s hull. I stare out toward the growing light and the open ocean. I'm being dramatic. Melancholy for sure. But if I can't be out there, I like to remind myself it's not that far. Whenever we figure out Stef's situation, I can go back to it.

I've worked my whole life on boats, crewing for other people. I've fished halibut, salmon, and crab. One summer I worked on a big commercial pollock boat, but the grind was relentless, and after I nearly got swept overboard one night in the middle of the storm, I decided to stick with smaller boats and captains I knew.

Last summer, I even bought my own boat. It wasn't much to look at. Rusty, with patched fiberglass. But it was mine, even if last year's fishing season was one of the worst in memory. Between constant repairs and poor catches, I didn't have much to show for it in the end. Then Stef came back. I worked odd jobs through the winter, plowing snow and painting houses. But in the end, the boat had to go, because Stef needed the money and the boat was costing me more than it was worth. Still feels like I lost something though.

A soft curse sounds behind me. A tall, dark shape in an over-sized coat stands on the dock a few feet away. He must have slipped on the same wet spot that nearly took me down.

"Watch your step," I say, taking a slow drink of my coffee. The heat settles into my bones, and for a moment, I don't feel so depressed about the whole situation.

The figure swivels toward me like he didn't know I was there until now. "Sorry. I didn't mean to bother you."

I shrug. "No bother. Want some coffee?" Whoever he is, if he's trying to get away from the bedroom antics in the staff rooms, the least I can do is offer him some caffeine.

The lamps on the dock don't cast much light. They're some kind of solar-powered LED that doesn't strain the lodge's power system. It's only as the man comes closer that I recognize the tall bodyguard from the plane.

"You have coffee?" His voice is deep, but it ticks up hopefully at the end.

I raise my mug to cover my surprise. "It's nothing fancy. Not like they have inside."

The man laughs softly. He's wearing the same parka from the day before. It's still out of season, but in the cool air before the sun comes all the way up, it isn't quite as ridiculous.

"I'm allergic to hazelnuts," he says.

Hazelnuts. That's what that taste was. Harper will shoot steam from her ears—or possibly just shoot someone—when she finds out her guest has been inconvenienced by their designer coffee.

"Simpler is better, I always say."

He stands at the rail, hesitating for a moment. "Permission to come aboard?"

I salute him with my mug and go into the cabin to pour another one. The boat shifts as he steps onto the deck, and I almost wish my back wasn't turned just to see if he took one long step down like he did getting off the plane. A man that in control of his body always holds a certain appeal.

Still, when I come out, he's standing on the starboard side, overlooking the inlet.

"Cheers," I say, handing him his mug. For a minute, nerves spark in my chest because I'm probably supposed to say something more professional. *Courtesy of the Wild Eagle Lodge. Please enjoy.* But he doesn't wait on ceremony.

"Cheers," he says with a smile, then takes a sip. He closes his eyes and sighs. "It's good."

I preen before I can catch myself, and I turn out toward the horizon again. "You're up early." Am I allowed to comment on a guest's sleeping habits? Am I supposed to let him be the first one to speak? Apparently, Harper's training has taken hold more than I expected.

"Couldn't sleep," he says, and I remind myself he's not the VIP. Maybe he doesn't know what the rules are here any more than I do.

"Jet lag?"

He peers at me with a quirk of his lips. "From California?"

I shrug. "Is that where you came from?"

"From—They didn't tell you—" The man frowns. "You don't know who—"

"Don't worry about that. They made me sign one of those damn nondisclosure documents. I mean"—I wave an arm over the side of the boat—"look at where we are. Who the hell am I going to tell?"

The man sighs. "Yeah." He doesn't look happy about it, and I can't figure out why.

"You done this long?" I ask, trying to fix my blunder.

"Done what?"

I shrug, searching for words. "The thing . . . you're doing. Here. With the guy you came with."

"The guy?" The man laughs, more of his features visible as

he turns to look out over the water. "What exactly do you think we're doing?"

"Your job. Protecting him or . . . whatever. He's someone famous. Or powerful. That's why they made me sign the NDA, right? So that I can't tell anyone I saw him nearly fall out of a plane?"

The man laughs again, but it's more genuine this time, less like he's laughing at me.

"Yeah, we all pretend not to notice his antics. Better for career longevity. He can be a bit . . . feisty."

"I'm Jack." I hold out a hand, and after a moment's hesitation, the other man shakes it.

"David. Nice to meet you."

"You go by David or Dave?"

He tilts his head for a minute, like he has to think about it, but he finally takes a sip of his coffee and says, "David."

"And your boss's name? Or am I really supposed to call him Mr. Morgan? Fishing boats usually aren't that formal." I'd keep his real name to myself, but I'm a little curious now. And really, it's not like I have anything of value Harper can sue me for.

But David shakes his head. "Sorry. I'm not at liberty to say."

Fair enough. Not that knowing his name would have helped. We clearly travel in very different circles. With my luck, David would tell me who his boss is, and I would only be able to give him that vague "ooh" people use when they don't actually know what's going on but are too embarrassed to say anything else. No point in looking like an uncultured hick before the day has fully started.

Especially since, as the sun rises up over the edge of the ocean and sparkles between the trees, the morning light reflects off David's face, and with every passing minute, it becomes clear he is a good-looking man. We mostly watch the water, drinking our coffee, but it gives me an excuse to examine him quietly. His dark hair with its shaved sides has lost some of its carelessness from the day before, combed down now into soft waves that glow with a bit of red in the sun. His skin is tanned, which makes sense if he's from California. His nose is straight, his lips wide. His eyes are dark, but the brown holds a warmth that makes me think there'll be more color to them when the light is brighter.

And when did I start swooning over someone's eyes? Though maybe crushing on a VI-VIP's bodyguard is less against the rules? He's only sort of a guest. When you look at it from a certain way, we're both basically staff. Our paychecks come from different bank accounts, but David's not here because he chose to be any more than I did.

He turns like he can feel me staring. "Something wrong?"

I take a risk and hold his gaze, and he doesn't blink.

I say, "No. Been a while since I've done this."

"This?"

Stared at a hot man and wondered what his stubble would feel like rasping over my skin. I chicken out and go back to the horizon. "Watched the sunrise."

"You do them well here."

"That we do."

I go back inside and pour us both more coffee. It's still early, but I'm being hospitable, and that's what I'm here to do, right?

"Come on," I say, and he doesn't ask any questions, instead following me up to the flybridge. He manages the ladder pretty well, even with the mug in his hand.

From here, ten or so feet off the deck, we can see even farther, and for the first time since the plane dropped me off here, I'm proud to have something to share. We turn the seats so we can face the stern and out to the ocean. A gull sails low along the water, wings curved to hold itself steady as it looks for a meal.

"You work here long?" David asks, and I like that he can make conversation but doesn't need to fill all the quiet spaces.

"We only opened yesterday." I don't add "for you," but he drops his gaze and smiles quietly, so he probably knows it anyway.

"And what did you do before?"

"I'm a fisherman." Was. I don't mention the other odd jobs I've done. Anyone who fishes has cobbled together a career from other stuff in the off-season. Along with plowing and painting, I've also worked in construction and collected garbage. None of it's ever really stuck. Nothing except being out on the water. "We're all fishermen in my family. My uncles. My dad."

David nods. "My dad was a miner."

"Really?"

David blinks at me, then shivers, even under his heavy coat. "Wow. I haven't talked about him in a long time. I don't know what made me think of him now."

Well, I'm not one to pry. "Forget I said anything."

"No." He scans the water in front of us, but his frown says he's gone deep inside himself. "I dunno. He was always the outdoorsy one. Loved hunting and fishing. He'd probably think a place like this was too nice. If your fishing lodge isn't ready to fall over in a stiff breeze, is it even worth the trip?"

I laugh at that. "Sounds like we'd get along."

"No." He glances at me, and his brown eyes have gone hard. "He's a racist, homophobic asshole, and I'm assuming you're not."

Well then. "When you put it like that . . . I had my first boyfriend in high school. Would be hard to be homophobic at this point."

He scowls into his empty mug and doesn't reply for a minute. Finally, he hands it back to me. "Thanks for the coffee."

"My pleasure." Something has changed, and I'm sorry for it. I was enjoying his company, but if it's about his dad, that's not something I can make better.

He climbs wordlessly down the ladder from the flybridge,

and the employee manual probably says I should follow him. Maybe even walk him back into the hotel. But I stay where I am because he clearly wants space.

He doesn't turn until he's made it up to the dock in one long step. David shades his eyes as he looks up at me on the bridge. "I'll see you later."

"I'll be here. It was nice to meet you, David."

5

DAMIAN

EXTRA*tainment Insider!*
Close Encounters with Damian Marshall Through the Years

More information is coming out about the recent run-in between Shadow League *star Damian Marshall and the film franchise's director, Anderson Lind. According to patrons at the bar where the two met, Marshall had been there for some time before Anderson arrived. Bar staff say Mr. Marshall is a regular who always keeps a low profile.*

It's been a few years since Marshall has been seen in public like this. He's better known for frequenting private parties and exclusive clubs, but fans who have met him have always said he's happy to stop for an autograph or a picture, and he's made a reputation for himself in Hollywood as the consummate gentleman.

@darealesttea on Twitter says, "Met @DamianMarshall in Saigon a couple of years ago. Nicest guy. He smelled so good."

@ladyX423 also reports meeting the star. "Don't hurt my boo @DamianMarshall. He let me do this prom pose with him at Comic Con for a photo. Best Day Ever!!"

Although the actor has never brought home an Oscar, he made headlines two years ago when he helped Best Director winner Amelia

Wilson up the stairs to the stage at the Kodak Theatre when the director tripped on her vintage Oscar de la Renta dress.

Why Marshall's behavior has turned frosty remains unknown.

———

I FIND my way up to the third floor and stumble down the hall to Vin's room, giddy with excitement, and pound on the door with shaking fists.

From the other side of the door comes a tortured groan. "What?"

"Open up!"

"Are you dying?"

I roll my eyes and bang again impatiently. "No."

"On fire?"

"No."

"Is anyone else on fire?"

"Vin, come on. Open up, or I'll—" I'm cut off when the door swings open. Vin is wrapped in a fuchsia and turquoise robe. His hair is in his face, and he only has one eye open.

"What is it?"

"We're going fishing." I push past him. The heavy drapes over the floor-to-ceiling windows are down, and I yank them back, letting the bright glow of the rising sun flood the room. "God, it's beautiful here. The sunrises are amazing."

Vin's sitting at the edge of the bed, arms and legs crossed, expression dripping with disdain. "Who are you and what have you done with Damian?"

"I'm serious. Come look."

Instead, Vin moans and flops face-first onto the bed, his open robe spreading over him in a jewel-toned puddle.

"What time is it?" he asks into his pillow.

"Just after six. Come on, get up!" I pull open a dresser and toss a shirt at him.

"After six?" Vin rolls to glare at me, letting the shirt drop to the floor. "They don't even start serving breakfast until seven. I'm not doing anything until I've had coffee and whatever the equivalent of a smoothie is around here!"

I crawl onto the bed next to him, ignoring him as he grumbles and scoots out of the way, and pick up the bedside phone.

"Good morning. Front desk, Marci speaking," a female voice on the other end of the line says.

"Good morning. It's Mr. Morgan," I say, giving the alias Ivy uses when booking us into hotels. Vin stomps off toward the shower in his shimmering robe.

"Yes, good morning, sir. How are you today?" Her voice suddenly has that breathless quality like she'd do anything I ask, whether that's go for a swim in the freezing water outside or hike deep into the woods to find me freshly picked berries. It's the tone I get from most people, but after my conversation with Jack, it feels extra weird.

"I'm fine. Thanks for asking. Would it be possible to have breakfast served early?"

Thirty seconds later, after a lot of very perky reassurances that an early breakfast will be no trouble at all, I hang up. "All set. Get a move on!" I bounce at the edge of the mattress, kicking my heels against the oak bed frame.

"I still hate you," Vin calls over the sound of running water.

"You'll hate me less when I tell you who I met."

"Curtis Hollingsworth?"

I snort. Although now that I think about it, Jack the fisherman had a certain resemblance. Curt and I were in the first *Shadow League* together. Might have screwed around a bit, but not publicly. He was nice to look at and had a legion of fans who hovered outside the hotel for a chance to see the back of his head. Jack is red where Curt is blond, and a little younger too. And there was something about Jack's face that said he was less prone to smiling than Curt was, but still . . . not a bad likeness.

Vin pokes his head out of the bathroom, eyes wide. "Hollingsworth is staying here?"

I blink, caught somewhere between a memory of me and Curt in bed on a rare day off and a fantasy of me and Jack rolling around in the big bed upstairs. "What? No. Nothing like that."

"Oh." Vin pouts, and I roll my eyes. Vin so isn't into the burly Viking type.

I am though. But that isn't the point. Four-poster fantasies aside, I can't seduce a unicorn, and Jack is definitely one of those.

"I couldn't sleep, so I went for a walk." I didn't realize when I got dressed that there really wasn't anywhere to walk to. We're on a floating hotel in the middle of nowhere. It backs onto a shoreline that's basically dense forest I didn't feel brave enough to try on my own when no one knew where I was, so I could only go as far as the end of the dock.

"And you came face to face with a Sasquatch?" Vin is still sulking, but he's also getting dressed, so we're making progress. We'll grab something to eat and get back to Jack as soon as we can. I can't wait for Vin to meet him. Of all the things I thought I'd find up here in the middle of nowhere, someone like Jack hadn't even made my list.

"No. Better than a Sasquatch." I can barely control my grin at the thought of the quiet man on the fishing boat who offered me coffee and conversation with no other agenda. Not after the last ten days of endless questions and requests for comments. Not after the months—hell, the years—of cameras and cellphones and people asking for a photo or a hug when the last thing I want is to be touched by another stranger. I told Roberta I wanted to be famous, I just didn't realize I'd have to give up so many pieces of myself—from my sexuality to my personal space —to do it.

Of course, there's a chance I'm wrong about what happened this morning and it'll all spectacularly blow up in my face, but with everything else that's gone sideways lately, I believe Jack was genuine.

I hold the hotel room door open, trying to hurry Vin along.

"Nothing's better than a Sasquatch," he says as he slides his shoes on.

"Yes, there is. Vin, I think I met someone who doesn't know who I am."

———

As WE COME DOWN the grand staircase that leads to the hotel's main lobby, a few staff members scurry by. They keep their eyes down as they've no doubt been trained to, though one young woman can't help herself and turns at the last second, staring at me with wide eyes like she's seen a ghost. I get that a lot.

Encounters with fans typically fall into one of three categories. There are people who do their best to keep their cool and fail. Usually if they do manage to say anything, it's a stammered "Hi. I love your movies," and then they hurry away.

Then there are the superfans. The ones who scream and cry and beg for a selfie and talk to me in a way that always leaves me a bit uncertain as to whether they understand Damian Marshall is not the same person as Dex Russo, the mafia son trying to reclaim his life in the *Shadow League* movies. These fans can get overwhelming, but they're mostly harmless.

And finally, there are the weirdos. They're like the first group in that they don't approach, but these ones hover, watching. It's downright creepy, especially when it goes on for more than a minute or two. Sometimes people don't realize they're doing it. One woman was so enthralled, she tried to follow me into the men's room at La Patrie in New York City, then burst into tears when a waiter asked her where she was going.

Others, well, I don't know what they're doing, but there's always a chance they're building up an idealized impression of me so they can then send me streams of letters or social media messages about how we're meant to be together after the time we almost met while I was waiting in line for coffee at a Starbucks in Pittsburgh.

Honestly, I haven't been inside a Starbucks in a couple of years. The risk isn't worth it. One look at my social media DMs is enough to explain why. Not that I manage my own social media anymore. I stopped after the first *Shadow League* because it was too much to keep up with and not good for my mental health. The things people feel comfortable telling you when there's a few phone screens between you is truly weird and frequently disturbing. I've received everything from marriage proposals to death threats, pictures of strangers naked to some truly intrusive questions about my sexual preferences. And I don't just mean my orientation. There was one guy who seemed determine to figure out my preferred type of sex toy by sending videos of himself demonstrating how each was used. Ivy sent me the highlights before she finally blocked him. I asked Roberta if any of her other clients had the same problems, and she waved it off, saying it was the price to pay in the industry.

Still, the staff at the lodge is well-trained to pretend I'm just another guy. Except for Jack. He wasn't playing along. I know what that looks like. He honestly believed every word I told him.

Of course, all of it was true. The name on my birth certificate is David Morgan, and my dad is a racist bigot from the backwoods. It's just not the story I give most people. Or anyone, really. Not since my career took off. To everyone except Vin and Roberta, I'm Damian Marshall, movie star. People want to talk about my movies, my international adventures, and how I feel about getting snubbed at the Oscars last year. No one wants to hear about my childhood growing up as a gay kid in the middle of nowhere.

The main dining room is silent as we enter, but a crash and muffled shouting comes from the kitchen. A woman in a Wild

Eagle polo shirt and khakis walks us to a table, then hurries into the kitchen when we ask for coffee. Although she repeatedly reassures us that it's no trouble we showed up early, the ruckus coming from behind the kitchen doors leaves the impression that someone has been caught off guard.

This is only reinforced when the blonde woman who met us on the dock the day before rushes into the dining room, stopping short when she sees us. I've forgotten her name, but she's definitely the one in charge, and she can't be happy that we've caught her staff unprepared.

"Mr. Morgan, good morning. I trust you slept well."

"I did!" I say, putting on my best sunny smile, while Vin grumbles low words that end with something like "could still be asleep."

The server reappears with a French press and two mugs on a tray. She doesn't meet the blonde manager's eyes as she sets them down on the table, and the coffee splatters over its spout and onto the white tablecloth. For a second, she looks like she might panic under her manager's scrutiny.

"I'll have an egg white omelette, whole grain toast, butter on the side, and whatever meat or sausage your chef wants to put with that," I say before someone starts breaking dishes to relieve the tension growing in the room.

The server writes my order down with shaking hands and glances at Vin, who stretches back lazily in his chair.

"Fresh fruit. Yogurt. Granola if it's gluten free."

She writes it down too and rushes away. The manager—she's close enough that I can read Harper on the gold-plated name tag pinned to her shirt—watches the whole thing with a tense frustration that makes me sorry for the rest of the morning shift. If their granola isn't gluten free, it will be tomorrow, and no doubt our rooms will have the luxury equivalent of extra mints on our pillows and towel swans on our beds tonight.

She gives us an apologetic smile. "I'm sorry. I didn't realize you'd be up early. The kitchen will—"

"It's fine." And it is. As long as we don't wait two hours for them to cook an omelette and slice the fruit, I don't care that they weren't ready for our early service. Still, I can throw her a bone to smooth things over. "But since you're here, there is something I'd like your help with."

She squares her shoulders, no doubt relieved to be back in familiar territory. "Of course. What can we do for you?"

"Fishing. My agent said her office had booked a fishing charter while I'm here."

"Absolutely. Your agent already gave us your information, and your nonresident fishing licenses are taken care of. We have a few guides on staff. If you tell me your preferred fish, I can have one of them ready this afternoon, and—"

"No. I'd like to go this morning." Why spend more time in here with all these people practically bowing and scraping when I can spend more time with Jack?

Her eyes tighten ever so slightly in the corners. "Of course. This morning. I'll see who is—"

"I've already met him."

Her lashes flutter. "Who?"

"The fishing guide. Jack. Red hair. The strong, silent type?"

Her smile never falters. "Jack. Of course."

"He makes good coffee."

That finally cracks her composure entirely. "He made you coffee?"

"I'm allergic to hazelnuts."

"You—" Her breath catches before she exhales slowly and smooths down the front of her shirt. "Excuse me."

No doubt she's off to yell at the catering staff and then probably the concierge for not double-checking with Ivy about allergies.

Vin tsks. "She's off to shred her pillow with a butcher knife over that one."

Our meal is served, and I'm surprisingly hungry.

"Wait until you meet him," I say, laying into the omelet. The sausage is apparently some sort of artisanal caribou something or other that sounded fun, but it's kind of mealy. "He really doesn't know who I am. He thinks you're the VIP."

Vin waves a careless hand as he picks at a blueberry. "Honey, I'm the most important VIP there is."

"Of course you are."

"So what do you want to do?"

"About what?"

"Your new fishing friend who has recently returned from ten years in space? We need to make sure he's not fooling." The arch to Vin's eyebrow says no good can come from what he has in mind.

"I'm pretty sure we can trust him."

He snorts. "Like Felicia?"

Oh. Felicia was my personal assistant for about thirty-six hours a couple of years ago. Roberta hired her based on her impeccable resume that included working as a PA for a number of other actors and LA socialites. She even had friends who she'd set up to pretend to be references when Ivy called. The first day was good. The second day, when Felicia's photographer boyfriend hopped my fence to take pictures of me while I was working out with my trainer in the pool house . . . not so much.

Still, the idea that Jack is someone who needs testing doesn't sit well with me. Surely that's the hotel's job, not ours. But vetting Felicia was Roberta's job, and look how that turned out.

"What do you have in mind?" I ask.

Vin grins devilishly as he drains his coffee in a single gulp. "I'm pretty sure it's time for Horatio to go on a little trip."

"What? Horatio? No, come on."

He pouts. "Why not?"

"Because your Spanish accent is terrible."

"How do you know this guy is for real? What if he takes us out on the water and then refuses to bring us back until he gets a naked selfie with you or a lock of your hair?"

"He's not like that." The idea that he could be makes my stomach turn. Being careful and making sure everyone is vetted before I put my trust in them is exhausting. To learn that Jack was lying this morning, that he was playing some game to fuck with me . . . I'm not sure I could handle the disappointment right now.

"What if I do the Greenpeace bit? He thinks I'm someone important, right?" Vin asks. I wince, but I can see where he's going with this, even if it makes me uncomfortable. Is it okay to confirm someone's not lying by lying yourself?

Still, the Greenpeace thing is pretty harmless.

"Fine," I say. "But no accents."

Vin crosses his heart. "No accents. Just call me Mr. Morgan."

6

JACK

For lack of anything else to do, I'm on page one hundred twenty-seven of the *Hawk*'s fish finder manual when Harper comes marching out of the lodge and directly to where I'm tied off.

"You had a guest this morning," she says, hands on her hips. She's out of breath like she's run part of the way or is controlling the urge to scream. "Playing barista, are you?"

"I wasn't supposed to serve him coffee?"

"You didn't tell me."

It's after seven o'clock. The lodge is only now gearing up for the day, and I'm still the only one down here by the water. Was I supposed to run to Harper's room and wake her up the second David left the boat?

When I don't reply, Harper glares at me. "They want to go out today."

I blink. "Both of them?" David seems like a good guy, but I still can't imagine his boss really wanting to go fishing.

She doesn't acknowledge my response. "I'll tell Mr. Morgan you'll be ready to go by eight o'clock." Then she spins on the heel of her still-unblemished boot and marches away again.

Shortly after her departure, there's a flurry of activity as the kitchen staff shows up with enough hampers of food to feed an army of people for a week—though somehow all of it disappears neatly into the cupboards and cold locker in the galley. Then Luis, who is head of recreation services, insists on going over some kind of safety checklist that includes everything from what I would do in the event of an onboard fire to a medical emergency to getting lost at sea, even though the forecast is clear today and I don't imagine we'll go anywhere offshore.

After that's settled, there's a brief pause where I go through all the food and double-check my bait and gear. I'm closing the dry locker when shouting comes from the dock. I stick my head outside, and David is walking toward me, once again in his parka. The shouting is coming from his boss behind him, who is back on his phone, staring off into the distance from behind a pair of weird, green-tinted glasses.

"Yes," he says. "I told you that is unacceptable. We won't consider anything less than seventeen million. No. No. You listen to me, jackass—" His point is cut off abruptly by whoever is on the phone. I'm impressed he even has cell service out here.

"Good morning again." David's voice is friendly, and his smile soft as he grins over the stovepipe collar of his coat.

"Hi." I step forward and lift a hand. "Welcome aboard."

David takes it as he steps down, but there's no tension in his grip. He must be pretty fit if he doesn't need any support off the dock.

His boss, however, is a different story. He's still on his phone as he approaches the *Winter Hawk*. I start, half expecting him to walk off the dock and drop the three feet of open space onto the deck, but it seems David is prepared for this sort of thing. The way he catches the smaller man under his arms and sets him gently down speaks of a lot of practice.

Maybe being a bodyguard isn't just protecting a client from

bad guys with guns like on TV? Maybe it also means keeping your client from killing himself when he isn't watching where he's going while taking important phone calls.

"No. No, that is not what we agreed to." Despite his near accident, he's still speaking without missing a beat. "It is nineteen thousand hectares. Do you know what the Greenpeace freaks would do to me if they found out I was speaking to you?"

"Everything all right?" David asks behind me, making me jump. For such a big man, he moves softly, even on a metal boat.

I straighten. "Harper says you want to go fishing."

David smiles, bigger this time. He has the whitest teeth I have ever seen in my life. "This is a fishing boat, isn't it?"

It sure is. The nicest one I've been on. And getting better for the company that has joined me.

I squash that thought because David is working, and I'm supposed to be too. "Got a preference?" I ask, glancing quickly at the man on the phone. Technically, he's the guest, right? I should be asking him these questions.

"A preference for what?" David asks with an arched eyebrow that makes me heat under my fleece. I haven't flirted with anyone in a while, and that one question, coupled with David's smile, squeezes something in my gut that hasn't been touched for what feels like years. I dig my nails into my palms to ignore the shiver of interest that ripples up my body. I'm not so hard up that I'm going to jump on top of an innocent question asked by a man I've just met who I'm supposed to be taking care of.

Instead, I clear my throat. "For fishing."

David runs a hand over the back of his neck, almost like he was also caught off guard. "I used to fish walleye as a kid."

"And your boss? Should we ask him?"

David glances at his boss, who is still yelling into his phone. "Mr. Morgan will be busy for a while. Let's get going. Wherever you want to take us is fine."

"You won't find much walleye up here," I say. "Mostly salmon, halibut, or rockfish if you know where to look."

"Hey!" His boss's nasal voice cuts through the conversation.

David winces but glances over my shoulder. "Yes, Mr. Morgan?"

"Are we going? I could be inside having this conversation where it's warm." Like the day before, he's vastly underdressed for what we're about to do. His blue pants are back and rolled to his ankles, and his green boat shoes are still pristine. He's swapped out the pink beach ball shirt for a white collared one, worn underneath a bright blue sweater.

"Can I get you some warmer clothes before we go?" I ask because one of the things Luis made me talk about was what to do if any of the guests get hypothermia, and once we're out on the water, that sweater won't cut it. "There are slickers, floater coats, and boots in the cabin."

Mr. Morgan smacks a hand to his chest. "This is cashmere!"

I'm not sure what that proves other than that it's still completely unsuitable for a day on the ocean. On instinct, I square my shoulders. This is the kind of guest I was afraid of. He's not going to appreciate anything about today. Instead, he'll complain that the water is too wet and the sun is too bright.

Behind me, David makes a strangled noise and steps by me to put an arm around Mr. Morgan's shoulders.

"Why don't you wait inside the cabin? You can call Horatio, and we'll let you know if we see anything interesting."

"Anything interesting?" Mr. Morgan's voice is full of disbelief. "Do you know where we are? What would there be to see?" His voice pitches up, and his next questions come in a long string of pointed Italian—or is it Spanish?—that I don't understand, but at least he allows David to guide him into the cabin. I climb the flybridge, and Mr. Morgan's tirade is mercifully drowned out as I fire up the engine. The *Winter Hawk* has two big outboard motors that roar to life on the first try, and I have to stop the reflex of turning the key in the ignition a second time—something that was required for my old boat to start every time.

We motor quietly out toward the mouth of the inlet, keeping the engine down to a dull purr. Motion catches my eye, and David appears down below. He's traded his heavy coat for one of the bright yellow Wild Eagle windbreakers in the dry locker, and he smiles when he spots me on the bridge. I pull the brim of my ball cap down a little farther and tell myself it's windburn from picking up speed that makes my cheeks heat. David points one finger upward, a silent request to join me, and my hands tighten on the wheel.

I have one job—to keep these people happy—so I nod, even if the confined space of the flybridge suddenly feels cozy. I turn my attention ahead of me, steering us beyond the spit and out into the surf.

David climbs up, taking a seat beside me. "I borrowed a coat. I hope you don't mind."

I glance at him, keeping my hands on the steering wheel as the swells pick up beneath us. "That's what they're there for."

I stare ahead, trying to conjure up the kind of person David —and more specifically, Mr. Morgan—expects me to be. Personable and good at conversation. Eager to serve.

"Your boss is . . ." Yeah, that's not a good place to start.

Beside me, David smiles at my poor attempt at small talk. "Mr. Morgan, the sixth richest man in Massachusetts."

"You mean California."

"What?" His grin turns confused.

"This morning you said you flew up from California."

His eyes tighten in the corners for a second before he says, "We did. We were in Palo Alto for a conference. Then he decided to come up here."

"What does he do?"

David stares out at the horizon. "Real estate. Land develop-ment. Together with his husband, the other Mr. Morgan, they own half the available mineral rights this side of the Mason–Dixon."

I search for something to say. You can't be a born and bred Alaskan and not know a little something about mining and mineral rights. But those conversations often get heated, and while Mr. Morgan's mention of "Greenpeace freaks" makes it clear what side of the argument he's on, I can't say for sure where David's convictions lie, and for whatever reason, I want him to like me. Maybe so today's trip is even remotely tolerable since it's clear Mr. Morgan isn't going out of his way to be friendly.

While I'm considering all of this though, David has already moved on. "So where are we headed?"

"Are you sure we shouldn't check with your boss? It's his dime." A day of fishing at the Wild Eagle Lodge is more than a dime, but whatever.

David shrugs. "Mr. Morgan would rather be on a beach right now."

"So why isn't he?"

"The two Morgans are . . . having a rough spot. So the other Mr. Morgan took the house in St. Barth's, and my Mr. Morgan is . . ." He grins. "Proving a point. So wherever you want to take us will be great."

I shake my head. I'm not getting involved in some kind of international marital dispute when I could be fishing. Hell, with the engines on this boat, I could be at home in under three hours. I'd like to see the look on Mr. Morgan's face when Stef and Robbie descend on him and his cashmere sweater. But Harper probably wouldn't be keen on that plan, and if I upset Mr. Morgan, I can kiss my payday goodbye, and that will be the exact opposite of the homecoming I want.

I glance at David, who's got his head tipped back in the breeze.

I can think of a few other things I'd like to kiss.

The seas roll under the gleaming boat, and I turn her toward the waves.

"Well then, let's get fishing."

7

DAMIAN

E XTRAtainment *INVESTIGATES!*
      IS DAMIAN MARSHALL'S CAREER IN TROUBLE?

Following recent run-ins with director Anderson Lind, Damian Marshall has left Hollywood. He was spotted early yesterday morning at a private airfield boarding a jet. His representatives could not be reached for comment about his destination. Given his recent behavior, unnamed sources close to the actor believe he may be seeking treatment for an undisclosed mental health condition. Will this impact his ability to continue with production of the next Shadow League *film?* Shadow League: Through Darkness *has been generally panned by critics and continues to struggle at the box office as international receipts come in. Asked about the future of the franchise, executive producer Cedric Oberman said, "We're very proud of what we've accomplished with* Shadow League *and its sequels. We want these movies to continue to be a success and are considering all our options before we move into production." Oberman refused to comment on whether one of these options would be moving ahead without the film's star as they explore new stories in the same universe. More details to follow as they become available.*

———

I'M ASTONISHED. It's not a word I use often, but in this case, it's the right one. I spend an hour sitting next to Jack as he confidently navigates the boat along the coast, and in that time, I tell increasingly elaborate stories about "Mr. Morgan" and his antics, and never once does Jack look at me with anything other than utter trust. I watch. I wait for the moment. The double take where he finally catches the right light or the right angle and his eyes widen and his mouth drops open before he collects himself and tries to be cool. But it never comes.

He literally has no idea who I am.

How is that even possible?

Since I first arrived in California, I've done my best to keep my feet glued to the ground. The first few years, when I heard more nos than yeses, when Vin and I took turns month by month sleeping in our shitty apartment's one bed while the other one slept on a leaky air mattress on the floor, it was easy to stay humble. But even when I hit my break, when the paychecks started rolling in and the media and the public clamored for my attention, I tried to stay grounded and remember what real life was like.

But it's been years since I've been able to go anywhere—*anywhere*—without being recognized. I was nearly crushed in a mob of fans at a bazaar in Morocco. I had the scare of my life when a woman climbed through my hotel room window in Bangkok, not to attack me or seduce me, but to steal a piece of my clothing to sell on the internet.

There's nowhere in the world where someone doesn't know who I am.

Except, it seems, right here on this boat with Jack the fisherman.

"Do you like movies, Jack?" I finally ask when I can't take it any longer.

Once, a few years ago, I was at a charity gala talking to an elderly woman who, for a moment, also seemed to not recognize me. She even blandly asked if I'd been in anything she'd seen when I told her I was an actor. But then her eyes went huge in her carefully Botoxed face when I listed a few of my more recent roles.

"That was you?" she asked. "My granddaughter has a picture of your naked bottom on her cellphone!"

As do many people. One of the hazards of taking your pants off in a blockbuster.

But the point is, even though the woman didn't recognize my face, it appeared that she'd recognized my ass from a single grainy screenshot.

Would Jack recognize my ass?

I look him up and down, from the coppery red hair on his chin to the width of his chest in his Wild Eagle jacket and on down to the heavy thighs that perch on the edge of his seat. I really wouldn't mind much if Jack got to know my ass. Not at all.

"I don't watch many movies," Jack says, bringing me back to my question.

"No?" I can't squash the excitement that's beating inside me. "What was the last movie you saw in the theater?"

Jack's face scrunches up, highlighting the lines and creases on his skin that happen when a man works outdoors for years. I like them a lot. "I took my nephew to see that fish movie a few years ago when I went to visit my sister."

"The fish movie?"

"Yeah. You know the one. The fish gets lost, and they have to get it home."

"*Finding Nemo*?"

"I think so."

"That was like twenty years ago."

"No. It wasn't that one then."

There was a sequel, or at least I'm pretty sure there was, though I couldn't say how long ago it was. My schedule doesn't allow for a lot of movie viewing apart from appearances at premieres, and my presence isn't often requested at family-friendly films. But still, if that was the last movie Jack remembered seeing . . .

"Nothing more recent?" I prod, still waiting for the other shoe to drop.

Jack shrugs. "The closest movie theater to where I live is a four-hour drive. I don't get there very often."

"But you have Netflix, right?" The resort has Wi-Fi, proving that there is internet in Alaska.

"I like documentaries more." He doesn't take his eyes off the horizon.

I wait. Hold my breath. Expect Jack to turn to me with a big smile and go *Surprise!* But it doesn't come.

To Jack, I'm David.

Well, not really. David was a scared, closeted teen from a village in North Dakota where he was related by blood to half the residents and by marriage to the rest.

The David Jack thinks he knows is a bodyguard for an eccentric real estate mogul.

I've succeeded at tougher roles though. The bionic alien hybrid in *The Outerlands*, for example. I was almost nominated for SAG Award for that one.

The point, though, is that Jack doesn't know Damian the movie star. And that means he doesn't know about Cannes. He hasn't seen the endless loops of memes and videos in which I called Anderson a fear-mongering slobber donkey. He doesn't know what my ass looks like and doesn't think he's owed any amount of my time or attention, but somehow that leaves me wanting to give it to him even more.

The boat slows.

"We're here," Jack says, all honest grins as he stands and gestures for me to climb down the ladder to the deck below.

"We're where?" We're surrounded by open water. The shore is visible in the distance, a green-brown line of trees with the endless gray and white peaks of mountains looming behind them, but it would be a hell of a swim to get there. Other than that, it's all water.

Jack follows me down the ladder, and holy shit if the view toward shore is beautiful, the view of Jack's denim-clad ass as he makes his easy way backward down the ladder is its own kind of picturesque.

They sure grow them nice in Alaska.

Oh, knock it off. It's easy to get infatuated with someone like Jack. All I wanted to do was escape, and whether he knows it or not, Jack is offering me even more than I could have dreamed of. But he's a guy trying to do a job, and I shouldn't take advantage of that. Spending a few hours with him making small talk about fish and sunrises is enough.

Before I can embarrass myself further, the door to the cabin opens and Vin comes out, eyes narrowed.

"Why did we stop?" he asks, voice thick with his nasal Boston accent. The Greenpeace bit is one he dreamed up several years ago at Comic Con, right before the second *Shadow League* film came out. I was trapped in an endless line of bloggers and critics who all wanted "just one minute" of my time, and it was only Vin hollering at the imaginary Horatio on his phone about rain forests and endangered baby seals who caused enough of a commotion that I was able to slip out a staff door and make my escape on a passing golf cart.

"Mr. Morgan, I think we're going to fish."

"Fish?" He spits it out between clenched teeth and tense lips like the word is offensive to him.

"Yes." I have to bite down on my smile at the incensed look on Vin's face. "Our guide thinks this is a good place to try."

Vin strides across the deck until he's standing chest to chest with Jack. Or actually, it's more like forehead to chest, since Vin is several inches shorter than Jack, but that doesn't stop him from glaring up at the bigger man.

"Now you listen to me," he says, poking a finger toward Jack. "We came all this way to see the big Alaskan fish, yeah?"

Jack blinks a few times. "Okay."

"Not like we haven't seen fish before. You should have seen the size of the tuna I caught in front of the house at Martha's Vineyard last year."

My toes curl in my shoes as I try to hold in my laughter. He sounds like such an entitled prick.

"I'm sure it must have been very impressive." Jack doesn't sound impressed. He sounds pissed. Like he doesn't care he's staring down the ninth richest—or did I say he was the sixth?— man in Massachusetts.

"Oh, it was." Vin holds his arms out to show the size of the mythical tuna, still glaring up at Jack. "So you'd better show us something as impressive."

"That's the plan." Jack gives me a glance that once again makes me wonder if we're even talking about fish anymore.

Vin at least seems content. "Good. Now you and David fish. I have to call Horatio back."

Jack glances from Vin to me and back again. "You're not joining us? What about the tuna in—"

"No!" Vin gives a little hop to punctuate his outrage at the suggestion and nearly clips Jack's chin with the top of his head in the process. That's my cue to intervene.

"Mr. M." I set a hand on Vin's shoulder and tug him back gently. "Why don't you go sit up top and get a little sun?"

"Sun?" Vin is clearly going for his best soap opera performance today. "You call this sun? Do you know where there is sun? In St. Barth's. Do you know who's in St. Barth's? My Emilio!" His voice wavers on the last word like he's about to cry, and I widen my eyes, silently begging him to rein it in a bit. But I also make a mental note to let Roberta know she should be sending him out for auditions.

Vin winks, then spins on his heel, flouncing to the ladder

and climbing up. I take a step back so I'm shoulder to shoulder with Jack. We watch silently until Vin is settled in one of the tall chairs, his back to us as he continues to mutter to himself about "Emilio."

"Your boss is a bit high-maintenance," Jack says softly. The crow's feet at the corners of his eyes crinkle, and I can't tell if he's amused or annoyed.

"He's an acquired taste."

He stares at me like he knows bullshit when he smells it. "He really came all this way and he's not fishing?"

"He's not . . ." I scrub a hand over the back of my neck, trying to figure a way out of this. "Maybe he's humoring me."

"You?"

I try to keep my shrug casual. "He's not really into fishing, but I told him I wanted to go, so he said he'd make it happen."

Jack glares up at the bridge, but he's still keeping his voice down. "And now he's going to hang out there?"

I don't know what to say. "With money comes certain privileges?"

Jack laughs in acknowledgment. It's a quiet sound low in his chest, and it hits me in exactly the same place.

"He reminds me of my brother-in-law."

"Yeah?" I say.

He shrugs. "Well . . . ex-brother-in-law. Almost. I think his family has a place on Martha's Vineyard too. You know the type. Their money opens doors everywhere they go, and they forget how real people live."

My growing amusement fades. If he knew who I really was, would he think the same thing about me?

"So how do you want to do this?" Jack asks like nothing we've said is worth a second thought.

"Do what?"

He takes down one of the fishing rods lined up in a rack. "Do you want the hands-on version, or do you want to sit back and let me do the work?"

Okay, seriously. That's a pickup line, right? Either he's fucking with me . . . or he wants to be fucking with me.

But still, he's staring with that same blankly expectant expression like he didn't just ask me if I like to take charge in bed any more than he's asked me any of the usual crap people want to know, like how I remember all those lines or if Dex really is secretly in love with his best friend, Leon Martinelli.

In case you're wondering, he's not. Dex is straight as a rail. It's something that's been drilled into me for years by the studio PR team because the question comes up at every single con and panel I've been to, and we can't risk alienating our fan base—or that's the fear anyway.

As I watch Jack though, I've never felt so off-balance in my life, and it's not the boat rolling underneath my feet.

"Uh, I think I'd like the full experience," I say, voice rougher than I mean it to be.

And yet again, Jack nods like nothing is amiss. He lifts hinged metal panels in the floor and pulls out nets, a curved hook, and a few tools I don't recognize. To one side, he sets out a bucket of jiggling fish guts.

"What's that?" I ask, taking a step back. We're under a wide-open sky, but even with a good breeze blowing past us, the stench of rotting fish makes my eyes water.

"Bait." Jack methodically hooks fish heads and skinned ribs to the end of lines with no more interest than if he was making a sandwich. When he's done, he stands back and gestures to the rods mounted along the boat's railing. "Would you like to do the honors?"

It's been a long time since I went fishing, and back at home, it was much more of the beer-in-a-tin-boat kind of fishing than the rig Jack's got going here, but with a little guidance, we let the lines reel out. The fish guts disappear below the water, and everything gets quiet.

"I'll get the coffee brewing," Jack says. "You want some?"

Hell yes. I want everything Jack is offering, even if he doesn't know it. I trail after him toward the cabin like a lost puppy. Like if he gets too far away from me, the spell will be broken, and he'll suddenly realize who I am. I can't have that. I thought this place would basically be a forest prison, and instead I've found the best gift I could possibly imagine.

I practically bump into him as he turns suddenly at the cabin door.

"Whoa there," he says, strong hands on my shoulders. He might still have fish guts on them and I can't bring myself to worry about it.

"Sorry," I say, flustered by my strange neediness.

"You okay?"

"Yeah, fine." This close to him, I can't quite make myself look him in the eye.

"You stay out here," he says.

"Why?"

"If the lines start spooling out, someone needs to be ready. You wanted the full experience, right?"

More than anything.

"Uh, yeah."

"Good. Now go take a seat, and I'll be right back."

His big frame disappears through the door, and I feel like I've lost something.

However long I'm up here, I'll spend as much time as I can with Jack. Roberta was right. Alaska will be good for me.

8

JACK

For all my misgivings about being a fishing guide, my first few hours aren't terrible. Mr. Morgan stays up on the flybridge, periodically shouting into his phone and more frequently shouting at us that he doesn't have a signal. David answers all his questions and commands patiently, and I don't have to deal with him very much. The wind has come up as we drift farther offshore, and eventually Mr. Morgan finally accepts that his cashmere isn't going to cut it and takes my offer of a coat, but otherwise he keeps to himself. Harper will probably give me shit for spending more time with David than with our VIP, but whatever Mr. Morgan came up here for, it obviously wasn't to fish.

David, though, seems to be enjoying himself. He keeps checking the lines even though there's nothing to do now but wait, and he asks a lot of questions about me and the industry, listening attentively while I give him the basics of what we might catch out here.

"The halibut can get to be over a hundred pounds," I say. David's eyes widen, and he grips the end of his rod tighter. I laugh and put a hand on his back. The muscle beneath my palm is solid. "No rush. We'll know if we land something like that."

Except we aren't landing much of anything. The boat has all the bells and whistles, and I've got five rods running, but whether it's the bait, the sunshine, or the wind, the fish aren't interested in what the *Winter Hawk* has trailing behind her.

"So how long have you been doing this?" David asks.

"My whole life."

"Born and raised in Alaska?"

"Yup. I crewed on different boats for a while, then finally bought my own a couple of years ago." And sold it as soon as there were enough hours of daylight to show it to a buyer this winter. I'd hoped it would be enough for Stef and Robbie, but an old boat like that isn't worth much. Hope is worth less.

"Do you ever think about doing anything else?"

He sounds like Stef. Like I have options without a college degree. Like I haven't tried to find new things to do, only to have life drag me back to the small town I grew up in over and over.

But I can't say that when she's the one who needs my help now, just like it doesn't do me any good to brood in front of the guests, so I force a smile as I ask David, "I like being on the water. What about you? Are you from the Northeast too?"

He shakes his head. "North Dakota."

"No shit?" I don't mean to curse—that's on page seven of the employee manual under the heading Standards of Professional Speech.

"Yeah." He grins crookedly. "Not what you were expecting?"

"If you don't mind me saying, I feel like North Dakota might be even harder to get out of than Alaska."

He laughs. "Not that hard. You get on a bus and never look back."

And have a family you won't miss, based on what he said this morning. That's the hardest part for me. Alaska is far from everything, and my parents are getting older. Stef was gone for more than a decade, and even though she's back now, she doesn't have any room to take on more responsibility.

"David!" Mr. Morgan's voice cuts through the air before I can get too down on things.

David turns with a tight smile. "Yes?"

"Where are the fish? You said we were going to have a nice day fishing, but where are my fish?"

David laughs, but his amusement doesn't reach his eyes. "I'm sure we'll find some, sir."

Mr. Morgan spins back in his chair, green deck shoes braced against the console as the boat rocks. "I don't like to be disappointed, David."

I reel in a few lines to check the bait and whisper quietly, "Is he always like this?"

David checks over his shoulder before he leans in so he can't be heard. "This is him on a good day. The thing with the other Mr. Morgan . . . it's ugly. He didn't want to come up here, but it seemed best to get as far away from the scandal as possible."

"What scandal?" I ask, and David straightens immediately, face going blank. "Are you okay?"

"Yeah, it's fine." He tugs at the bottom of his jacket. "Sorry. I shouldn't have said anything. But this isn't his scene at all. He likes to live his vacations vicariously whenever possible, unless it involves sun and alcohol."

"So he takes you all over the world, and you get to have all the fun? That's a pretty sweet gig."

"Something like that. Most places aren't quite this isolated, so I have more to look out for." He looks like he wants to say something else, but before I can ask, one of the lines runs out with a hiss. I leap forward to catch the rod before it pops out of its mount at the same time David does, and we wind up in a tangle of arms. I stare up at David's eyes as the rod strains in our hands. His pupils dilate as he studies me too.

But he shakes his head and steps back. "It's all yours."

"No, no." I motion toward him. "It's your trip. Come take it."

"It's fine. I'm sure there will be more."

"Oh *my God!*" Mr. Morgan calls from the bridge. "Stop dancing around each other and get me a damn fish!"

I clear my throat. The line in the reel continues to feed out. Whatever's on the other end is big and moving fast. I hand the rod to David.

"Don't fight with him. He'll let you know when he's ready to come in."

He takes it, setting himself with his hips and shoulders square to the side of the boat. "What are you, the fish whisperer?"

"Just trust me."

The line plays out. Every time David's fingers twitch toward the reel, I shush him and tell him to wait. A fish this big, whatever it is—trying to bring it in before it's ready to stop fighting will only wind up with a snapped line.

The rod bends and jerks in David's hands. He keeps checking in with me out of the corner of his eye.

Eventually, the tension in the rod slackens.

"Now."

David must have been waiting like a sprinter. I've barely closed my mouth and he's reeling. He works so fast, hand flying, pulling on the rod until it's curved again, that I don't even have a chance to shout the warning as it dips and swings to the right, banging against one of the flybridge's supports.

The rod snaps straight.

"What happened?" David gasps with wide eyes.

"Broke the line."

He frowns, looking confused. "But I did what you said."

I nudge him gently with my elbow as I take the rod from him. "There will be other chances."

"You sure about that?" David's voice drops, and I have to clear my throat because I'm staring again. I'd been expecting a season of bored, rich tourists. Maybe a couple who actually came for the fishing, and a couple more who thought they knew what they were doing and wouldn't listen when I tried to help them bring in their catch.

David is none of those things. And the way he speaks to me and watches me, I'm never sure if he's talking about fishing or something else entirely. Of course, the "something else" is totally off-limits, but out here on this perfect boat away from Harper and her rules, it feels tempting to at least imagine it.

"Da-David." Mr. Morgan voice is so soft and high that I don't hear it at first.

"That's why we set out multiple reels," I say.

"David."

"So you think we'll catch something else?" David's face is full of hope. Fishing will break your heart over and over, but even though we've just met and I wanted so badly to resent him and his boss for being here, I can already tell I'll do my best to help him enjoy this trip, even if his asshole boss hides up top the whole time.

"Do you—" My question is cut off by the sound of violent retching. I turn in time to see Mr. Morgan leaning against the rail as he pukes over the side.

"Oh shit." David rushes to the ladder as Mr. Morgan lurches toward the open back of the flybridge. I stumble forward too because a fall from there is a hell of a lot farther than the step down from the dock this morning. But just as Mr. Morgan is about to teeter over the edge, the boat rocks against a wave, and he stumbles back into his seat before flinging himself at the rail to throw up again. David scrambles up the ladder with the same long-limbed grace he seems to have for everything.

"I don't feel so good," Mr. Morgan says when David reaches him.

"Yeah, buddy," David says, putting his arm around his shoulders.

"It's so wavy up here."

"We'll get you home."

"Why is it so wavy? It wasn't wavy before. It was sunny and warm and—"

David makes a soft noise, rubbing his boss's back like he's trying to calm an angry child. It's a weird thing to do. I don't know much, but back rubs also didn't seem like something in the bodyguard job description.

Mr. Morgan throws up for a third time, but at least nothing comes out but a thin trail of spittle that hangs in the wind for a second before he wipes it away.

One of the reels spins out, and I cut the line quickly, then bring in the others while David helps Mr. Morgan down from the bridge.

"I need to lie down," Mr. Morgan is saying. His face is the color of drying putty, and the sight of him shivering against David makes me feel a little queasy too, because now I'll have to explain to Harper how I took her VI-VIP out fishing and got so distracted by his friendly and attractive bodyguard that I didn't even notice he was getting seasick.

"You should stay out here," I say as they head for the cabin. "I'll get you some water, but it'll pass faster if you can see the horizon."

He looks miserable, all his bravado wiped away, but he hunches down on a bench while I go to get him something to drink.

We don't bother with sightseeing. David stays down on the main deck, and I drive from inside the cabin. Fortunately, the wind blows away the scent of puke, but I wince every time we hit a wave harder than I mean to. I radio the lodge letting them know our VIP is under the weather, and there's a whole troop of them waiting on the dock for us when we pull in, with Harper at the head of the line.

"Oh, Mr. Morgan," she says as David helps his employer off the boat. "I'm so sorry. Did everything not go well on your expedition?"

I bite back a snort because what we did was barely a morning out, much less an expedition, but I'm supposed to be playing the concerned guide here.

"It's fine," David says. He glances once at me. "Seasickness is no one's fault."

Harper is watching me with pursed lips that say she disagrees. Well, she can certainly do that, but how was I supposed to know? There's probably a lecture coming my way about guest care standards, but for now, she follows David and Mr. Morgan up the dock still offering apologies, and I'm left to hose down the boat.

Unfortunately, even cleaning up puke doesn't take as long as I want it to, and pretty soon it's midafternoon, and I once again have nothing to do. This is both the easiest and most boring job I've ever had. I kind of want to wander to the resort and see if David's looking for something to do. We were having a nice time up until the end.

Instead, I gather up the sandwiches and other food we never got around to eating and carry them inside to the staff dining room. It's mostly empty when I walk in, but Marci is there as I set the tray down.

"Hey!" She hops up, putting down the book she'd been reading. "How did it go?"

I glance around, half expecting that she's speaking to someone else, but the only other person in the room is a man whose name I don't know but I think works in housekeeping. He's got a pair of big headphones on and pretty obviously doesn't want to be disturbed. I should get a pair of those.

"Uh, not bad," I say.

"What's he like?" She roots through the plate of food, grabbing a bunch of carrot sticks and a sandwich overflowing with soggy-looking vegetables like eggplant and zucchini.

"Who?" I ask.

"You know." She drops her voice because she no doubt is

also waiting for the ghost of Harper to appear and tell us to stop gossiping. "*Him.*"

"Mr. Morgan?" I say, and Marci nods eagerly. She sits down and bites into her sandwich like we're settling in for a long chat, but I only shrug. "He's okay. I dunno. I think people like that have forgotten how to interact with normal people, you know?"

She looks disappointed. "What did you talk about?"

"Not much. He spent most of the time on his phone."

It's funny. If we'd avoided the whole seasickness thing, I'd have told her what an utter asshole he is, but he looked so terrible by the end, it's hard to be mean to him now.

"Oh." Marci sets down her sandwich, picking at a slice of eggplant. "Well, that's not nearly as much fun as I wanted it to be."

"Sorry to disappoint you. He's another rich guy who wants a swanky vacation without having to give up any conveniences."

Okay. Maybe I don't feel that bad about him after all. I grab a sandwich—it looks like roast beef, and I can deal with that—and head out of the staff room. I'm back to resenting being here, so my idea about keeping an eye out for David feels like a bad one. We both may be doing a job, but he's still a guest, and I can't expect him to spend time with me just because I'm looking for something to do.

9

DAMIAN

EXTRA*tainment Exclusive!*
DAMIAN MARSHALL HITS THE BEACH IN IBIZA

Escaping growing rumors that he's come to a crossroads in his career, Hollywood's favorite leading man Damian Marshall is reportedly staying at an exclusive villa in Ibiza. The Spanish island known for its celebrity-watching and nightclub scenes may seem like an unusual choice for a star trying to keep a low profile, but Marshall has frequented Ibiza in the past. He is believed to be staying at a vacation home belonging to model and actress Savannah Blake with whom Marshall shared an onscreen kiss in The Outlerlands. *Could this be the start of a new romance for the perennially single star?*

————

SO THAT WAS NOT FUN. Vin's got some kind of uberseasickness. He throws up for another hour after we get back inside. I try to keep an eye on him at first, but after a while even I'm starting to feel queasy. Every time I get halfway out of his room though, Vin makes sad puppy noises that end in more retching. I wind up lying on a lounger outside on his balcony, scrolling through news sites and looking at the latest bogus stories about me.

Apparently, I'm in Spain. I hope Savannah doesn't mind the imposition. She was fun to work with, but we aren't nearly so close that I'd ever feel comfortable showing up unannounced. Still, Ibiza would be better than sitting here wincing every time Vin rushes back to the bathroom with a hurried slam of the door.

But this is what friends are for, I guess.

And really, I owe him. Things had been going so well right up until Vin lost his breakfast. Jack had bought into the Mr. Morgan persona hook, line, and sinker, and I could be . . . Well, I don't know if I was being totally myself, but it felt closer to who I think I am than any other version of me has felt in a while. Jack's either completely oblivious, or he needs to come back with me to California, because he's the best actor I've ever met.

And now I'm stuck out here like a princess in a tower, waiting for her handsome fisherman to rescue her, and instead all I've got is Vin, who finally emerges late in the afternoon looking shaky but human. He's wrapped up in a Wild Eagle monogrammed robe that's so fluffy it practically swallows him, and he's gingerly sipping a bottle of sparkling water. He sits down at the edge of the lounger, then pouts and squirms until he's snuggled up against my chest.

"We need a blanket," he says, shivering.

"You should go back inside," I say, wiping his hair away from his forehead. His skin is clammy, and he smells vaguely of sweat. Later, he's going to be humiliated that I saw him like this.

"No. Fresh air is good." He sighs and nestles in farther. I'm aware of how intimate the pose is, and to the outside world, it would raise all kinds of questions, but I can honestly swear nothing is going on with us and never has. Well, there was that one time not long after we first met when we both sneaked into a premiere party because Vin knew one of the guys working security. We got completely wasted and made out in our tiny apartment when we got home. The morning after was hella awkward when we both admitted we had zero chemistry without alcohol to help us along.

But aside from that, there's nothing romantic going on between us. Vin's a great friend, sounding board, and partner in crime. Nothing more.

"I'll call Ivy in the morning," he says.

"What for?" I ask.

"She'll find us somewhere else to stay. Somewhere that isn't . . ." He burps softly. "Floating."

Twenty-four hours ago, the idea of leaving was pretty much everything I wanted. Going back to California. Pretty much anywhere with a reliable cell signal so I could torture myself by refreshing social media and news feeds, looking for any new headlines with my name in them.

Now, though . . .

"We don't have to go," I say. When Vin looks up at me with a confused frown, I continue quickly. "I mean, obviously if you're not feeling better, we'll have to talk about it. But you were okay yesterday, right?"

"I guess."

"Weren't you?" I'm not a complete asshole. If he's been putting on a brave face over his queasy stomach since we landed, that's not fair to him.

"Yes. No. I mean, yeah, I was fine." He sits up, squinting at me. "But I thought you hated it here."

That was yesterday. Today, I got to spend a few hours with someone who treated me like a human being instead of a hero or a commercial asset. Anywhere else we go, it'll be all the usual bowing and scraping or the steely professionalism that leaves me feeling isolated.

"I want to stay. If nothing else, the views are nice."

Vin laughs softly. "Yeah, I saw you checking out the views earlier."

Clearly he's feeling better. "I have no idea what you're talking about." I push him away so I can stand up and go to the balcony, trying to create some space between me and my lies.

He swoons backward into the cushions I abandoned, draping a fluffy arm over his forehead dramatically. "Oh, Jack. Tell me more, Jack. Please hold my rod, Jack. Is it too tight, Jack? It's so big, Jack."

"Shut up!" My face feels like it's on fire.

Vin pouts. "You were so adorable, making puppy eyes at the big, strong fisherman."

I'm struck with equal parts horror and excitement because if Vin noticed, maybe Jack did too? And if he did, he certainly didn't seem bothered by it. Unless his openness was more professional courtesy than actual interest.

God, being with him, even talking fish for a couple of hours . . . I could get addicted. Half the news sites say I'm hiding a substance abuse problem anyway. Why not make Jack my drug of choice? It doesn't hurt that he's easy to look at, but beyond that, I want more time with him. He can explain to me the different kinds of bait he uses or how to tell where the best fishing spots are. I really don't care as long as he'll let me be David with him.

Like he knows what I'm thinking—because he almost always does—Vin says, "He really has no idea who you are, does he?"

"Nope." Something like excitement rushes over me.

"So when are you going to tell him?"

And because even after all these years I still think I can outsmart Vin, I ask, "Tell him what?"

He folds his hands into his sleeves like a Jedi. "Damian."

"Why do I need to tell him?"

"Uh, because we're adults, and it's the adult thing to do?"

I hate it when he gets all mature and shit.

"What does it matter? It's fishing."

"Uh-huh." He sips his fizzy water with a knowing smirk.

"It is," I insist. "We're here for twelve more days, and then we go back to LA. If he thinks I'm a bodyguard named David and doesn't talk to me like the sun shines out of my ass or ask me about Cannes every ten minutes, what's the harm?"

"The harm is that you think it feels real, and it isn't. You're playing another role."

I stride up and down the length of the balcony. "So now you're a psychologist on top of everything else?"

"Well, one of us needs our head on straight, and apparently it's not you."

"Look." I hold my hands up. "As long as it's only fishing, I'm not saying anything, okay? If it starts heading anywhere else though, I'll come clean. Does that work for you, oh wise teacher?"

He arches an eyebrow. I really don't want to fight with him about this. Finally, he jabs an accusatory finger at me. "I'm not going back out on that boat."

"That's fine." Suits me better actually. The Mr. Morgan ruse would only work for so long with Vin there in person.

"Which means you have to keep your promise like a big boy without mummy watching over your shoulder."

"You're too self-involved to be anyone's mother," I say, rolling my eyes.

"But you'd like Jack to be your daddy, wouldn't you?"

First thing I'm doing when I get back to LA is finding new friends.

———

THE FOLLOWING morning starts off with the unexpected whir of the electronic lock on my door.

"Hey! I'm okay. I don't need housekeeping." I struggle to sit up, still half asleep.

"Oh, come on. It's me." Vin pushes into the room with a sunny grin on his face. It is, unfortunately, the only sunny thing going on. It's raining outside. Big fat drops of water splash onto the balcony, which is already more puddles than planks.

"How did you get a key to my room?" I ask.

"Ivy authorized it," Vin says. "Now come on, get up."

Oh, I'm up. I leap out of bed and tackle him, wrestling until I can grab the extra key card from him. He squawks a protest, but he doesn't try to get it back.

"I take it you're feeling better?" I ask.

He was already mostly recovered last night, but we took it easy, ordering room service and playing pool in a games room we found on the second floor. Vin hates playing pool. He says his arms aren't long enough. I still let him win half the time.

"Better, because I have proof that Hollywood has not forsaken you." He holds out a telltale envelope. It's weird to see it here out of its usual context. Normally, it comes with a guy in sunglasses who sits in my front hall, waiting for me to read it before he takes it back and disappears in an inconspicuous car.

"Is it the script for *Shadow League 5*?" I ask, suddenly very awake and reaching for the envelope. I don't care if it's as bad as the last movie. It's a sign that things are about to get better.

"I don't know," Vin says, sitting at the edge of the bed. "I got a call from the desk saying it had arrived. Oh, and there was a note." He holds out another smaller envelope. On it, written in blue ink, are the words *read me first*.

Well, that can't be good. When Roberta sends me scripts while I'm on location, they never come with a disclaimer.

Dread fills me as I hold my hand out, and Vin places the second envelope in it.

"Did she really fly this all the way out here?" I ask as tear it open.

"More like she emailed it to the hotel, they printed it off, and wrote the note by hand for authenticity."

In fact, the handwriting on the note is not Roberta's. And it's short. All it says is *Just think about it. They want you for Joe.*

I have a bad feeling about this. I already have a role in *Shadow League*, and his name's not Joe.

I flip through the script. Joe is not on the first page, but sometimes they like me to make an entrance, so they gave it a scene or two before they introduce my character. I keep flipping. Not in the second scene. But there he is in the third. In fact, Joe is—

He is—

I drop the script. It hits the floor with a solid thunk.

"What?" Vin asks.

"This is a joke, right?"

"What is?"

"Have you read this?" I point at the paper on the ground.

"No. What is it?"

"It's—it's—" It's insulting. No, it's a dare, and that's the worst part of it all. "Did you know she was sending this?"

"I don't even know what it is." Vin collects the dropped pages and glances down at the cover. "*Beloved Cove*. That's a terrible title. Who wrote it? Anyone good?"

I might have glanced at the writer's name, but I've already forgotten it because it doesn't matter. I won't be doing this film.

"Tell Roberta to go fuck herself." She probably sees it as some kind of image rehabilitation, but sitting here in exile, it feels manipulative.

Vin makes a strangled noise. "I don't think that's in either of our best interests. I like being alive too much."

"Then I'll do it." I grab my phone from the nightstand, but I only have enough time to see I still have no reception before Vin yanks it out of my hand.

"What are you doing? You can't call her right now. Not like this."

"Then you call her. Tell her I'm not taking it. What happened to the formula? I'll stay up here for the rest of the year if I have to, but she can't make me do this."

"Why?" Vin flips quickly through the pages.

"Scene three." I slump onto the sectional sofa around the fireplace.

Vin's gaze flicks over the page. He reads a second, then a third, which is farther than I got.

He laughs—the fucker—and flips one more page. "This is actually really funny. I think I've read this before somewhere. Or something like it."

"It's ridiculous. She can't seriously want me to consider it."

"I think you'd be great at it."

"What?" I lift my head off the back of the sofa to glare.

"I mean, a rom-com would be a departure, but maybe that's what you need. In Roberta we trust, right? She wouldn't steer you wrong."

"I can't."

Vin snorts. "I mean, you're not Sir Laurence Olivier, but I think your range can handle this."

"It's—" I swallow the words. Vin will be pissed if I say it out loud.

And of course, because Vin knows me better than anyone, he narrows his eyes and sits uncomfortably close to me. "It's what?"

I shudder. Time for the lecture. We're literally trapped in a floating hotel that requires a tin can plane to reach civilization. Even if I don't tell Vin now, I can't avoid it forever. Better to rip off the Band-Aid.

"It's the gay best friend."

Vin gasps, hand on his chest. "Do not splatter your internalized homophobia all over me."

"Internalized—"

"It's the twenty-first century. No one cares if you're gay."

"I—" I swallow. I might legitimately be sick over this. This reaction, the way I've hidden behind the persona I created for myself since coming to LA, is not something I'm proud of. At first, it had been a can-neither-confirm-nor-deny sort of thing. I was trying to keep my options open. I even had one potential agent—not Roberta—tell me I'd never get the kind of roles I wanted if I was public about my sexuality. I told him to go fuck himself, but the advice stuck with me, especially after the first rumors about *Shadow League* being interested in me started floating around. I am the face of the most successful (until recently anyway) and most hypermasculine movie franchise in the world. I have action figures, for God's sake. Everyone knows me or wants to know me, and judges everything from the way my hair is done for interviews to how many times I'm seen eating at the same restaurant. If I was out publicly, the way I'm perceived by everyone from producers and directors to the media to the fans would change. Pair that knowledge with a closeted childhood and adolescence in a small rural town and it would be a big hurdle to get over.

Vin sits back down next to me, head on my shoulder. "Honey. It'll be okay. I promise. Step into the light."

I sigh. So unfair. Straight actors take gay roles all the time. Some of them even win Oscars for it. Taking the part Roberta is suggesting won't out me.

But she wouldn't have sent it if she wasn't trying to send a message along with it. It's clearly time for a change—but is it because it's the right choice, or because she can't salvage *Shadow League* and we have to get ahead of it and make it look like it was my idea?

"Fucking Anderson," I mutter because he's the reason any of this is happening. Somehow he's got all the power, and I'm left doing damage control.

Vin reaches between us, pulling my head down so my cheek rests against the stiff swirl of his hair. The product he uses smells like pineapple, which never seems out of place in California but is so strange in our cedar and fur surroundings.

I make an unhappy sound, and Vin presses a finger to my

lips, shushing me. "You don't have to make a decision today. About Anderson or about the script. But I'm also not calling Roberta until you've slept on it. And read it. The whole script. It's been a while since you did a comedy. You might like it."

I kiss his pineapple-scented hair. "You're an amazing gay best friend."

He pats my cheek. "Honey, I am the best kind of any best friend. Now, what do you want to do today?"

"We're going fishing."

"No." He groans. "Did you miss the part where I spent yesterday afternoon turning my insides into my outsides?"

"They've got to have pills for motion sickness around here somewhere," I say.

"But it's raining." Vin points at the window where the world is all misty gray. But the puddles on the balcony are still, with not a single raindrop rippling their surface.

"Not right now."

"Damian." He slumps his shoulders as he whines, and I get it. If I were him, I would be reluctant to get back on the boat after yesterday too, but I want to see Jack. Want to have conversations with him about fish and mountains and whatever else he wants to talk about.

Vin purses his lips but finally flicks an irritated hand at me. "Fine. Go."

"You're not coming?"

He laughs. "Not in a million years. I'm staying in the hotel until the plane comes to take us home."

Well, shit. Now I feel like a dick leaving Vin behind, but he must see it on my face, because he puts a hand on my shoulder. "I have a bunch of stuff to do for Roberta anyway. But here." He presses the paper to my chest. "If you're spending the day hiding from your problems, at least take the script. Get Jack to read the sides with you or something."

"He won't want to read a script with me."

Vin purses his lips and arches an eyebrow. He pushes the pages at me harder, like if he keeps going, they'll stick to my body.

Finally, I sigh. "Okay. I'll take it." Maybe I'll let it conveniently blow overboard. But Vin would get the front desk to print off another copy and make me read it in front of him.

Whatever. Time to find Jack and pretend my problems don't exist.

10

JACK

You can tell Mr. Morgan really isn't here for the fishing because days like today are great for it, especially if he wants to try something closer to shore. The rain keeps the waves down, which will help his seasickness.

But by nine o'clock, there's still no sign of anyone on the dock. Even Harper has stayed inside. I clean out my coffee pot on the *Hawk*, make sure all the hatches and lockers are closed, and I'm about to pull my hood up when motion catches my eye.

David is walking toward me, hunched in his puffy parka, hands stuffed into the pockets.

"Is that really the only coat you brought with you?" I ask.

He huffs a single laugh. "They said I was leaving for Alaska in twenty-four hours. I forgot it's not winter here all the time."

"Really?"

"I mean, I've never been up here. I guess I thought—"

"No," I cut him off. "I meant is that really how your job works? They say 'we're leaving in twenty-four hours' and you pack a bag?"

He glances down at me, brow furrowing like he doesn't understand the question, before he finally shrugs and says,

"Rich people. You know how they are. They tell us to jump, and we say how high."

I laugh. "Yeah, fair enough. My brother-in-law comes and goes whenever he wants, even though it's a hassle for my sister and their son. No consideration. Thinks he's the most important person in the world."

"Right." David clenches his jaw and I make a mental note to stop talking about Graham. He doesn't deserve the airtime anyway, and David doesn't want to hear about my family's problems. "So are we going fishing or what?"

"Oh." I glance toward the hotel. I didn't get any specific marching orders from Harper this morning. No one's been by with trays of sandwiches or gourmet snacks. "What about your boss?"

"He gave me the day off. He's staying in bed to mope about embarrassing himself in front of the staff yesterday, so I'm free to do what I like." He steps down onto the boat, and really, who am I to argue with him? He may not be *the* VIP, but he's still a guest, and if he wants to go out for a few hours, I can't really tell him no. But I must make a face or something, because he laughs and asks, "What?"

"Not knocking your day off or anything, but that proves my point. He buys the whole lodge out because he's pissed at his husband and then doesn't use any of the amenities, even though there's a whole staff waiting to do things for him."

David laughs again, but he doesn't sound as amused this time. "I guess you're right."

I still probably shouldn't be talking down his boss though. Inevitably, it'll get back to Harper and I'll have hell to pay. "Make yourself comfortable."

"Where are you going?" he asks when I put a hand on a piling and step up to the dock.

"Just going to get a few supplies. Sit tight."

He doesn't say anything else as I hurry off to the hotel to

stock up. Bait from the fridge in the recreation supply room. A dry pair of socks from my room—then a second pair because I didn't notice what kind of shoes David was wearing, but I can almost guarantee they'll be soaked through by the time we head home. A loaf of bread and some smoked salmon—I try to ask for deli meat but the cook looks insulted at the very idea—from the kitchen. I stop in the recreation office to let Luis know we're heading out, but there's no one around.

The drizzle has started again as I head down to the boat. David's gone inside to stay dry, but he re-emerges when I approach. He's traded the parka for one of the Wild Eagle slickers again, and he makes no complaints as I hand down the bucket of gooey bait. He helps me shove off from the dock and settles onto one of the benches in the cabin as I turn us out toward the open ocean.

The water's a bit choppy as we head out, so I stick closer to shore. David doesn't seem to mind though.

"You don't get seasick?" I ask.

"Nah. Iron constitution." He wraps his knuckles against his stomach. He's taken off the slicker, and it's the first time I've seen him without a coat on. He's wearing a long-sleeved Henley that hugs his shoulders and broad chest, and the material stretches nicely as he touches it.

I pull us farther away from land, pushing the engine to keep us on top of most of the chop. David leans into the thrust, tipping his head back, and I have to swallow to clear my suddenly dry throat.

During staff orientation, they let me take the boat out for a day to scope out potential spots to bring guests. Of course Harper had a checklist of things to look for. Great fishing grounds, obviously, but also things like "views of the mountains," which is pretty much everywhere here, and "a beach fit for a picnic," which turned out to be easier said than done since the shorelines here are often marshy, and "good places to see wildlife," like I'm some kind of moose or bear whisperer that can conjure them up on a whim because someone like Mr. Morgan has had enough of fishing and wants to see what else Alaska has to offer.

But while I was exploring, I found a bay that pretty much had all three, along with some decent fishing. It was farther out than my checklist said I was supposed to go with guests, and it was past dark by the time I got back to the lodge, which earned me a lecture about guest safety and sticking to the schedule because apparently when there were actually guests to ferry around, my delay would have forced chef Marc-André to recook his caviar soufflé after the first one had fallen before anyone was ready to eat it. I may have said something about people not coming here for his damn soufflé, which earned me an extended conversation the next morning about making sure guests had a "cohesive" Wild Eagle experience.

But today it's me and David. If I go faster than I normally would, he doesn't seem to notice, and what Harper doesn't know won't hurt her.

"I shouldn't have said what I did before," David says at one point, pitching his voice over the engines.

"What's that?" I ask.

"About rich people getting what they want because they can."

I shrug. "Your secret is safe with me."

"He's not a bad person though," David says. "It's a weird life. Everyone around him is always saying how great he is, how important he is."

I snort. "Sounds terrible."

David presses his lips together, and I have to remind myself yet again he's still a guest and insulting his boss isn't the best idea.

He says, "I think it's easy to lose perspective when you're surrounded by all those people. Like no matter how hard you try to stay grounded, your view of what's normal shifts, you know?"

I can't say I do, but instead, I smile and say, "Look, if you're worried I'll say something to your boss when we get back, I won't. You keep what I said to yourself and I'll keep your secret too, okay?"

He frowns, lips pressing together. I don't really know what else to say to make him feel better. Finally, he says, "Deal."

"Perfect. We're just two normal guys out looking to fish. No problem."

The rain has stopped again by the time we round the last curve of land, and the bay I've been looking for sits in front of us.

"Oh wow," David says, and I brighten at the way he leans forward in his seat. I bring us in a little way so we're out of the worst of the chop, then kill the motor. Ahead of us, the mountains stretch in a straight blue-black line capped in white where the snow won't melt until deep into the summer. No bears or moose are along the shore, but a line of black murres skim along the water's edge before heading out to the open sea.

"No one else knows about this spot," I say.

"In all of Alaska?" David gives me a wry smile.

"Well." I can't help but smile back. "Maybe a few others. But we're a long way from anything. We get to spend the day exactly how you want to."

"Been a while since I had a day off," he says.

"Yeah?" I say as I set out the rods and bait the hooks. "What do you like to do when you've got some time to yourself?"

David follows me as I work, but it takes a couple more rods before I realize he hasn't said anything. I glance up and he shrugs.

"Guess it's been longer than a while."

"You never have a day off?" I ask.

"I, uh." He scratches at his chin. "Vin and I will go out for brunch sometimes."

"Vin?"

He smiles. "My best friend. He knows all the places that'll give you bottomless mimosas and a quiet table in the back."

"That doesn't sound so bad."

His smile widens. "Must sound pretty fussy for someone who lives up here."

"Nah," I say. "A mimosa's one of those drinks with the umbrellas in it, right?"

David laughs. "It's orange juice and champagne."

Well, any hope I had of not looking like a hick has evaporated. I let the lines out, trying to keep busy so I don't have to look him in the eye.

"You have any family?" I ask.

"No." He backtracks when I glance at him. "I mean, I wasn't born in a lab. I have parents and siblings, but we don't really talk."

"That's too bad."

"Not really," he says flatly, then lets out a long sigh. "They thought I had a choice between them and being gay."

My hands spasm as I set the last rod in its holder, and it nearly tumbles into the water. When I turn my head, David's watching me carefully.

"Being gay isn't a choice," I say.

"No," he says. "So I chose not to see them anymore."

"Guess there was a choice after all." When I straighten again, David's standing next to me, eyes on the shore. I should say something, even to change the subject, but instead I go for honesty.

"My mom was nothing but supportive when I came out. My dad thought being bisexual was some kind of phase. But I've been out since my teens, so I think even he has to admit it stuck."

David laughs. "Dads, right?"

"Yeah." But I'm not thinking about my dad. I'm thinking that David's gay, and we're all alone on this boat, and I'd be kidding myself if I said I wasn't attracted to him. Except nothing can happen. Harper would have my balls. And just because he's gay doesn't mean he's attracted to me too. For all I know, he might be one of those "sorry, I'm not into bi guys" weirdos who always make me want to punch something.

Still, as he grips the rail, it's hard to look away from him. He's back in the yellow rain jacket, but it's easy to see how toned his legs are under his jeans. Even his hands are perfectly tanned and strong.

"So . . ." I say, then realize I was about to say something inane like "What should we do now?" when really, there's nothing to do but wait for the lines. It'll take some time for the bait to stream into the current and bring fish to us, so until then, we're two guys on a boat a few hours from anyone else who knows us.

"Well, what about you?" David asks.

"What about me?"

"What do you do when you're not taking people out fishing?"

Oh. I didn't realize we were going to talk about me. That really wasn't what I was thinking of. And none of it sounds very exciting when David's traveled all over and my idea of a good time is taking apart an outboard motor to figure out why it's smoking.

"I like to spend time with my sister and her son. They moved up from Massachusetts actually." I smile, trying to ignore the awkward feeling that comes with talking about my personal life. "Maybe you know them."

He frowns. "Why would I know them?"

"Because they lived near Boston, and you live in Boston, and . . ." My confidence in what was never a very good joke falters. "You know what, never mind. I—"

"Oh! Oh, right, because—" David says quickly.

"No, it's fine. I was only—"

"No. My fault. I wasn't thinking—"

We trail off at the same time, words drifting out over the water. His gaze is on me, and I'm having a hard time tearing mine away. He's magnetic. I can't say why, but every time he speaks or moves or breathes, I want to know him more.

The boat rocks and I take one stumbling step toward him before I can steady myself. He seems to catch his breath.

Before I can say anything though, one of the reels whines as it spools out.

David laughs softly to himself. "Someone's ready to go."

I can't tell if he's talking about me or the fish.

11

DAMIAN

EXTRAtainment UPDATE!
DAMIAN MARSHALL VANISHES

Damian Marshall, previously reported to be in Ibiza following a public blowout with director Anderson Lind, has vanished. It's now unclear if he was in Spain at all. Since leaving Los Angeles last Thursday, the star has not been heard from or seen officially in several days.

"Mr. Marshall is a private citizen entitled to time to himself" was the official statement from Ivy Sinclair, assistant at Feuerstein Talent, Marshall's agency. No further comment was offered.

———

THIS IS EXACTLY what I needed. The salt air blows away the tension that rode on my shoulders like a demon as I headed out of the lodge earlier.

But in its place is a different kind of tension. The unresolved sexual kind. In his knit cap and flannel shirt, Jack is every inch the rugged bear that usually drives me wild. When he asked me what I like to do for fun, I drew a complete blank. Partly because it's been such a long time since I had a day off that I've forgotten what it is to go out for fun's sake and not because I've been paid to make an appearance or because Roberta says it'll be good for my career. And part of my mental vacancy was because, as I cast back to the years before everyone knew my face, all I could recall were nights out with Vin at gay bars in WeHo. I was a nameless, faceless struggling actor back then, and on more than one occasion I wound up in a bathroom or even going home with a big, strapping bear who would pull my hair and ask me if I liked it rough. I don't remember their names any more than they remember mine, but I remember the pressure and the heat as they pounded my ass or told me to tip my head back so they could fuck my mouth, and it's easy enough to put Jack's face on those memories and imagine what it would be like.

It's weird, I know, and yes, I'm avoiding my issues—and in particular the script that's currently folded into the oversized pocket of my parka—but the way Jack's looking at me as he stumbles toward me says he's feeling the tension too.

Which is why it's such a pain in the ass when one of the fishing rods reels out, and he goes back into business mode, stepping past me to grab for it, watching the tip dip and bob with an air of quiet competence that's as attractive to me as the rest of him.

"What kind of fish do we get here?" I ask.

"Mostly rockfish, I expect," he says, his eyes on the water. His jaw is set, and I can see him on a red carpet, beard neatly trimmed, staring down the cameras as everyone wonders where this strong, attractive man came from. He's got a presence that makes people like him right away. Something about him says you can trust him.

Like I trusted him when I told him I was gay. It's been a while since I've said the words out loud. If he ever finds out who I really am, he could sell my revelation to the media and never have to work again. But for now, he didn't make a big deal out of it, like he hasn't made a big deal out of anything. Because to him, I'm David, and David can be anyone he wants.

And if he wants to flirt with Jack a bit, he can do that too.

Though the way he's so thoroughly unimpressed with "Mr. Morgan" leaves me uneasy. He clearly likes David, but I'm not so sure how he'd feel about Damian.

The fact that I'm talking about myself in the third person is a clear indication how twisted up this is all becoming in my head.

The rod curves, and Jack leans back, gripping it hard.

I whistle softly, trying to focus on the present instead of potential messy what-ifs in the future. "Looks like a big one."

He grunts. "Maybe forty pounds."

I open my mouth to say something quippy but, still distracted, nothing comes. "Is that . . . is that big?"

He grins as he glances at me. "Depends on what you wanna do with it."

Oh, it's going to be like that, is it?

He steps back, holding out the rod. "You take it."

"But—"

"Your vacation. Your catch."

But unlike yesterday, he doesn't move away when I take the rod from him. He gives me enough space so I can stand square against the rail and reel the fish in, but he only leaves a few inches between us. Enough that when the boat rocks, our shoulders brush for a second before we lean away from each other again.

Whatever's on the other end of this line, it definitely feels solid, and for every foot or so I bring in, I have to pause and let the rod go slack again. My shoulders burn.

"Hard work, isn't it?" Jack asks.

"I'm okay." But within minutes, I'm breathing hard, which is embarrassing. I work out every day. I've had contracts specify how much weight I needed to lose or gain for a role. Roberta always strikes that clause out during negotiations, but then I do the diet or change my gym routine to hit the weight anyway. But my standard regime is about looking good shirtless and being able to keep up with the cardio demands of running across the same rooftop a dozen times in a row while the director of photography gets every camera angle he wants.

Reeling in a giant prehistoric fish for what feels like an hour is not on my exercise rotation, but maybe it should be.

"Are you sure I'm doing this right?" My biceps and traps are on fire.

"You're almost there," Jack says.

"Forty pounds," I say. Even my voice is straining now.

He shrugs. "Maybe eighty."

"That's twice what you said before."

"Hard to tell. Water does weird things to guessing how big a fish is."

"Are you fucking with me now?"

He doesn't say anything, but the telltale twitch of his lips practically has me throwing the rod overboard so I can tell him exactly what I think of his sense of humor. It takes two to fuck, so he better be careful what he wishes for. Instead, I manage to twist enough that I can lash out with my foot, nearly connecting with his shin before he dances away at the last minute. His laugh is a big, strong thing that hits me in the gut, and I have to turn back to the rail, not because of the fish I'm now convinced weighs almost as much as I do, but because I'm halfway hard in my jeans, and that's not something Jack needs to know about.

Unless he wanted to . . .

But before I can examine that thought too closely, or worse, say something I'll regret immediately, the rod jumps again in my hand.

"A little help here?"

I lose my grip on the line, and it zings out with a whine. Jack's on me in a second, gripping the rod and tucking the butt of it under my arm pit.

"Hold on tight." His voice is close behind me, and I'm torn between leaning into the rail, even though it's already pressing painfully against my hips, and leaning back against him, even though he hasn't given me permission to do so.

"I'm okay," I say, even though I'm breathing hard as I start to bring in the line again.

"You got it?" His hand is on my elbow, and my heart's beating fast.

The rod bows, and I nod shakily. "Yeah. I'm good."

"Okay. Just let me know if you need anything."

God, do I need him. I didn't know when Roberta said I was being sent away how badly I needed someone like Jack. Someone who would talk to me like a human being. Someone who doesn't want anything from me. It's too bad he'd feel differently if he knew who I really was, but for now, I'll take the break I can get and go back to being Damian when Roberta says the coast is clear.

Oblivious to all of this, Jack's standing just beyond my shoulder giving careful, patient instructions.

"There you go. Keep the rod out or you'll snap the line. Take your time. He'll try to outsmart you."

"He's a fish," I say through gritted teeth.

"He's basically a dinosaur." Jack gives me a knowing wink when I glare at him.

Finally, a flash of white appears beneath the surface of the water. Jack whistles softly as he leans over the side to get a better look.

"He's also a big boy," he says appreciatively.

"Rockfish?" I ask, throwing my whole body backward to gain some ground as the fish struggles to escape.

"No. Halibut. We don't usually see them this big so close to shore. Your license won't let us pull it in."

"Why not?" I feel like I've been through the toughest boot camp of my life. Seriously. Guys trying to bulk up for a shoot should skip the gym and come fishing for a few days.

"We're only allowed to fish big halibut in designated areas up here, and this isn't one of them."

"So this has all been for nothing?" Despite my mounting disappointment, I'm still reeling. The fish is huge, easily four or five feet long. It's dark green and spotted, and it glares at me with bulbous eyes like it's really pissed off I've interrupted its meal.

"If you want to take a picture or anything, now's the time to do it," Jack says.

And yet again, his offer only reminds me how utterly normal all of this is to him. If I were a tourist looking for a few days of fishing, of course I'd want a picture, and that's exactly how Jack is treating me. I want to bathe in his disinterest, and the desire makes me wonder if being Damian Marshall has been worth it all these years. I got the career I wanted but had to become someone else to do it. The question leaves me uncomfortable.

"I think I left my phone at the hotel," I say.

The fish is alongside the boat, its giant fin rippling just at the water's surface.

"Hold on to that rod," Jack says as he pushes me gently to one side and leans over to the water. He's got a pair of solid-looking bolt cutters, and he grabs hold of the long hook extending from the fish's mouth with a confident hand while he cuts the fish free.

We stand quietly for a minute, watching the dark shape slowly descend back into the ocean. I'm still breathing hard, and I really would love nothing more than a massage right now. I'm about to make a crack about whether or not that's part of Jack's job description when, very softly, he says, "Look."

I glance up, and at the edge of the forest ahead of us, a rock moves. Except it's not a rock. It's a hump of brown fur the size of a compact car, until it raises its head, showing off two round ears and a square snout, and I swear I can hear the thing grunt even though we're more than a hundred yards away.

"Whoa," I say as the bear makes its way through the tall grasses.

"Looking for a snack," Jack says.

I glance at him, but his face is perfectly neutral, so I bite down the joke about how I'd let the right bear eat me up any day.

"Shouldn't it be hibernating or something?" I ask.

"You really do think it's winter twelve months of the year up here, don't you?" His eyes positively twinkle, and it really isn't fair for him to have a skill like that while I'm trying to behave myself.

"No." I fidget, trying to think of a comeback. If only Vin could see me now. I'm practically scuffing my feet on the deck like a teenager with a crush. I don't know if he'd tell me he's proud of me or be too embarrassed to associate with me ever again.

"They don't have bears in North Dakota?" Jack asks. Does he take a step closer to me, or is it the motion of the boat bringing us together? On the shore, the bear lumbers back into the woods.

"Oh, they have bears," I say, fighting not to lick my lips and give the game away. "Big ones." My dad had one skinned and laid out in the living room. A couple others were more like baby bear cubs in training who let me suck their dicks behind the bleachers after wrestling practice.

Speaking of lips, have Jack's always been that pouty? Is he doing something different? Does he even know he's doing it?

His knuckles graze mine, and part of me feels the thrill of excitement that comes when I know someone wants to kiss me. The other part of me tells me to behave myself, because whether he knows it or not, I'm the guest, and Jack is the employee, and if one of us winds up wearing the fallout from any shenanigans we get up to, it's him. But that part is being drowned out by the first, which is arguing very loudly that we're hours from the hotel, so who would know if fishing leads to kissing?

"David," Jack says, and his voice has gone rough.

"Uh-huh," I say, and it's so weird and so good to hear him use that name. My real name. I close my eyes.

Then he spits on me.

"Wha—" I start to say as my lids fly open again. Another drop of water splashes on my nose. Then another. And another. None of them are coming from Jack. All of them are coming from the sky. And about a million more follow immediately, descending with a sound like deafening static.

"Oh no," Jack says, and I can't tell if he's disappointed Mother Nature ruined our first kiss or pissed at the way the water is running down the insides of his jeans like I am, because trust me, it is not a fun feeling.

The moment's gone. We run back into the cabin, feet slipping on the deck as the water pummels us. We're laughing, and I'm shivering, and I'm so glad Vin's not here, because his cashmere would be toast by now.

"Here." Jack opens a cabinet and pulls out a fluffy towel with the hotel's logo monogrammed on it. He takes one for himself, burying his face in it, which leaves me a moment to admire the way his clothes cling to his body—arms, shoulders, thighs—before I have to wipe my face off too or he'll catch me staring.

As I come up for air—marginally dryer than I was a second ago—I have to project to be heard over the downpour going on around us.

"Do you think it'll rain long?"

Jack's squinting through the window. The mountains and the shore have disappeared. Everything is gray.

"Probably long enough. We should head back to the lodge." He goes to the magic cupboard again and this time, instead of towels, pulls out a couple of gray sweatshirts and passes one to me. "I can't do anything about your pants, but a dry shirt will help. And I've got dry socks around here somewhere. Sorry the rest of our trip was ruined."

"No, it's fine. It was great. We saw a giant fish and a bear. It was totally worth it for—" The end of my sentence gets cut off when Jack tugs his soaking wet sweater and the shirt underneath off and over his head.

Yup. Totally worth it for the bear.

He's broad and strong. Hairy belly. Muscular arms that have nothing to do with a personal training plan. They don't grow them like this in Hollywood. He turns as he pulls the dry shirt over his head, and even his back has a dusting of hair on it that would get him kicked off a shoot and sent straight to the aestheticians, but all I want to do is press myself against it and cuddle into him.

Jack sits on one of the benches, removes his boots, and glances up like he can't smell the hormones pouring off me like a rainstorm.

"What's wrong? Doesn't it fit?"

I'm still clutching the shirt to my chest, and now there's a wet spot along one side because I'm basically a human puddle. Ninety-nine percent water and lust. That's me.

I pretend I'm on set as I pull my shirt off. It's only awkward the first ten or so times. Then you get used to the rush of cold air and stop blushing when a grip somewhere beyond the camera lets out a low whistle. I struggle into the dry one with no finesse at all, and I'm annoyed when I finally get my head clear and Jack's rummaging under the console, because apparently my striptease was unworthy.

Until he turns around and hands me a pair of woolly socks that practically make me moan.

"Are extra socks a standard part of my VIP package?" I ask.

Jack peels his own socks off without looking at me. "I'm glad your boss isn't here. He could probably fit both feet in one of my socks."

And my brain goes off on another cosmic voyage as I think about that tidbit of information. These are *his* socks? I unroll them and yup. They're huge. You know what they say about a man with big feet.

Jesus, I should throw myself at him and be done with it. Would be less painful than this waiting and hoping he feels the same pull I do.

But he's all business as he gets the boat's motor going. "You sit tight," he says, and that doesn't sound like a pickup line. It sounds like he wants me out of the way.

The rain has lessened some as we pull away from his fishing spot, but it's still coming down hard enough that there's no question of us staying. I'm sorry for that. Whether he was flirting or toeing the line of friendly professionalism, I was having a good time.

My heavy coat swings on the hook where I stowed it this morning. The big envelope sticks out of one pocket, beckoning me. Time to come back to the real world where I have a career to think about.

Except a banging noise from outside makes us both jump. Jack swears as he glances over his shoulder.

"What's wrong?" I ask.

"I left one of the lockers open."

"Want me to go close it?"

"No, you'll get wet all over again. Come take the wheel."

"You want me to drive the boat?"

"It's not hard." He steps aside like he did when he handed the fishing rod off to me. "Just like driving a car. Hands at ten and two and keep us going straight. I'll only be a minute."

Sure. Sure, I can do this. I drove a speedboat through the canals of Venice in a high-speed chase. I can drive a fishing boat in a straight line with nothing around us but water.

There's a spatter of rain on the back of my neck as Jack opens the cabin door, but it doesn't last long before he closes it again. I try to watch him, but I have to twist my whole body, and the boat veers off course for a second. Jack has to grab hold of a rail to keep from falling, and I mouth "Sorry" before I turn my attention back to the water ahead of us.

A particularly big wave rolls up, crashing over the front as the boat slams down so hard I nearly bite my tongue. The impact jars me all the way up my legs into my hips and back. With one hand on the throttle, I glance over my shoulder. Should I slow down? Jack said to keep going, but—

Where is Jack?

The rear section of the boat isn't particularly spacious. It has a lot of gear, but a big guy in a rain jacket shouldn't be that hard to see.

"Jack?" I say, even though he would never hear me from in here.

I slow the boat down as my heart beats faster than the drum of raindrops overhead. We rock in the churning water, but at least we're a long way from anything, so I don't have to worry about where we drift as I throw the cabin door open and stumble outside.

A long leg extends from the other side of the benches and lockers.

"Jack!"

But the only answer I get is a soft moan.

12

JACK

Well, this is embarrassing. Here I'm supposed to be the experienced guide, and now I'm lying on my back staring straight up at a ceiling of dark gray clouds while the rain tries to drown me, and I can't seem to bring together the where-withal to get out of the way.

"Jack?" David appears, and he at least blocks some of the rain. "Are you okay?"

"Slipped." My voice is hoarse. We hit a wave and the damn thing knocked me off my feet.

David manages better and gets the locker door secured.

"Can you sit up?" he asks, looking concerned.

"Yeah. Just banged my elbow on the way down."

Except I still can't seem to move.

"Jack?"

"Yeah?" I blink and turn my head so I can see David more clearly.

"Oh God." He reaches down, and when he touches my temple, it burns.

I hiss. "What's that?"

"You're bleeding."

"I am?" I touch the throbbing place, and my fingers come away slick and red. "Shit. Must have hit my head too."

"Can you move?" David asks.

"Yeah." Finally, my limbs remember they have a job to do. "I'm just stunned."

The embarrassment gets worse as David helps me sit up. We're both soaked again. I only did up a couple of snaps on my jacket, thinking I wouldn't be out here long, and he doesn't have a coat on at all.

"New boat like this shouldn't be so slippery," I say. All that fresh decking. Lots of surfaces for me to catch onto, and yet here we are.

"We'll bring it up when we get back to the lodge." David loops one of my arms over his shoulder and hoists me up with a grunt.

"I'm fine," I say, but it's actually hard to make my feet go in a straight line, and I can't tell if it's the bobbing boat or the head injury.

Inside the cabin, David helps me sit down on one of the benches.

"I don't suppose you've got any more dry clothes?"

"In the cabinet over there," I say, wincing when I try to motion with my chin and my whole head pounds instead. "No more socks though."

He gives me a dark smile, but he goes digging until he finds a couple more sweatshirts. And to think I rolled my eyes when Luis said there were clothes stocked in the dry locker as well as a first aid kit beneath the sink in the boat's small bathroom.

David doesn't even look at me as he sits down so our knees are touching. He grabs the hem of my wet shirt. "Lift up your arms."

"I can undress myself."

"I don't want you to knock that cut more than we have to."

He's got a point, because it still stings like a son of a bitch as the collar rides over my skin. There's a red smear down the side of the shirt, and David glances from it to me before he balls the shirt up and presses it to the side of my head.

"Ow." My eyes water.

"Just hold that there. You're bleeding a lot, but it doesn't look deep."

I do as he says and try to laugh because he looks so worried. "You do a lot of first aid as a bodyguard?"

He glances up at me as he digs through the first aid pack, and the dark shade to his eyes says he doesn't find this funny. Water drips off his hair.

"You should get changed," I say.

"I will in a second." His voice is all business now. He grabs hold of my chin and turns my head. "Look that way."

I can't see what he's doing, but the wrestling of wrappers says he's found what he's looking for. I curse at the cold sting of alcohol as he dabs at my head.

"Sorry. I need to see how far it goes."

"So you can what?" I ask. "Stitch me up?"

He presses at the side of my head. His lips are still thin as I turn back to look at him.

"Will I live?" I ask.

"I put some Steri-Strips on it to try to stop the bleeding." He holds up my ruined shirt. "But I guess we'll have some explaining to do when we get back."

"Occupational hazard." I'm already feeling better, though goose bumps are raising up on my skin in the cool air of the cabin. I shiver, and David's expression focuses intently on my chest. I let him look. Something happened outside before the rain started. I felt it, and the way he didn't step back from me said he was feeling it too. Risky. But who would know out here?

Finally, he hands me a dry shirt, then turns his back so he can put the other one on.

"How far to the lodge?" David asks.

Good question. The engine is still idling, but we're definitely bobbing in no particular direction. The rain has let up some, so I can at least orient myself against the shore in the distance.

"Couple of hours," I say. "We'll take it a little more carefully until the weather gets better."

David scoots up close to me again, and even if I weren't chilled through, I would still be able to feel the heat radiating off him. He touches the side of my head, apologizing when I flinch.

"Just wanted to make sure they were really stuck down."

The weather doesn't improve. On a clear day, I'd let the engine open up and stick close to shore where we might find some calm spots, but everything is choppy bordering on sloppy, and I don't know this shoreline as well as I would if we were closer to home, so I can't say for sure how far out any shoals and rocks might extend. It's a slow, bouncy ride. My head is killing me. David finds some ibuprofen in the first aid kit, and I down it with one of the sparkling wild berry drinks stored in the cold locker. I nearly throw it all back up because the drink tastes like synthetic cherry, and I hate that.

"Are you okay?" David asks. He's so worried about me he's been leaning against the cabin door just behind my shoulder the whole way, even when I tell him he can sit down.

"Fine."

"You're sure?"

I try to pull up all my hours of Wild Eagle training. The guest comes first. But in truth, the ache that's spreading from my ear all the way over the crown of my head is my priority. "Actually, no. I'm having a hard time concentrating. Can you take the wheel for a bit?"

He leaps up instantly, and I sag down to the bench.

"You're not okay," he says.

"I've had worse. Just need to get off the boat so the world stops moving."

David squares his shoulders and sticks his gaze to the horizon. He's got a mission. He even opens up the throttle a little farther, and the added whine of the engine makes me close my eyes, but I know it'll be worth it when we're back at the lodge and I can lie down.

"Can you—" He clears his throat, and when I open my eyes again, he's watching me with a worried expression. "Can you keep talking though? Or something. Just so I know you're conscious."

"What do you want me to say?"

"I don't know. Tell me about yourself. Have you been anywhere but Alaska?"

"Just to visit my sister when she lived in Boston. And I went to college in Oregon for a year," I say, trying to focus on anything else but my head.

"Really?"

"Yeah. I thought I might be a teacher, but it didn't work out." I spread a palm on the table and force myself to open my eyes. David's alternating between watching me and watching ahead of us like he's afraid if he looks away for too long, I might keel over. "My dad got sick, and I had to come back up here to help out."

"Is he okay?" David asks.

"Yeah. He had prostate cancer and needed about a year of treatment, but he got better. It took a lot out of him, and he's retired now. He'll go out with his buddies, but he doesn't fish commercially anymore."

"And you didn't go back to school?"

I shrug. I had plans. First Oregon, then the rest of the lower forty-eight. Maybe California, maybe Texas. Stef pushes me to go back, but school costs money and time, and I always feel like it'll end in another crisis that drags me back home. "I like fishing. Like being close to my family. My sister started having some problems with her marriage. She left her husband and moved back up here. It seemed easier to stay and work on the boats. I get to spend a lot of time with my nephew. He's great."

I wait for David to argue. Stef's pointed out more than once that I could get my teaching degree in Alaska. But it's not the same. I had a vision. Going south, seeing more of the country. It didn't work out . . . which was what I was trying to explain when I started telling David this whole story.

"So you've never been anywhere else?"

"Not really. I'd like to see Europe one day. Maybe Hawaii." Though all of that assumes my brain stays safely between my ears, and right now it feels a bit touch and go. "What about you?"

"You know. Work keeps me moving all over."

"What's it like?"

He gives me a bleak smile. "I wish I could say, but I don't get the chance to play tourist."

"That doesn't sound like much fun. You don't have one place you'd want to go back to?"

He doesn't say anything to that. He just watches me worriedly as we bounce along the water.

Even with David pushing the engine as much as he's comfortable, it takes a long time to get back. Closer to three hours instead of two. I take over the wheel as we come around the edge of the cove, and they must have known we had a problem, because there's half a dozen staff standing at the end of the dock. I brush the *Hawk* against the boards a little harder than I mean to, and David puts a hand on my shoulder. We stare at each other for a long time before I finally kill the engine.

"We made it," he says.

"Thanks to you."

For a minute, it feels like we're back on the ocean with the bear in the distance and almost no space between us. I have to look like a mess, but I want to ask him if maybe, when I get myself together again, we could see if we can close this distance even more.

"Jack? Jack is everything okay?" Harper's voice cuts through the closed cabin door, killing what might be left of the moment. I go to open the door and stagger halfway there, leaving David to push past me and do what I can't.

"We could use some help," he says.

What follows is a flurry of activity. Harper's in my face asking me over and over if I'm okay and how many fingers she is holding up? I'm ferried into the lodge like I can't get there on my own, no matter how many times I say I'm fine. And honestly, as soon as I'm on solid ground, things get immediately better. The spinning stops, and the pain in my head goes from being a pulsing thing to a steady ache. But Harper won't hear any of it, instead herding me into the staff dining room and shouting orders. Somewhere along the way, David disappears.

It's only after I've had a conversation with a virtual doctor in Anchorage that they leave me alone. The doctor says there's a chance I have a concussion, but short of flying me off the property, she can't confirm. Harper's given instructions on how to monitor me, and even though I swear I'll be okay, she sends me to my room and says she'll be back in two hours to make sure I haven't slipped into a coma.

"It's the middle of the afternoon. I won't be sleeping for hours."

She jabs a finger at me. "You took off with a guest without telling anyone where you were going, and you came back with a head injury. You're lucky I don't ship you out of here."

Hard to argue with that.

But once she's gone, the only things I want to do involve sleeping or leaving this room. I need to go back down to the boat and clean things up. I should find David and make sure he's okay—though why he wouldn't be okay is unclear and maybe related to my nonconcussion. I could go back to the dining room because I'm starving. It's midafternoon, and I haven't had anything to eat since before David and I left this morning.

But there's every chance Harper is standing outside my door waiting for me to sneak out.

I call Stef.

"Hey, what's wrong with your screen?" she asks, instead of "Hi" or "How are you?"

"I don't have the camera on," I say.

"Why not?"

Oh, this was a bad idea. I needed something to distract myself, but this was the wrong solution.

"Because I might have a concussion, and the doctor said to stay away from screens."

"Jack!"

"I'm fine." I slump down at my little desk.

"Turn it on."

"Stef, it's fine. The doctor said—"

"Turn it on. I want to see you."

The glare makes me squint, but when I turn the desk lamp on, it gets easier. Stef leans in so her face gets distorted, and I can see most of her forehead and not much else.

"You look like shit."

"Thanks."

"What happened?"

I tell her. About the rain. The bear. About falling and hitting my head. I leave out most of the details about David. She does the appropriately sisterly thing and laughs her ass off.

"Do you know someone named Morgan?" I ask, mostly to get her to stop howling before Harper comes to see what the noise is.

Stef frowns. "Is that a first name or a last?"

"Last. Some kind of real estate bigwig in Massachusetts."

She shakes her head. "Those aren't really the social circles Graham and I traveled in. It was all doctors and nonprofits. Why? Is he the entitled asshole who made you go fishing in a storm?"

"It wasn't storming when we left." And also, despite all the fuss, I noticed Mr. Morgan wasn't waiting on the dock when we got back. Jerk. "Never mind," I say. "Speaking of entitled assholes, have you heard from Graham?"

She makes an annoyed face. "No, but I ran into Mrs. DeLuca from the public school. She said they need to hire a PE teacher for the fall." The way she raises her eyebrows expectantly makes my head hurt more.

"Stef, I don't have a teaching degree."

"From the way she was talking, I don't think that'll be a problem."

I don't want to have this conversation right now. "How's Robbie?"

We talk for a few more minutes. After we hang up, I sneak out—Harper is nowhere to be seen—and grab some food from the kitchen. My head doesn't hurt as much as before, and I take that as a good sign. Back in my room, I doze for a while until a soft knock comes on my door. Harper, back from wherever, and no doubt checking to make sure I'm not bleeding out of my eye sockets.

"I'm fine," I call.

The knock sounds again, even softer than before, like the knocker can't make up their mind if they should go away or not. Finally, a voice says, "Uh. You have a visitor."

Not Harper. Female, but someone else.

I grunt as I pull myself to my feet. The sleep helped. I pop a couple more ibuprofen on my way to the door.

It's Marci. She's shaking when I open the door. She blinks rapidly and opens and closes her mouth several times.

"What's wrong?"

It takes her a few more tries before she manages to stitch the words together.

"He wanted to see you. Insisted."

"Who?"

She steps aside, moving awkwardly, and a tall shape takes her place.

It's David.

"Hi," I say, blinking as I take him in.

He smiles. "Can I come in?"

13

DAMIAN

EXTRAtainment INVESTIGATES!
WHERE IN THE WORLD IS DAMIAN MARSHALL?

In the case of the disappearing movie star, the mystery remains. Instead of facing his fans and supporters, Damian Marshall has dropped off the map. While rumors swirl, everyone from former co-stars to users on social media has weighed in on the actor's where-abouts. He's been reportedly spotted everywhere from a guerilla fashion show in Tokyo to a Buddhist monastery in Nova Scotia, Canada. But while hearsay abounds, the Marshall camp remains silent.

Anderson Lind, director of the Shadow League *franchise, was one of the last people to see Marshall in public. He says, "I hope wherever Damian is, he's taking the time to look after himself and reflect on his career in Hollywood. This is a tough business, and taking time away can be good for everyone."*

Still, the question remains. Where in the world is Damian Marshall?

———

I TRIED to give him some space. I honestly did. The hotel staff took over as soon as we docked, and I went up to my room, figuring Jack was in good hands. But within thirty minutes, I couldn't sit still. I tried to check some emails but instead wound up on news sites again, reading about the growing media manhunt to determine my whereabouts and Anderson giving fucking soundbites like we're friends. The silver fish on the wall gave me a sympathetic look, like "What can you do?"

I went down to Vin's room, but he was on a call with Roberta, and as soon as she saw me in the corner of the screen, she shouted "Damian! Did you read the script I sent?" and I couldn't get out of there fast enough. I found the fitness center and ran on the treadmill until my legs ached, then sat in the hot tub until my head swam. Vin was still on his call, and even after I'd showered, I couldn't settle.

So I go down to the front desk. The young woman working turns bright red as I walk up to her, and I give her a minute to compose herself before I speak.

"H-Hello," she stammers.

"Hi."

"Can I . . . can I help you?"

And now it's my turn to feel uncomfortable because I'm about to ask for something personal. Not for a custom fishing expedition or a meal made entirely of macrobiotic foods or for someone to redecorate my room using only the color white. Not that I've ever asked for either of the last two, but right now I'm feeling super vulnerable.

"I want to see Jack," I say. She blinks like I've spoken in a language she doesn't understand. "Please. I need to know he's okay."

He scared the shit out of me. When he asked me to take over driving the boat, I half expected him to be dead or at least unconscious by the time we got back to the hotel. And he held it together, but now I'm envisioning him bleeding out slowly somewhere without anyone knowing.

Clearly I've been in too many movies and have lost touch with reality.

"Oh." The woman at the desk looks around uneasily. Her name tag says she's Marci.

"Marci. I'll feel terrible if he's really hurt. I was the one who asked to go out this morning even though the weather was bad. If I could see him to know he's okay, I'll feel a lot better."

Marci's still glancing around like she's worried someone will overhear us. She bites her lip, and finally she says, "I want to play charades."

"I'm sorry, what?" I know all those words, but none of them make sense in context.

She stands up straighter. "I could get in a lot of trouble taking you to see him. Guests aren't allowed in employee areas. So if you want me to show you where he is, I want you to tell Harper that you want to play charades with the staff, and then I want to be on your team."

That . . . I've had stranger requests. And as they go, a party game at a wilderness fishing lodge is far less weird or intrusive than the people who want to hold my hand, or have a piece of my clothing, or keep the plastic cup I drank from while on a panel.

"Why?" Now I'm having visions of her rigging the game so I have to act out something insensitive or incriminating and a video of it will wind up on social media before I've even managed to get back to California.

She smiles. "Because I want you to have the best Wild Eagle experience ever. And I'll never be able to tell anyone, but I'll know I got to act with Damian Marshall, and that's pretty amazing."

I can't tell if she's lying or if her life's ambition is to have me make a fool of myself for her entertainment, but ultimately, I can't really see a huge downside to this.

"Uh . . . sure. I'll make it happen."

Vin's going to hate me. He hates games like that. Mostly because he's super competitive but also terrible at any kind of game with a time limit. He gets stressed and freaks out, and then he gets pissed when he loses.

"Deal." Marci holds out her hand to shake, and I give her my best movie star smile when I take it, just to watch her squirm. She goes bright red again, but she puts out the Back in Five Minutes card on the desk—even though I'm her only guest, so who else needs to know she'll be back?—and motions for me to follow her.

I half expect that when we go through the Staff Only door it'll be like walking around the back of a soundstage where suddenly the world becomes shadows and plywood. But the staff area looks pretty much the same as the rest of the lodge. Maybe less art on the walls, but otherwise it's all familiar. We go past a lounge with a bunch of sofas and a dining room that looks downright welcoming and cozy. A few staff members pass us, but they all keep their gazes down, and Marci says something breezy about me wanting a tour and no one seems to be too bothered about it.

It's only as we reach the last door at the end of the hall that a flicker of nervousness shivers its way through me, and I wonder what I'm trying to accomplish here. But Marci's already knocking, and Jack opens the door, and despite the fact that she was bold enough to demand games from me not five minutes ago, suddenly Marci can't seem to think of anything to say.

Time for me to step up.

"Can I come in?"

Jack moves aside, Marci disappears back up the hall, and I let myself into the room. It's smaller than I would have expected, plainer than the common areas we passed. It's also dim, with the blinds drawn and only one light on at the desk.

"Sorry," I say. "Were you sleeping?"

"It's fine. I'm supposed to be staying awake in case it's a concussion anyway."

"Ouch." One of my co-stars had a similar injury trying to jump from a moving bus to a truck on a shoot a few years ago. It had all been done as safely as possible, but he'd still missed the landing, caught his head on the door frame, and caused the whole film to be shut down for a month and a half while he recovered.

Jack waves his hand though. "I'm fine. The doctor said she didn't think it would be a problem, but Harper's not taking any chances." He washed his face sometime along the way, because the blood that had crusted into his hair and at his temple is gone.

"How's the cut?"

"Good." He smiles. "The doc said whoever patched me up did a good job."

I can't help the way I puff up under his compliment. "Thanks." We don't have to talk about the way my hands shook, and my heart still barely feels like it's slowed down since I found Jack sprawled on the deck.

"You might have to get someone else to take you out tomorrow," he says.

"What? No." The words come too fast.

He arches an eyebrow and sits on the edge of his bed, motioning for me to take the one chair at the desk. "I'm flattered you think so highly of me."

"I do." I flush. "I mean . . . You've been great. And anyway, I think there's some kind of staff game day tomorrow if the weather's still bad." That sounds unimpressive. I stare down at my hands, astonished that I'm lost for words. I can charm my way through any interview. Ad-lib on the busiest red carpets. And yet, ever since Cannes, I feel like I'm always two steps behind. Always playing catch-up and doing damage control. I don't know who I am anymore.

Except when I'm with Jack. He doesn't ask anything from me, and the space it creates around us is intoxicating.

"Was there . . ." I say slowly, trying to choose my words carefully. "Back on the boat, was there like . . . a moment? Did you feel something?"

He's probably going to tell me he felt the rain soak him to the bone and then the jar of every wave I drove us through as I tried to get back.

Instead, he folds his hands in front of him, and says, "Yeah. I think so."

I lean back in my chair, and he watches me with steady eyes. I have to carefully clear my throat before I speak again.

"To be clear. When I say I felt something, I don't mean an overwhelming appreciation for nature and all its bounty."

Jack's lips quirk up. "No. That's not what I meant either."

My ears are flaming. "You want me to say it, don't you?"

He crosses one foot over his knee. "Think I do, actually. Might have a head injury after all. You should probably spell it out for me."

And the crinkle at the corners of his eyes and the knowing twist of his mouth is enough to have me tugging at the collar of my shirt.

"Tension," I say. "Of a sexual nature. Between you and me."

His speculative gaze has me shifting in my seat, subtly making room for the way my dick swells in my pants. The way he tugs his bottom lip between his teeth for a second says he notices, and that doesn't help my situation at all.

"Yeah," he says before he has to clear his throat. "That's what I was thinking too."

"And would you—" I start to say.

"No."

My question screeches to a halt so fast I nearly bite my tongue. "Oh."

He gives me an apologetic smile. "Look, I know you're not the very important VIP. You're not even here because you want to be."

The last few days, things haven't been so bad. But the longer he keeps speaking, the more I want out of this room. I got caught up in my head and some kind of fantasy of what could be between us, maybe even a place where I could tell Jack who I really am and he would be okay with it, but everything coming out of Jack's mouth is the unvarnished truth.

"But you're still a guest," he says, "and Harper's pissed at me already. I can't risk this job. My family is counting on me."

And wow. Doesn't that leave me feeling like a presumptuous asshole?

"I understand." I push up to my feet. "Sorry to have bothered you. I hope you feel better."

"David." He looks unhappy, but even him calling me by the name that's mine but isn't proves how wrong all of this is. I got carried away.

"No, it's okay. I shouldn't have brought it up. Sorry."

He half follows me to the door, or maybe he stands and the room is so small that it feels like he's following when really there's nowhere else for him to go. I don't know, and I don't stick around to find out.

The hall feels as confined as Jack's room did, and I nearly bump into someone halfway back to the main lodge.

"Oh, Mr. Morgan. Are you all right?"

It's Harper. The woman who would fire Jack if she caught us together, and she's too close for comfort.

"Everything is fine." I keep using that word. Nothing is fine. "I got turned around."

"Oh." She turns on her best professional smile, and it's so artificial compared to all the ones Jack has given me that I resent her for it, even though she's literally doing her job. "The main lobby is this way. Let me show you."

I make my escape as soon as plausibly polite and bolt for my room. I need a minute—maybe an hour—alone to get my shit together.

So of course Vin is sitting in the living room.

"Hey, you're back," he says with a distracted wave of his hand.

"How did you get into my room? I took away your key."

He holds up another white key card. "The girl at the front desk gave me another one. I told her you lost yours."

Marci is off my charades team.

"So." Vin folds his hands over the back of the sofa and bats his eyelashes at me. Asshole. "Where have you been?"

"Nowhere," I say too quickly. "Just walking around."

He arches an eyebrow. "Visiting your man?"

"Did Marci tell you that too?"

Vin sprawls out on the couch, an arm over his brow like a silver screen starlet. "You know me. Always make friends with the staff. Marci's a sweetheart. She loves your movies, but not in a weird way. Just a fan who is excited we're here."

I sit down next to him, lifting his legs so they rest on my thighs. "Well, I'm glad you two are BFFs, because she negotiated a game night, and she and I will kick your ass."

He pouts. "She told me about that. Don't think I won't get you both back for this. At least Jack will be on my team. That'll hurt."

"I don't think he will be." I stare up at the ceiling, trying to figure out why I feel like I've lost something.

"Why not?"

"Let's say I overestimated my appeal."

"Shocking." He blows air kisses at me until I push him off the sofa with a thump. Doesn't stop him from laughing, even if he's doing it from the floor.

"You love it, don't you?" he says. "That he treats you like a regular guy. Probably even that he said no to you like you're someone who ever hears the word no."

"It's not like that," I say. "And I hear the word no a lot. Got turned down for that dog movie last year, didn't I?"

Vin snorts. "You didn't want to do a family movie anyway. You were trying to make a point to Roberta."

Well, yeah. I was trying to prove that my brand extended beyond explosions and car chases, but the plan had been for me to turn them down when they offered me the role, not for them to say they thought my high-profile reputation would distract audiences from the dog. When Roberta heard, she patted my cheek and told me to trust the formula.

"You can't control everything," Vin says.

"I know that."

"And pretending you're someone you aren't doesn't solve anything."

"I'm David."

Vin rolls his eyes, then the rest of himself as he wiggles and squirms until he's able to get to his feet. Even standing in front of me with his hands on his hips, he's still only a head taller than I am sitting down.

"You're Damian Marshall. Maybe it still says David on your birth certificate, but you haven't been that person in a long time."

"Well, what if I don't want to be Damian anymore?"

He throws his head back with a sigh that's moved beyond world-weary into galactically weary. "You've only ever wanted to be Damian. You're pouting because Jack doesn't want you, and your shitty ex has made being Damian a little bit harder. Guess what? Being anyone is hard. You don't want to do the work."

I nearly point out that Jack does want me, he just wants his job more, but that's not really his point. And spending time with

Jack is a fun distraction, but it won't magically solve my problems.

I glance at the pages Vin was working through when I walked in.

"Is this my script?" I ask.

"You should read it. And call Roberta. She has some ideas for how we can get you back into Hollywood with limited fuss."

Limited fuss sounds good. We can pretend this whole thing never happened. Someday, Jack will figure out who I am, but by then this trip will be a fun story he can talk about at parties. Two fishing boats passing in the night. That's all we can be to each other.

14

JACK

I don't have a concussion. By the end of the evening, with a full stomach and enough ibuprofen, I'm feeling pretty close to human. Still, Harper insists on knocking on my door every two hours through the night. I try to tell her I'll be okay and she doesn't need to keep waking us both up, but she insists. Her presence at least means that most of the midnight sexual antics from my neighbors are kept to a minimum, but I also don't manage to get more than forty-five minutes of consecutive sleep before she's back again. In some ways, I miss the creaky springs.

My own springs remain silent. Because I said that was the right thing to do.

We'll blame the head injury—concussion or not—for my questionable decision-making.

Harper's clearly not firing me. It would have been easy enough to announce she's putting me on a plane to get my brain checked out and then use my absence as an excuse to hire someone else. Instead, she's knocking on my door at two in the morning to make sure I haven't slipped into a coma, in case her VI-VIP and his bodyguard want to go out tomorrow.

The same bodyguard I turned down less than twelve hours ago.

I finally fall asleep around five. The sun is already halfway up. My last thought is *I hope David finds decent coffee without me.*

I wake up in the afternoon. The blackout shade has done its job, and my room is still almost entirely dark, though when I raise the shade, it turns out it's also pouring again, so there wasn't that much light to block in the first place.

I call Stef, but she doesn't pick up, so I send a quick email letting her know I made it through the night, then strip and take a long, hot shower since apparently my services aren't needed today. The Steri-Strips stay in place, and I can't help but remember the gentle pressure of David's hand on my face as he patched me up.

If I'd let him, he would have touched me more. Maybe even other places than my head.

I towel off and tell myself to get it together. I learned a long time ago that the right thing and the thing you want only line up half the time. And anyway, David will be gone soon, and it won't matter anymore. I'll be on to the next VI-VIP, and all they'll want is for me to find them the biggest fish I can.

The staff lounge is empty when I go looking for food. So is the staff kitchen. I slap together some bread and cold cuts, and the whole time I'm eating, not a single person appears.

Did I sleep through an evacuation?

When I walk out into the main part of the lodge, the front desk is unattended, which seems like a huge lapse in service on Harper's watch. I go to the front door, and the world outside is completely gray and drenched. The *Hawk* is tied up at the dock, and no one is around.

A shout comes from the second floor. It's followed almost immediately by cheering, and I can't help myself when I take the first step up and then the next, curiosity drawing me toward the sound.

The second floor is what Harper calls "the social floor." One wing has guest rooms, but the other, over where the dining room is, has an open space where guests can hang out in the afternoons when fishing is done. It's got leather couches, a pool table, a bookshelf on one wall, and a chest of board games for people to play on days like today when it's too wet to go outside.

As I come up to the top of the stairs, there's a small party going on. Maybe sixteen people are squashed onto various couches. Harper is perched on the arm of one of the chairs, looking as meticulous as ever, but her smile creases her cheeks in a way I haven't seen before. One of the waitstaff from the dining room—I think his name is Rick—is standing in the middle of the crowd, waving his arms excitedly, then hopping on one foot, while people shout at him and laugh.

"An apple a day keeps the doctor away!"

"Always look on the bright side of life!"

"What goes around comes around!"

"Get two pizzas for the price of one!"

The last comment has the whole room dissolving into hysterical laughter while Marci stands up abruptly and shouts "Time!" Rick puts his hands on his hips and glares at the people around him.

"You're all the worst," he says. "The answer was obviously 'bad moon rising.'" This declaration only leads to more laughter as Rick pouts and Marci strikes a big X on the paper flip chart that's been set up off to one side.

"Okay, who's next?" Harper asks, clapping her hands brightly. Even when everyone's having a good time, she can't help herding them all like ducklings. There's a lot of finger pointing and a lot of "No, I already went!" and finally a voice behind me says, "I don't think Jack's had a turn."

David's standing behind me. He's holding a full coffee mug in each hand and gives me a smile that nearly has me reminding him we're not alone, but before I can, people are back to cheering and yelling.

"Yeah! Jack, come play." Marci tugs on my hand.

"No, no. It's okay. I just wanted to know where everyone was."

David's behind me, close enough that if Marci lets go, I'll stumble into him and most likely get two cups of coffee dumped on me for my trouble. I continue to protest while Marci leads me into the circle, and David skirts around me to hand one of the mugs to his boss, who says something I can't hear to David, but he only shakes his head before he goes to stand behind the couch where Mr. Morgan is sitting.

"Come on," Marci's saying. "It's a friendly game of charades. You can be on my team."

"No!" Harper says, her expression bright again. "We're short a player on our team. Jack, you're with us."

I don't know how this has happened. Maybe I have a concussion after all, and this is all some trauma-induced hallucination. But the next thing I know, I'm standing in the center of the group and Marci is handing me a bowl with a bunch of folded slips of paper. I take one and stare at it so long that someone laughs and asks, "You know how to play charades, right?"

Everyone's watching me expectantly, and I don't know the names of at least half the people in the room. And for once, I feel bad about it. I've resented them because I've resented being here, but right now, as they're huddled around and clearly having fun together, I can see they're not all the blank robots I assumed they were. They aren't co-opting this experience. If anything, I've been spoiling my own experience by not getting to know them. We're all trying to do a job. They're just more committed to enjoying themselves than I have been.

"I know how to play."

I glance at David. I hold out four fingers.

"Hey." Harper snaps her fingers. "Wrong team. Eyes over here."

They try. I'll give them that much. But knowing how to play charades doesn't mean I'm any good at it. They get the first word pretty easily, but after that it falls apart pretty quickly.

"Me Tarzan, you Jane!" Harper shouts.

"I'll be back!" someone else calls.

"That's not four words." A young woman—maybe her name is Nadine? I guess I should know this—says.

"Sure it is. I will be back."

"That's not how he says it."

"Can we focus, please?" I say as they all start repeating "I'll be back" in terrible accents, then laughing.

"No talking," Harper says. She's staring at me so intently it's like she's trying to see inside my brain since clearly none of my acting is helping.

My blood pressure is rising, and the side of my head aches. I can't help myself when I check over my shoulder. David's watching me, lips pressed tight together to contain his smile or his laughter or both.

This is humiliating.

But everyone around me appears to be having a great time, regardless of how I'm doing.

"Thirty seconds!" Marci calls from her spot by the flip chart.

I square my posture. My team leans in like I'm about to make a great revelation.

Instead, I hold up four fingers again.

"Four words," they say in unison.

I point at my chest.

"Me," they all shout.

And that's where I get stuck again. I try my best, waving my hands at the floor trying to show them what I mean, but they all start shouting random words again.

"Splatter."

"Tail."

"Fart!" Harper shouts it so loud she nearly falls off the couch, and then everyone is laughing again. I grind my teeth in frustration.

"Time!" Marci calls. Everyone around me groans while the other team whoops.

"That was awful," Nadine laughs.

"It was really hard," I say. I'm out of breath. "The last word especially was—"

"Ah, ah." Marci steps in front of me. "Don't give it away. The other team has a chance to steal the point now."

I laugh. "Good luck to them."

We turn, and seven heads are all down and whispering, but David's still watching me, completely amused at my expense.

"Well?" Marci asks.

Rick says, "We think it's—"

"Me and my shadow."

All eyes go to David, whose smile has spread to his eyes as he calmly folds his arms across his chest. When he doesn't say anything else, his whole team swings back to me.

"So?" Rick asks. "Is that what it was?"

"Uh. Yeah."

This sets off a whole new round of exclamations. David's team claps him on the back. My team shouts objections.

"How the hell did you get that from what he was doing?" someone asks.

"Where was the shadow?" Harper asks.

I do the thing again where I try to wave my hands at the floor to indicate my shadow. Both teams break out in laughter, and this time I'm annoyed.

"I honestly thought you were farting and trying to hide it," someone says.

"I thought he was finger painting."

"Shadow's the easiest word there," Marci says, "You should have just pointed at Da—"

"Okay!" David stands up abruptly. "I think it's my turn."

"David." From the sofa where he's been sitting by himself, Mr. Morgan also stands up. "I need to speak with you."

The room gets quiet. David's watching me nervously for some reason. Harper's also got an eyebrow up as she glances between us. Mr. Morgan is looking anxious and making not-so-subtle meet-me-over-there motions toward David.

"But I was going to say—" Marci starts again.

"Jack, how's your head?" David says.

More staring. Someone giggles. I don't know what's going on, but I put my fingers beneath the Steri-Strips. "It's sore, but I'm no worse for wear. Thanks for asking."

An awkward pause follows. Mr. Morgan is still standing, David's eyeing Marci, who appears to be doing complex math in her head. Harper's still ping-ponging between me and David in a way I don't like.

Outside, a clap of thunder makes us all jump. The lights flicker and go out, and everyone groans.

"Something must have hit the generator," Harper says.

"Bar's open!" Mr. Morgan claps his hands. "First round is on me!"

A cheer goes up, and Harper protests for a minute, but either she's more worried about the generator or she knows it's a losing battle—or maybe I've read her wrong this whole time and she knows to trust her staff—because everyone heads out of the lounge, and she goes with them.

I walk to one of the front windows. Thunderstorms this early in the year are rare, but they're no joke. The water in the cove is churning, white caps forming as the wind pushes water in from the ocean. The *Hawk* bobs at the dock, straining against her lines.

"Everything okay?"

I nearly jump out of my skin at David's voice behind me. He's a tall, shadowed shape in the darkened room, but there's enough daylight that I can still see the way his shirt stretches tight as he slides his hands into his back pockets. It takes everything I can do not to lick my lips and stare at his fly.

"Yeah. Just wanted to check on the boat."

He comes up next to me, looking out the window. "Still there."

"Yeah." I clear my throat and wonder if I've passed Harper's concussion protocols thoroughly enough that I can grab one of those drinks Mr. Morgan is paying for downstairs.

"You sure you're not hiding up here so you don't have to explain your atrocious charades skills to everyone else?"

I laugh in spite of myself. "*You* knew what I was going for."

"You could have made finger puppets. Shadow? Seriously?"

"Who came up with those anyway? They were terrible. Isn't charades supposed to be like movie titles or something?"

"But you don't know movie titles," he says, making me laugh again.

"Yeah, that's fair."

We watch the rain come down, leaving silver trails on the glass. I start when a finger brushes the side of my head.

"Sorry," he says. "You're really okay?"

"Nothing a few more days and some sleep won't fix." I go to touch the cut and brush against David's fingers instead. We both freeze, and the drum of raindrops on the window matches the drumming of my heart in my chest.

My throat's still dry, and we're standing less than a window's width apart. David's shirt has a piece of lint on it, and I reach unsteadily for it, only to stop halfway when his breath catches and his whole frame goes still.

He's so close. So tall. I rest my fingertips against his chest, and he's warm beneath the soft cotton.

It feels like it takes forever to get my gaze to go from his torso up to his chin, then farther up until I find his lips. His stubble has gotten thicker over the last few days, shadowing his jaw and framing his mouth.

"Jack."

It would only take the gentlest puff of air to stop me as I lean in—to remind me why this is a bad idea—but I don't feel anything. Just the hungry pull toward him that's been there since the first time he stepped onto my boat.

His breathing quickens in the second before our lips meet, then he goes completely still again. I said no before, and he's waiting, letting me call the shots. The hesitation and the anticipation are brutal.

David's mouth quivers under mine, then his whole body seems to melt as he kisses me back. I put my hands on his sides and, as he steps toward me, grab fistfuls of his shirt to pull him in closer.

I said I didn't want this, but I was lying. Up here, alone and out of view, I want this very much.

He moans softly as I nose against his stubble. He smells like mint and leather—probably some fancy soap they've stocked in his room. It feels like forever before he finally touches me, but then he wraps his long arms around my back and closes the last few inches between us.

"Jack," he says again, and I can't tell if there's more to the thought or if he wants to make sure he has my attention, which he absolutely does. I catch his bottom lip with my teeth, and David growls as he presses his hips against mine.

The lights come back on with a pop and a hum that has us both stumbling back. Downstairs, a cheer comes up from the bar. We're still alone, and it would be easy enough to pick up where we left off, but something doesn't feel the same in the bright light.

"You okay?" he asks, and I should ask him the same. He's breathing hard, and part of his shirt is stuffed into the waistband of his jeans.

I try to ground myself back in reality, but it's hard when David throws a quick glance around us before he steps into my space again and drops his head so his lips are right by my ear.

"You changed your mind?"

I nod jerkily. This close, I can't think of why I said no in the first place.

"Tomorrow? We'll take the boat out?" His voice is soft and hopeful, and I can't help it when I press my thigh between his legs and let him grind up against me.

"Tomorrow," I say. I both do and don't know what I've agreed to, but the smell of him, the heat of his body so close to mine . . . I guess we'll find out.

Tomorrow.

15

DAMIAN

EXTRAtainment *INVESTIGATES!*
IS DAMIAN MARSHALL GAY?

While the whereabouts of actor Damian Marshall remain a mystery, more information is coming to light about his altercation with director Anderson Lind. A source close to Lind, who has asked not to be named, says the two were in a relationship during the filming of Shadow League: Through Darkness. *Although Marshall has never publicly confirmed his sexuality, Lind was previously in a relationship with model Aleksander Dyatlov.*

Could the scene in Cannes have been a lover's quarrel?

———

I'M HORNY. Like so much. I wake up in the morning and my dick has pitched its own tent in the buttery soft sheets, and there's even a damp spot at the peak that I'm not proud of, but I can't really blame my anatomy for getting carried away.

I nearly got called out yesterday. Marci pointed at me, and she was about to tell Jack that if he needed the word "shadow" all he had to do was remind us all I was in *Shadow League*. I couldn't let that happen. Not in front of everyone. Even Vin knew that would be bad for everyone. Then we were alone, Jack and me, and my adrenaline was still up. He was so close, and I tried to give him space, but he wouldn't take it.

The press of Jack's lips on mine stayed with me a long time after we went our separate ways yesterday. The brush of his beard. His hair was coarse and wiry, and I want him to drag it all over every inch of my body.

So yeah. Horny and hard as a rock, and I'm not really sorry.

Okay, maybe a little sorry when the telltale whir of a key card in a lock is my only warning before the door to my suite swings open and Vin walks in.

"Hey!" I roll over to hide the evidence. "What the hell?"

"Get up. Roberta's calling in five minutes."

"Tell her I'm sleeping." I bury my head back under a pillow for emphasis and grind my dick down onto the mattress until it hurts, hoping it gets the message that now is not the time.

"Yeah, you need to be here for this."

"Vin!" I groan, but it turns to a shriek when he yanks the comforter from the bed and cold air hits my naked skin.

"Well, good morning to you too, sailor," he says with a smirk.

"What happened to boundaries?" I grumble as I get to my feet. The chill in the room does nothing to kill my erection, but you know what? Fuck it. Nothing Vin hasn't seen before, because despite my complaint, we really do have no boundaries. I march off to the bathroom while Vin makes a mess clearing stuff off the coffee table.

At least the cold shower does the trick, but once my libido calms down, my brain starts working. California is an hour ahead of us, but even still the workday has barely begun there. I'm pretty sure Roberta's been getting by for decades on three hours of sleep and the premium vodka she imports from Kazakhstan, but she doesn't usually do calls with clients until the afternoon. If she's up this early, Houston, we have a problem.

"What's going on?" I ask as I come out of the bathroom.

"Damian, is that you?" Roberta's voice crackles over the speakers of Vin's laptop. She is the pinnacle of Palm Springs chic in a magenta tracksuit and a satin scarf tied around her head. I'm sure the tracksuit cost thousands, but I've never seen her look so casual.

"Yeah, I'm here." I slide onto the sofa next to Vin.

"Okay, good." Her gaze slides away from the screen, and she speaks to someone I can't see. "No, I'm on a call. Yes, with Damian. No, I told you. I need to talk to Cedric Oberman. I don't care if he's in Germany. It's after noon there. He has no excuse."

I go cold. Cedric was the executive producer behind the last three *Shadow League* movies. If Roberta's trying to connect with him, things can't be good.

"Everything okay?" I ask.

"Damian"—Roberta turns back to me, voice rasping—"I want you to know, whatever you read or hear in the next few days, it's not a done deal."

"Okay," I say slowly. "Is that the good news?"

"I'm speaking with Cedric as soon as Ivy can get hold of him. They can't drop you because—"

"Excuse me, what?" I glance at Vin, and he gives me an apologetic shrug that says he knew this was coming.

"There's a rumor going around the studio is recasting the part. Some nonsense about bringing new blood into the franchise."

"Recast?" I leap to my feet. "They can't do that. I have a contract."

"And that contract has a good behavior clause, and it's possible they could say your recent behavior has not been a good reflection on the studio or the franchise."

"That clause isn't for this," I say, pacing. "It's for assholes who get charged on domestic abuse cases or post racist shit online. I was sexually harassed and threatened, and I defended myself. That's the opposite of bad behavior."

"I know," Roberta says patiently, "and I need to be able to tell Cedric that when I speak with him."

I freeze midstride. Outside, the sun is well above the horizon, streaming a beam of pink and orange light over the water like nature's perfect spotlight. Jack's boat bobs at the dock. He might be down there already. We had plans today. Good plans.

I slump back down next to Vin. "You're asking my permission to admit I had a relationship with my director who is a man. That I've had relationships with men before."

"Only to Cedric, and under the utmost secrecy. I need him to understand—"

"It won't be just to Cedric," I say. "You know it won't. A secret is only a secret if the rest of us are dead."

"I don't think that's how the saying goes," Vin says softly, but he stops when Roberta and I both glare at him.

"Damian," Roberta says. "This is your career. You were born to play the hero, but the only way you get to keep doing that is if you let me tell them you were the victim here."

I put my face in my hands. This is impossible. It's not fair.

"What if we don't?" I ask. "What if they recast it?"

"No," Vin says. "You can't let them do that."

"Just, what if?" I ask again. "Give it a little time for the gossip to move on to the next story. People forget. Right? Tell them I'm reprioritizing my career. In a year, you start taking calls again."

"And what will you do for a year, honey?" Roberta asks. She's not looking out for her paycheck. I know she isn't. She's genuinely concerned about what I'll do with twelve consecutive months of free time when I haven't had more than a day to myself in years.

"Maybe I'll stay up north," I say. With every second, the sky is turning bluer, and the ocean sparkles as the trees cast long shadows. The whole experience is breathtaking.

"In Alaska?" she says.

"In Alaska?" Vin asks, squinting so hard he's going to have wrinkles later he'll regret.

"Why not?" I fling an arm at the world outside. "It's nice here." I almost say something about the rest of the world not wanting me, but even I know that's getting melodramatic.

Roberta sighs. "Let me try to smooth things over with Cedric. They're looking for a scapegoat because the movie flopped and interest in the franchise is waning, and you're convenient. Cedric has to know that regardless of the names you called Anderson, the behavior clause won't stand up to scrutiny, which means they'll be on the hook for a lot of money over the next two films, even if they write you out."

I bite my lip at the thought. Not about the money, but rather the concept of not having *Shadow League* on my schedule anymore. It's taken up so much of my life.

"Sorry," she says. "We'll get past it. Did you read that script Ivy sent you?"

I drop back down. "Not yet."

"Even if things go well with Cedric, I want you to. Oscar Kane is attached to the project. It'll be good for both of you."

I'm about to ask her how a gay best friend rom-com fits with her formula, but Vin snorts next to me.

"What?" I ask.

"Nothing." He waves me off. "Don't worry, Roberta, we'll read it today."

She glances between us, perfectly painted lips pressed into a thin magenta line. I half expect her to say Ivy will be on the next flight north because clearly we can't be trusted to keep our shit together, but then Ivy herself appears at the edge of the computer screen, whispering something urgent to Roberta, whose expression changes immediately.

"I have to go," she says. "Don't worry. I've got everything under control."

"That's exactly the kind of statement that makes people

worry," I say, but the call has already ended. Vin and I stare at the blank screen in silence for a long time. I feel a long way away from wet dreams and an aching erection.

"You wouldn't really give it up, would you?" Vin asks slowly.

"What?"

"It's everything you've ever wanted from the first time we talked. Everything you worked for." He looks bereft, and I feel bad. We spent so many days and nights struggling, and Vin eventually went to the business side of the industry, but I know part of him has always lived vicariously through my success. He knows all the ups and downs better than anyone else.

"Would anyone notice?" I ask. "If I said I didn't want to do this anymore. If I wanted to disappear for a few years, do you think anyone would really care?"

He scoffs. "You aren't some midlist actor who's been on a cable cop show for the last eight years. You're Damian Marshall. No one will ever let you disappear."

His words make me shiver. We've been out of LA for less than a week, and already the idea of going back makes me queasy. How long have I felt like this? It's not just since Cannes. Maybe since the shoot? I knew the film was crap. It's why I hooked up with Anderson. Boredom. A career like this shouldn't bore me.

But Roberta's question about what I'd do for a year if I wasn't acting rings in my head, and the answer is, I don't know.

I grab the script off the coffee table.

"Okay," I say.

"Okay?" Vin asks.

"I'll read it." Maybe. I pick up the phone on the nightstand, and a chipper voice answers promptly at the front desk.

"I'm going fishing," I say, not bothering with introductions. They know who it is. "Can you have some breakfast sent down to the boat?"

"You're running away again," Vin says when I get off the phone.

"I'm coping. You banished me out here, and I'm doing the best I can." I rummage around for clothes.

"So you're leaving me here all day again?"

"You know you'll spend the day on the phone getting updates from Ivy anyway." Pretty sure this is yesterday's underwear but whatever. With any luck, I won't be in them very long.

"Fine," Vin says. "Marci and I are going to come up with all sorts of fun ways to embarrass you while you're out."

"Sounds good to me." I stumble as I try to put on my shoes, then realized I've skipped over my jeans entirely. Vin laughs, and I glare at him. He blows me a kiss as he scoops up his laptop and heads to the door.

"You'll tell Jack who you are today?" he asks with one hand on the doorknob.

I freeze with one foot in my jeans and nearly fall over again. Truthfully, I don't want to. It'll complicate what's between us when everything else is already complicated enough. But Vin's right, and especially if things get physical with Jack, he deserves the truth.

I'd complain, but Vin would point out that the common denominator in all my problems is me.

"Yeah," I say with a sigh as I finally finish getting dressed. "I'll try."

Then he's gone, and I'm by myself, and despite what happened with me and Jack yesterday, part of me really wants to climb back into bed and pull the blankets over my head. I can't believe I suggested I would quit. How did we get to this point? But the more time I spend here away from the crush of contracts and shoots and cameras, the more I'm starting to wonder how much of it I was really enjoying. Making movies is still the best job in the world, and I have Roberta and *Shadow League* to thank for that, but maybe I don't need to keep doing it the way I have been.

I leave the hotel and make my way down to the dock. Jack's waiting for me, and where I should be excited to see him, the sight of his smile as I step down onto the boat leaves me with an empty, sick feeling. I don't want him to treat me differently than he has.

"Hey," he says, and his eyes dart nervously from my face, then lower, then quickly over my shoulder like he's worried someone will catch him checking me out even though we're fifty yards from the hotel.

"Should we get going?" I try to step past him and wind up brushing against him instead. I can't help the way I shudder at how close he is coupled with the anxiety coursing through my nervous system.

"Probably a good idea." He brushes the side of his hand against mine in a way that would look accidental to anyone watching but absolutely isn't. I must make a sound or breathe funny or something because he pauses with only his pinky finger touching mine. "You okay?"

No? Maybe? I just said I was ready to give up my blockbuster career, so an existential crisis is warranted.

So of course all I say is, "Yeah, everything's great. Let's get going."

I'll let Vin yell at me later.

16

JACK

Something's up with David. Instead of sitting next to me up on the bridge as I take the boat out of the cove, he stays down below. He's got a giant stack of papers with him, and instead of sitting with me as we motor out, he paces anxiously outside, reading it. A couple of times, he nearly falls as the boat bounces, but his balance seems to be better than mine, because he always braces or grabs for a rail at the right moment.

There's a whole spread of breakfast things in the cabin. They brought it down right before David showed up, so I assume he ordered it. Pastries, fresh fruit, these little roll ups with egg and ham and cheese that have to be lukewarm already, but no one gave me any instructions for how to keep them hot. In any case, they go untouched. David stays outside reading and pacing.

Guess the kissing is on hold for now. Probably for the best, but I gotta admit I'm a bit pissed about it. I was ready to stick my neck out for him, and now suddenly he's got other things on his mind. Stef would probably tell me to get my head out of my ass, but I don't understand what's happening, and the emotional whiplash leaves me grumpy.

Since the plan has apparently changed, the least I can do is my job. We round a point of land and come alongside a wide bay. It's one of the officially designated fishing spots on the Wild Eagle recreation guide, and I had planned to avoid it to prove a point, but it's as good as anything. The winds are coming from the southeast, so they'll keep us from drifting too close to shore. I kill the engine and climb down from the bridge.

"Should I set up the rods?" I ask.

David glances up from his papers, squinting around him like he's surprised to see we've stopped. "What? Yeah, sure. Sounds good."

His answer only fuels my annoyance. I don't know what I thought would happen today. That we'd get out of sight of the lodge and sneak into the woods to fuck like bunnies? The whole authentic Alaskan experience? Okay, yeah, I know what I was hoping for, but it's not like I have a right to be pissed that it's not working out that way. It was never a good idea.

I rig up the gear, but even though it's only the two of us, no matter where I am on the boat, David seems to be there too. He's still pacing with his head down, muttering to himself, and whether I'm at a locker or setting a rod, he's in my way, bumping into me and generally being a nuisance.

"Do you mind?" I ask.

He glances up. "Sorry, what?"

"Forget it." I grab the bait bucket, turn, and he's there again. We collide, David's arms tangling with the bucket and our feet catching against each other, and the next thing I know, David's wearing a couple of gallons of salmon heads and fish guts.

"What?" he asks like he doesn't understand what happened. Pink fish flesh splats down onto his shoes. His shirt and the front of his jeans are soaking through. Whatever he's been reading is ruined.

"I'm so sorry." I reach for him, then catch myself. His mouth is open, and he drops the papers, slowly raising his hands from his sides like even *he* doesn't want to touch himself.

"Is that—"

"I've got dry clothes in the cabin." Except I don't, because we used all the spare shirts the other day when we got caught in the rain, and despite all their efforts at superior customer service, it looks like no one remembered to replace them. I guess he could sop up some of the mess with the pastries we haven't eaten.

When I come back out, he's got his shirt off. His back is to me, and the muscles ripple along his spine. I want to run my hands over them even with the pungent odor wafting from his general direction.

"What's the water temperature?" He's got his hands on his hips and squints toward shore while his hair falls in his face. It is unfair for one person to be so attractive, even when they smell like week-old salmon.

"About forty-five. Why?"

He nods and unbuckles his belt. "I can do that."

"David? What are you doing?"

He shucks off his jeans. His ass is framed in blue-gray boxer briefs the color of the sky, and the sight of them has me rooted to my spot, which is why I don't do anything when he glances once over his shoulder, says, "Haul me in quick, okay?" then reaches for the rail and throws himself overboard.

"Jesus Christ!" My feet unstick themselves in an instant, and I rush forward, but I'm too late. All I get is a face full of seawater as the splash comes up over the side. I can't see him in the water. It's all dark slate and bubbles.

Harper is going to kill me.

A white shape appears like a halibut rising to the surface, except it's David. His head comes up, and he flings water from his hair as he gasps.

"Holy shit, that's freezing!"

"What the hell is wrong with you?" I reach over and he grabs at my arm. The water that soaks through my jacket is painfully cold.

"It seemed like the thing to do," he says with a smile. He

kicks his legs, and I don't pull him in so much as he hoists himself up and back over the side. His skin is so pink it's almost red, and his underwear clings to his body. Despite his grin, he curls in on himself and starts shivering the second I get him into the boat.

"That was unbelievably dangerous. The shock could have given you a heart attack."

"Nah, I've done it in colder. It was fine."

I put an arm around him. He's icy. My heart is still racing at the idea of him never coming up from the water.

I get him inside the cabin where we're at least out of the wind. He may think he's fine, but his lips are bluish, and his teeth are chattering so fast I'm worried he'll bite his tongue off. I grab a towel from under one of the benches and throw it over his shoulders, rubbing forcefully to get his circulation back up.

"What made you think that was a good idea?" I ask.

"I wanted to get the fish smell off."

"There are other ways to do that." I cover his head with the towel and scrub to get the water out of his hair.

"Like what?" he asks when he re-emerges. "Not like you've got a shower onboard this thing."

I roll my eyes. "If you were really that desperate, I would've tossed one of these towels overboard and you could have washed off with that."

He blinks at me several times like his brain is so chilled he's struggling to make sense of the words. His lips are still trembling, but the color is coming back.

"Oh," he says finally. "Guess I didn't think of that."

I'm on my knees. My jeans are soaked through from where he's dripped all over the floor. David's got his hands shoved under his armpits, which to me says he's still cold. I tug the towel tighter around him.

"Scared the hell out of me," I mutter as I rub my hands over his arms. "I've got a responsibility to look out for you. If you hadn't come back up, I'd have—"

He kisses me.

David's hands on my face are ice cold, but his tongue as he presses it against my lips is warm and alive. I open up for him immediately, and he draws me closer, pulling me up and spreading his legs so I can fit between them. My thighs press against the edge of the bench, and it's uncomfortable, but it gives me something to lean against instead of falling into him completely.

"I didn't mean to scare you," he says between kisses.

"Well, you did." I push the towel off his shoulders so I can explore the muscles I was eyeing a few minutes ago. His skin is cool but warming quickly, and underneath he's all toned strength.

"Can I make it up to you?" He leaves my lips to nip at my chin through my beard, then moves farther down to mouth at my throat.

"Getting better already," I say, holding onto him as the boat rocks underneath us. Truthfully, I've nearly forgotten about his unplanned polar plunge. All I can remember now is the taste of him, the mint and leather smell from yesterday—now washed away—and the promises made when we were alone.

David's hands are on me, moving, exploring. He slides them under my shirt, then down my hips and around into the back pockets of my jeans so he can pull me closer. I don't really have anywhere to go in the confined space of the boat's cabin, but I do my best, finding every inch of him I can touch.

He suddenly stands, and I scramble to keep up with him. David backs me up until my ass hits the cabin's small table, and I have to put my hands down to keep from falling backward. He lines his whole body up along the length of mine, and the thick ridge pressed against my thigh is pretty unmistakable. He's wearing nothing but cold, wet underwear, which makes the enthusiasm of his erection all the more impressive.

"David," I say. "God."

"I'll stop if you want," he says. "I didn't mean to get out of my clothes so fast."

"If you're suggesting I'd have let you grind up against me while you were covered in fish guts, we probably need to talk about your common sense."

He laughs softly as he squeezes my ass. "I'm not sure I have any common sense when it comes to you."

"I have the exact same problem."

I tangle my fingers in the elastic around David's midsection. "These seem unnecessary."

He grabs my wrists and smiles. "Let's keep those on. One of us is overdressed here, and it's not me."

I push up on my elbows as David sinks to his knees, kissing along my thighs over the denim as he goes. He slides my boots off, and I work to uncurl my toes before they give me away. Socks next, and when he kisses the arch of my foot, I make a noise I've never heard before. He glances up with an arched eyebrow.

"You like that?"

"Did you think I wouldn't?"

He kisses me again, his thumb pressing into the tendon on the underside of my big toe, and I feel the sensation all the way up my legs and into my groin. I lie back, letting my head thump on the table as he repeats the exercise with my other foot.

"Gonna remember that for later," he says. I want to tell him now is fine too, but he's rising, pulling me to my feet, then lifting my shirt over my head. David growls appreciatively, and I can't help my laughter.

"You don't have to be nice about it," I say.

"What do you mean?" He runs his hands over my chest.

"Come on. Look at you. Then look at me." The differences

are obvious. David's body is perfect. Not a stray hair or mole anywhere. Not even a half-healed pimple or scars from teenage acne. His chest is cut, his abs defined.

"I see you," he says. "You're amazing." He kisses me, framing my face like he did yesterday, before his hands start moving again, exploring. Teasing. He pinches one of my nipples, and I arch into the sting.

"But I'm not—"

"You're real," he says. "Maybe the most real person I've met in a long time."

I'm about to ask him what he means, but I get distracted when he flicks my belt open, then starts working on my fly. He dips his hand inside my underwear, and I yelp. Despite everything, his fingertips are still freezing, and the sensation against the heated skin beneath my belly is almost painful.

I can't say we're graceful. Two tall men wedged between benches, a table, and gear. I bang a shin against the steering console. David stubs a toe. There's more cursing than is probably normal for this kind of thing, but there's some laughter too, and that's nice.

Finally, he backs me up until I'm pressed against the cabin door. David lifts my hands over my head and kisses me hard, holding me in place with his body, which has thankfully completely warmed up. His underwear is still damp, but it doesn't matter much as the space between us heats and he grinds against me, rubbing his dick along mine. I stretch up on my toes, trying to find the right position.

"David." I groan as he sucks at my neck. My shoulders ache, but when he lets go, I keep my arms overhead, letting him do what he wants. He pulls at my underwear, letting it drop to the floor, then he gets down on his knees.

"This okay?" he asks.

"Uh-huh." His hand isn't cold now as he takes my cock in his fist and strokes. I find the doorframe above me and use it like a tiny handhold, my nails digging into the wood as David looks up at me with big eyes, opens his mouth, and lets the head of my erection rest on his tongue. The anticipation is perfect and nearly painful. It would be so easy to shove my hips forward and push my way in, but I wait, and the puff of hot air from his laughter is my only warning before he closes his lips around me and sucks me down.

"Oh my God," I say. His mouth is warm and wet, his lips perfectly tight. He slides off with a pop and strokes me again, using his spit to keep his grip from becoming uncomfortable before he takes me back between his lips. He lets me run along the smooth inside of his cheek and then slides me deeper toward his throat. "David. Oh God, don't stop."

He's got one hand around the base of my shaft, and he moves the other up my body, fingers trailing over my skin until he finds one nipple and pinches it. The sting makes me hiss, but as he releases it, the pain radiates like heat over my skin, and I let go of my tiny handhold to grab his wrist before he can move on. I drag his hand back to my nipple, silently begging him to do it again. I whine when he does. The sting, coupled with the warm pressure of his mouth around my dick, makes my whole body shake and my thighs tremble.

"David." He must hear the warning, because he lets go of me, rising quickly to his feet to kiss me again. His mouth is hungry on mine, and I hiss when he slides a hand between us, stroking his dick along mine. I reach down to help him, and he purrs against my lips.

"You're amazing." He thrusts into our combined fists. The tight grip, the silk slide of his skin—I have nowhere to move, but I'm shaking from head to toe. I pinch one nipple with my free hand, and the sensation has my balls drawing up as I leak fluid that eases our movement.

"Gonna come," I say.

"Want you to." He puts a hand on the back of my head,

guiding me to the warm, dark space against his neck. He smells like sea and salt now, and I rock as he pumps against me. His breath is a storm along my back. I reach for my nipple one more time, but he seems to know what I want, because he tips up my chin to kiss me and instead takes my lower lip between his teeth, biting down enough to sting.

I'd speak if I could, but the wave of release crashes over me. Wet come splashes between us, and David thrusts faster, smearing it along our shafts and between our fingers. I kiss him, trying to thank him, and he groans deep in his throat before he freezes, hips bucking on their own as his orgasm takes him.

We're sticky when we finally part. I'm naked and softening and struggle not to turn away. I've never been totally comfortable being naked with someone else, but David leans back against the captain's chair, a glistening streak of come on his stomach and his cock on full display like he doesn't mind me looking at him.

So I look a lot.

"You okay?" he asks.

I nod.

David walks—swaggers?—back to the bench and picks up the towel we discarded what feels like days ago. His ass is spectacular. He grins at me as he dabs at the mess on his stomach. "Wanna do it again?"

This is the part where I should say no. I've scratched the itch, lived the fantasy, and now I should say it's probably best if we go back to something like a professionally hospitable relationship.

So of course the words that tumble out of my mouth are, "Well, not right now. I need a little time to recover. But later? Yeah."

He arches an eyebrow as he tosses the towel at me. I'm relatively clean, but I take a second to wipe off my hands before I go about finding my clothes.

David is still standing in the middle of the cabin with his hands on his hips though.

"Something wrong?" I ask.

"Well . . ." He glances around like he's waiting for a solution to present itself. "My clothes still stink like fish, and I don't really want to put that soggy underwear back on."

Shit. What do I tell Harper?

17

DAMIAN

E XTRAtainment UPDATE!
    Is DAMIAN MARSHALL OUT OF THE SHADOWS?
    A blockbuster film franchise lives and dies by its stars, but one franchise looks like it will try to go it alone, or will at least look different next year. After several weeks of rumors and speculation, it looks like the studio behind the Shadow League *franchise is preparing to part ways with its star, Damian Marshall. Although executive producer Cedric Oberman has yet to officially confirm, sources within the studio say Oberman's and Marshall's representatives are actively working to find a way to oust the star from his contract. Marshall rose to fame playing vigilante and former mafia son Dex Russo, but* Shadow League *fatigue has hit the box office, with the fourth film in the franchise already falling below the top ten performing movies this week. Whether it can revitalize its track record without Marshall on the marquee remains to be seen.*

––––––

MY SHIRT IS RUINED. The greasy fish stain down the front will never come out. My jeans are maybe salvageable, but the smell that comes off them when I pick them up makes me gag, so those are out too.

Jumping overboard was maybe not my best plan. I knew I could do it. I jumped into colder water while filming *Shadow League 2*, though that time I had a safety team ready to go with rebreathers and heated blankets instead of one terrified fishing guide. I hope I've made it up to him. I can still feel the press of his fingers on my shoulders as he came. He needed the release as much as I did, but I hope we get to do it again soon.

But first, there's the issue of my clothes, because while it may not be winter all the time up here, I still can't parade around Jack's boat naked.

Or can I? He probably wouldn't mind too much.

We finally find a pair of yellow fisherman's overalls and rain jacket. I look like I'm on my way to a nautical bachelorette party as the entertainment. If only the world entertainment media could see me now.

"I can't believe you're making us fish," I grumble an hour later.

"We're sticking to the schedule." Jack glares at me in a way that has me sweating inside my rubber outfit. "I'll already have to explain what happened to your clothes. We're spending a full day on the water, and we're bringing fish back like we're supposed to."

I shudder as too many old memories of days of forced fishing and hunting with my family as a kid bubble to the surface. They never quite break through though, because at the very top of my memories is the feeling of Jack. His hands on me. His mouth. The taste of him on my tongue and the rough sound he made as he came in my hand. He was everything I had hoped for. I want him again already, but he seems determined to play the conscientious fishing guide, and I know we crossed a line regarding his job, so if he wants some space, I'll give it to him.

"Not like we ever catch anything though," I say, even as I watch him cast the lines out.

"We've had a run of bad luck." He throws me a cocky grin. "But maybe our luck is turning."

"Well, I am wearing my lucky overalls." I smooth my hands over the yellow vinyl.

As it happens, our luck is turning. Within ten minutes, we have a bite, and Jack wastes no time hauling in a solid looking halibut that he dispatches with quick efficiency and throws into the locker. Next, he pulls in a bright orange rockfish with eyes that bulge out of its head. Every time he gets a bite, he offers to let me take the rod, but I'm happy to let him work. He's so in his element; it's nice to watch. A couple of years ago, I spent two weeks following a chef at a restaurant in Napa, learning every- thing she could teach me about fine dining for a part. The movie got shelved in the end, but those two weeks with Chef Alyssa really taught me a lot about the skill of people doing the thing they're meant to do. Jack's like that. He's meant to be here. Outside. Working with his hands. And possibly working alone. I can't remember the last time any part of my job involved soli- tude. There's always someone. Actors, directors, PAs, makeup artists. Someone's always touching you, talking to you, trying to get you somewhere on time.

"So I don't know," Jack says slowly, bringing me out of my head, "if this thing we're doing here includes talking . . ."

Speak of the devil.

I give him a smile. "It can involve talking."

"Well," he says thoughtfully. He's reeling in something that looks like it must weigh as much as a German shepherd, but he's doing it with calm movements when my heart would be racing. "It seemed like there was something on your mind before. When we left the lodge. If you needed to get it off your chest, I'm happy to listen."

Jesus, I don't deserve him. I slide up against him, pressing our shoulders together. He's still got both hands on the reel, but he turns to me, and I kiss him. His lips are soft, and his beard tickles my skin, and part of me wants to tell him to toss the rod overboard so I can have his full attention. But now that he's brought up the question, my brain starts spinning again about the conversation with Roberta, the script she sent . . . about basically everything.

Where do I even begin?

I know you think you know me, and I know I had your penis in my mouth, but there's something I haven't told you. My name is Damian Marshall. Somehow you don't know who that is, but everyone else on the planet does, and I'm hiding out because I couldn't keep it in my pants on set, and now my director is trying to destroy my career and the studio is turning me into their scapegoat to cover their butts. And I wish I could tell you the truth, but you'll hate the kind of person I am and think we don't have anything in common.

What a shitshow. I shudder at the questions that will follow. At how the way Jack looks at me will change as he understands who I am, and that I've lied.

I have to tell him. If we're having sex for a few more days before I go back to California, what does it matter if I'm David or Damian? Either way, he'll never have to see me again.

"Jack, I—"

"Oh Jesus. Look at this," he says. I peer over the side to see a churning mass of tentacles at the water's surface.

"Is that an octopus?"

"Sure is." His smile is the blinding excitement of a kid at Christmas. "We don't get these very often. Hold tight." He swaps out his hook for a wide net and bends down to scoop it up. The octopus is a baked orange color, and even though I can barely see its face, it's pretty clearly pissed about the situation. Frankly, I would be too if I had a hook in my arm and got dragged up from the bottom of the ocean. Jack sets it down gently on the deck, and the tentacles all wriggle in grumpy slow motion.

"Do we keep it?" I ask.

"No. Sometimes they get snagged on hooks, but they're not for eating. He deserves to go back to where he belongs." Jack pulls out a pair of pliers and cuts the hook caught in one writhing tentacle. We watch as the octopus slithers to the side of the boat and finds an opening that's probably meant to help drain water away but is the perfect size for a world-weary octopus. One tentacle, then another drips over the side, and finally the head slides under and disappears. I rush to the rail and watch it disappear back down to its home.

I deserve to go back to where I belong too. Not in shame or with lies, but as myself. Sure, there will be a few closed-minded gatekeepers in Hollywood who won't be so interested in seeing my name on their projects. Nervous producers and PR reps who are always muttering things about "the optics" without ever stopping to think whether those are issues and points of view we should be catering to. I'm Damian fucking Marshall. I've made more money in the last five years than anyone else in the industry. That's not all going away because I show up with a man on my arm at a premiere.

But there's a voice in the back of my head that says enough people might care. Fans who would say they felt let down or lied to, even though I never owed them anything. My family, who said being gay meant I'd never succeed. Angry news anchors and "family values" groups might make enough noise that things are hard for a while.

Though would it be harder than it is now? I'm a thousand miles from home, questioning everything and lying to the one person I want to be with.

There has to be a way to win this fight.

———

I HALF EXPECT Vin to be in my room again when I get upstairs, but it's empty. I'm showered and dressed in regular clothes again before I find the note that someone must have slid under the door.

Come see me. V

That's not good. The tension that evaporated with the touch of Jack's lips coils back up again. If Vin had good news, he'd be lounging on my balcony with a bottle of bubbly. If he's sending secret notes, I have to put on my serious face.

He's on a call when I knock on his door. He lets me in but doesn't invite me to join him at his laptop. He's got a pair of headphones on so I can't hear who he's speaking with.

"Yeah. Yeah, okay, he just walked in. No, he's been out all day. Doing what? Fishing, lying low, like Roberta told him to."

Not Roberta then. I don't know if that makes me feel better or worse.

"Okay," Vin says, throwing me a quick glance. "Well, let me talk to him, and I'll get back to you with a plan."

Plans are good, aren't they? If the conversation Vin was having was about how to break the news to me that I'd been kicked out of *Shadow League*, we wouldn't be making a plan. Unless it was a plan to crash the bar and toast the end of my career.

Vin shuts the laptop and pulls the headphones off.

"I hate these things," he says, fluffing his hair back up. "They give me a headache."

"I'm sorry to hear that. Who were you talking to? Did you talk to Cedric?"

"No."

"Oh."

"But I talked to Ivy who talked to Roberta who talked to Cedric." He looks me up and down. "What happened to you?"

"What do you mean?"

He squints, then sniffs the air. I put an involuntary hand to my throat. Vin gets right up in my space.

"You got laid, didn't you?"

"What? No. Can we get back to the matter at hand?" I push him off me.

The arch of his eyebrows says we're not done with this topic, but he goes to the small fridge built into the wall and pulls out a bottle of water. He takes a long sip before he speaks.

"I talked to Ivy who talked to Roberta who talked to Cedric."

"You said that already."

"And Cedric talked to Anderson."

Ugh.

I don't say it out loud, but Vin knows me too well, because he makes a sympathetic noise. "Yeah, I know. The good news is, he and Cedric are willing to keep you on the project."

I don't feel the relief I should. Maybe I really am ready to give it up. "What's the bad news?"

He wrinkles up his nose. Very little makes Vin uncomfortable, so this will be a wallop.

"They want you to make a statement with Anderson."

"What, like a press release? Is Ivy writing something up? I can look it over." The idea makes my stomach turn, but those generic things never say anything important, and then we can pretend this never happened. I can come back to LA and have a serious talk with Roberta about the future of my career and whether her formula is still working for me. Maybe she'll have a new franchise in mind, and we can keep going as we have been. Or else we'll agree to take a pause. Either way, no one has to know the whole backstory. I can come out when I'm ready, and not because Anderson forced my hand.

Vin's nose is still scrunched up to his eyebrows.

"Not a press release. More like they want you to go to *People* and give an interview about how it was all a big misunderstanding and how excited you are to be working together."

"What?" I leap up so fast I knock the bottle onto the floor, splashing water everywhere. "No way in hell."

Vin winces. "I told them that was what you would say."

"You want me to play nice with that asshole?" I can't. I can't sit next to him and tell the world everything is forgiven or that it was all a big misunderstanding in the first place.

"What I want is for you to stand up and tell everyone that he *is* an asshole, but you keep shooting me down, so what do you expect us to do? We're trying to save your career here. It's time for you to make some tough decisions."

You know what? He's right. Screw the formula. Screw Anderson—in the metaphorical sense anyway. I'll go on *Oprah* and answer her thoughtful and poignant questions and become the hero I was always meant to be. The studios can blackball me for being difficult to work with or whatever, but I'll know I did what was right for me.

But behind that conviction comes the sinking fear of what will follow. After the sanitized and controlled environment of an interview like that will come the fallout. The cameras, the shutters clicking a million miles an hour. The questions from paparazzi and random people on the street. The online hate. The fans who'll look at me in disgust or think I'm some token commodity to tuck into their purses. If it backfires—and there's no way to know until the cat's out of the bag—I'll be the thing my family said I'd always be: someone who couldn't hack it on their own terms.

Walking away will never be as easy as I want it to be. Vin was right this morning. After all, I'm Damian fucking Marshall. The world will follow me anywhere I go.

18

JACK

For once, there isn't a welcoming committee waiting for us at the dock when we come in. Things are finally going right. No sign of Harper lurking, waiting for a status report. But Marci is at the desk when I walk through, and she pounces on me.

"Hey, how did it go?"

"Fine." Gave him the red light special, but I leave that part out.

"What are you doing later?"

I glance around like this is a trick question. "Will this involve more charades?"

She laughs, shoving at my arm like we're good friends. "No, silly. Nate found a spot in the woods that'll be good for a bonfire. We're gonna sneak a few drinks and some marshmallows from the kitchen and go hang out. You want to come?"

A week ago, I would have said no. I had no interest in being here or socializing with the rest of the staff. And I still don't know who Nate is. But today? Maybe it's the last of the orgasmic afterglow, but hanging out in the woods making small talk doesn't sound so bad. If I have to be here all summer, I'll need a reason to enjoy myself here even after David leaves. I have to make more of an effort to get to know the people I work with. Otherwise it'll be very lonely.

"Sure. Sounds like fun."

Marci claps her hands like this is the best news she's heard all day. "Do you think you can get him to come too?"

"Who?"

Her eyes widen. "Him. Da—" Then her gaze drops down to the ground suddenly. "I mean, Mr. Morgan."

"Everything okay?" Harper has walked into the lobby and joined our little twosome.

"Fine." I tug at the zipper of my coat where it's done up to my chin, then ball my hands into fists because Harper can't know what David and I did on the boat by looking at me, but if I squirm like a guilty child, she'll find out one way or the other.

"Will you be going back out again tomorrow?" she asks.

"I believe so." Really trying not to think about what we'll do because it'll be hard to hide my face turning bright red.

Still, it would be nice to find a place with a little more room. Too bad I never found one of those beaches perfect for a picnic . . . or other things. They must exist. If Marci can find a place big enough for a bonfire, surely we can find enough space to—

I hop back like I've been burnt and both Harper and Marci stare at me with confusion.

"Sorry," I say. "Got a chill. It's drafty in here. I'm gonna go take a shower. I'll see you both later? At the bonfire, right?"

"Bonfire?" Harper asks, and I notice Marci's frantic motions signalling me to keep it a secret too late.

"Nothing. Sorry. I'll . . . I'm off to my room."

The last thing I see is Harper rounding on Marci, and I feel pretty bad about it. I didn't mean to share something I shouldn't, but blurting out Marci's secret is better than blurting out mine.

As I walk into my room, I see my laptop is open, showing an

incoming call from Stef. I scramble to answer it before she hangs up.

"Hello?"

"Hey." Her brown hair is piled up in a messy bun, and she gives me a thin smile. "How was your day?"

"Not bad. Nice weather." Got a blow job from an incredibly good-looking man, and I'm not allowed to tell anyone. I bite my lip to squash that thought. "How's Robbie?"

"He's good. Working on a dichotomous key for fish species identification."

"What's that?"

She shrugs. "Something he saw in a textbook, but he felt he could make a better one."

Sounds like him. I still don't know what a dichotomous key is, but I'm sure he'll make a fully illustrated version.

Stef undoes her hair, then quickly wraps it up again before twisting a loose strand of hair around one finger in quick, anxious motions.

"Everything okay?" I ask.

"Um . . ." She glances down and the wobble in her voice has me sitting up straighter. I unzip my jacket and shrug out of it.

"What's wrong?"

She grimaces. "Can't keep anything a secret from you."

"Stef."

I know my sister well enough that I can tell when she's struggling with something, but I also know if I push her, she'll tell me to take a long walk off a short pier, so I wait.

"Don't freak out," she finally says.

"Not freaking out, but I'm definitely worried."

She gnaws at her bottom lip, but she says, "Graham is flying to Anchorage."

"What?" My worry immediately turns to annoyance at the mention of her pain-in-the-ass husband.

"He texted me this morning. His team is done in Guatemala.

He was flying out from Guatemala City today and lands in Anchorage tomorrow. He wants to see me and Robbie."

"Is he going to sign the divorce papers?"

She shakes her head, and I'm angry before she even speaks. "He wants to get back together."

A small explosion happens inside my head. Everything goes white as the shock wave ripples through me.

"He what?"

She doesn't look happy about it. "He says he wants to talk. He's moving to Alaska, and he wants to try again." Her gaze drops from the screen before she says softly, "I thought I should let you know."

"Of course you should let me know. You're planning to tell him to sign the papers and get lost, right?"

"Jack." She tugs at a loose strand of her hair.

That's not the answer I was expecting. "You can't be considering this."

"He's my husband."

"You left him," I say.

Her brows pinch together. I can't believe she's defending him after everything she's been through, both since she came back to Alaska and before.

"I left because he was never there for me and Robbie. He's a good person. We fit together."

"He'd have to be in the same country for you to fit together," I mutter.

"Come on. I didn't tell you about this so you could get mad."

"Then why did you tell me? Did you think I'd be happy? Why are you so willing to forgive him?"

She swallows, and for a second, I think she's about to cry. I don't want to make my sister cry, I just want her to make sense.

But she says, "Because I love him. He's got a kind heart, and he's the smartest person I've ever met."

"Stef—"

"If he'll be around now . . . if he's willing to go so far as to move up here to be with us . . ."

I'm speechless. He's made everything so difficult for her. For years. Not just since she came back up north. And she's considering letting him do that again.

"But what about—" I start to say, but Stef holds up a hand.

"I don't want a lecture, Jack. I want you to let me live my life."

"Like you let me live mine?"

She reels back, and I didn't mean to say that, but now that it's out, I wonder if it's true.

"What's that supposed to mean?"

"I'm just looking out for you. Like you look out for me. The way you're always trying to find me a job. Telling me to leave."

"I never—"

"Well, now I'm telling you I think this is a bad idea."

"Jack. He's my husband."

I'm so frustrated I'm shaking. "Fine. Do what you want."

"I don't want to leave if you're mad at me."

"But you were happy enough to let me hang up my dignity and come work here."

She thins her lips. Even I know that was one step too far.

"Stef."

"I have to go," she says. "Robbie needs me."

"Wait. No."

"I'll call you from Anchorage."

The screen goes black. I curse and rub my face. I should call her back and apologize. I'd at least text her, but my phone has no signal.

She can't go back to him. Not that I have a say. But I was there when she came home from Boston. Exhausted. Heartbroken. He hurt her, even if it was just by never being there. She says he has a kind heart, but so does Stef, and she doesn't deserve to be treated like this. He doesn't deserve a second chance.

I'm not one for moping so I try and stay busy, but what is there to do really when you're on a floating hotel miles from home with no one to talk to? I go to dinner in the staff room, but everyone is chatting about the bonfire and laughing, and somehow it all feels too loud and too much. I'm not feeling like much for socializing tonight. They can enjoy their bonfire without me.

"You okay?" Marci asks, but her smile is too much like Stef's. Kind. Motherly. Like I'm the one who needs looking after, when all I was trying to do was look out for my sister.

"Yeah," I say. "Think I'll go to bed early. Got a long day tomorrow."

She winks. "With him?"

I don't know how she knows, but I leave before I say something I shouldn't. I've upset too many people already today.

In my room, there are no messages from Stef. She's probably on the road. I send an email telling her I'm sorry and wishing her luck. Hopefully she reads it.

I don't usually spend much time on the internet, but with nothing else to do, I find myself wandering through different websites. I look at boats—none that I can afford, even the ones that need a lot of repairs—and jobs I could apply for but don't want to do any more than this one. Eventually, I find myself on the University of Oregon's website, looking at their teaching program. It's too late for me to send them an email telling them I'm ready to come back. I'd have to apply all over again.

But it was never about teaching. Not really. It was about getting away. Oregon was the farthest I could imagine back then. A baby step. But maybe it's time to go farther. If Stef doesn't need me—

Okay. Time for sleep. Maybe that cut on my head is worse than I thought after all, because this is a train of thought I don't go down very often. I've always done what my family needed, because that's what family does. There's no shame in that.

Maybe it's time for me to make a change though. If I could do anything, what would it be?

My heart races when I come up with a big blank. Is it possible I've never actually asked myself this before?

Whatever. I won't get anything resolved tonight. Or probably over the next few days regardless of what Stef decides, because she'll be in Anchorage and I'm stuck out here. No point in getting ahead of myself. For now, I'll do the one thing I'm good at, and that's fish.

19

DAMIAN

E XTRAtainment *Insider!*
  Damian Marshall . . . King of the Rom-Com?

In an effort to save his beleaguered career, Damian Marshall is looking to make a change. The action star and leading man is taking his talents in a new direction: the rom-com! Rumor has it Marshall is set to appear in the upcoming film, Beloved Cove, *a rom-com by Tino Del Ray that has had Oscar Kane's name attached to it for the last several months. Where former child star Kane will land if he has to give up the part to a higher-profile actor remains to be seen.*

———

Vin and I have room service so I can continue my existential crisis in private.

"There's always theater," Vin says. We're on our second bottle of champagne. Not the smartest move, but sometimes the bubbles help.

"Please. You think after all those action movies, anyone wants to see me do Shakespeare?"

"There was a Spider-Man musical," Vin says, like it's the perfect solution, but then he giggles and drains his glass. "But it didn't do so well, so that's probably not the career move you want to make."

It feels like I'm running out of moves. The problem with Roberta's formula is, it only ever went in one direction. All or nothing. That's how it's always been.

Vin passes out on the couch at some point, an empty bottle curled up against his chest. I make my way to the bed, not bothering to take my clothes off. My sleep is full of weird dreams where Jack and I are walking a red carpet, but Cedric Oberman keeps stepping in front of the photographers to ask me if I've seen my parents because they're waiting for me.

I wake up late the next morning, and my head is playing host to what feels like a herd of stampeding elephants. Even my eyeballs hurt when I open them to find the bright Alaskan sun streaming through my windows.

I shower, trying to steam the champagne out of my pores. No idea where a place like this gets its water from, but I guess being one of only two guests has its perks since I never have to worry about running out of hot water. Then I call Vin.

"Hello?" He sounds like the elephants have moved down to his skull. I wasn't the only one drinking last night.

"What time did you leave?" I say.

"A couple of hours ago. You were snoring too loud for me to stay."

"Rude."

"What do you want, Damian? I was planning on being unconscious until well into the afternoon."

I pause. I don't know what I want. "Roberta hasn't been in touch today?"

There's a rustling, like he's checking his phone for new emails.

"No." He groans. "Ball's in your court."

Right. The interview with Anderson. My stomach curdles at the thought.

"We should read that script," I say. The parts I read on the boat yesterday didn't fill me with a lot of hope, but I wasn't even halfway through when Jack dumped his bait bucket on me. There's always a chance it redeemed itself in the last act.

Vin groans. "Shouldn't you be fishing or something?"

"I thought you wanted me to read that script?"

"I read it. It's not very good."

"Vin!"

He sighs heavily. "I mean, I get where Roberta was coming from, but I don't think this is the one to rebrand your career on. And also, my bed is still spinning. Go hang out with your Alaskan hunk for a few hours, and we can talk about it when you get back."

It feels a bit like I'm playing hooky as I head down to the dock. It's later than we've gone out the last few days, so I'm not surprised when there's no one around. I've brought the rubber rainsuit from yesterday to return, so I don't feel like I'm doing anything wrong when I climb down the ladder onto Jack's boat. I leave the pants and jacket in the closet they came from and close the cabin door behind me.

Jack is standing on the dock when I come outside.

"Good morning," I say, squinting up into the sunshine. I have to lift my hand to block the glare, and the second I do, I know something is wrong.

"Good morning." He doesn't smile when he says it. He looks tired, but not in the "well, at least we had a good time last night" way that I must look this morning.

"Everything okay?" I ask.

"Yeah." The word is clipped. "You want to go out?"

"Do you?" I ask, because the expression on his face says he wants to be pretty much anywhere but here.

"Let me get some gear."

It's not a yes or a no, and his posture as he walks back up the dock leaves me uneasy, but fifteen minutes later, he's back with what looks like a cooler of food, some dry clothes, and a pair of sunglasses that cover his eyes and keep me from reading him properly.

"Can I help with anything?" I ask as he pushes us away from the hotel.

He points to the flybridge. "Why don't you sit out here? It's a nice day. You'll enjoy the view."

Something is really wrong.

Jack takes the boat out to the ocean with a little more power in the engine than usual. The vibration shudders through me, mixing with my nerves. This time yesterday, we could barely keep our hands off each other, and now something's happened to completely change his behavior.

Does he know? Honestly, it's a miracle he hasn't figured it out yet. How no one has told him or that he hasn't spotted me online is a mystery. If he has, it would explain the icy feeling blasting off him, but honestly, Jack doesn't seem like he'd be big on the silent treatment when he's upset about something.

He takes us along the coastline for what feels like a long time. Every minute that goes by ratchets up my anxiety further.

Finally, the boat slows. I climb down to the deck. We're bobbing in the open ocean with the shore off to my right. I only get this nervous for auditions I really want and have no hope in hell of getting, which can't be a good sign. I hold my breath and wait for Jack to come join me. Watching him come out of the cabin and not being able to touch him is torture. His jacket is unzipped, and the flannel underneath looks cozy enough to snuggle up with. Like he knows I'm staring, he does up the zipper and folds his arms over his chest. He's still wearing his sunglasses.

He still looks unhappy when he says, "Do you want some coffee?"

"What's wrong?" I ask, because I'm done with giving him space. Just rip off the Band-Aid and let's have at it.

"I'll make coffee." But he doesn't complain when I follow him into the cabin. He sets a small kettle to boil on one of the propane burners, then goes about spooning coffee into a French press with the same quiet efficiency he does everything. I love watching him work. No fuss. No drama. No demands other than to be a decent human being.

A clatter makes me jump, and Jack hisses as he pulls his hand away from the kettle.

"Are you okay?"

"Just got a knuckle." He sucks his finger into his mouth, and I go weak at the knees because I'd rather he let me suck on his fingers. Or he sucks on mine. Anything but this frosty silence.

"I can get the first aid kit or—"

"I don't need a first aid kit, David." He shouts it like it's the fifth time I've asked him. "I just need . . ." He goes back to rattling around mugs and scoops of coffee.

"Did something happen?" I ask.

"You know"—he shakes his head—"it makes me so mad. I'm so sick of people who think their money and prestige gives them the right to just march in and treat people like their feelings don't matter."

Every single one of his words makes my heart sink.

"Jack, I should have—"

"Sorry." He pulls his sunglasses off and rubs his face. "I shouldn't unload my problems on you. It's not your fault."

"It—" My brain is already halfway through a breathless monologue of apology and begging. "It's not?"

"No." He hands me a mug like it's not a big deal. "I had a fight with my sister last night, and it's still bothering me today. I didn't mean to take it out on you, I—"

I crash into him, desperate to kiss him. Hot coffee slops between us, seeping through my shirt. I'll probably regret the burn in a minute, but right now I'm operating on pure relief and instinct. He stumbles back and I go with him, holding onto him until we crash into something and he grunts.

"Sorry," I say. "You were trying to tell me something."

"What was that about?" He smooths his hands down the front of his shirt and adjusts his pants.

"Nothing." I'm so giddy I'm shaking, and it's just as well I spilled my coffee, because I'd never be able to manage to drink it now. "You seemed upset, I wanted to make you feel better."

He grabs hold of my belt and tugs me forward so he can kiss me, just once. "Thank you."

I grab a roll of paper towel and go about mopping up the coffee off the floor. "Do you want to talk about it? That's a thing we do, remember?"

Jack laughs softly. "My sister is on her way to Anchorage today. Her ex-husband is flying in, and she's supposed to be meeting him there to hammer out the last details of their divorce, but now suddenly he's decided he's moving to Alaska so he can convince her to try again. She hasn't seen Graham in almost a year, and he didn't even come back to the States when she said she was leaving him, but now suddenly he's had a change of heart."

"Sounds complicated," I say.

"I said some things I shouldn't have, and she said some things that are maybe true but weren't easy to hear. And then I woke up this morning in this fancy place that looks nothing like what most people's lives look like back home, and where someone like your boss has a whole staff at his beck and call and doesn't even take them up on what we have to offer, and I was so angry that people like that can make up all the rules and we just have to play along."

Well, shit.

I take his hand. "Jack. I need to—"

"You asked me the other day where I'd go if I could travel, and I don't even have an answer. How sad is that?"

I'm caught between telling the truth and trying to soften the hurt on his face.

"What can I do to help?" I ask.

He looks devastated when he says, "You could kiss me again."

We go slower this time. No schedule. No agenda. Slowly, his kisses turn hungrier, his hands surer. I feel a surge of pride that I can do this for him when he's given me so much this week.

He's got a hand inside my pants before I have a second to breathe.

"Jack." I gasp as he closes around my cock.

"I want you." He turns us so he can back me toward the door.

"Where are we going?"

"Outside."

"What?"

"There's no room in here. I want to take you outside. Please. I need this."

Now. I should say it now. But I can't hurt him more. Not when his hands and his mouth are asking for so much.

I stumble as my pants slide off my hips, but I manage to get out onto the open deck without embarrassing myself. I take a quick glance around, but we're alone. There are a few boats dotting the horizon, but they're a mile or more off and moving away from us, and we've drifted closer to shore, so we're protected on the other side.

"Sit," Jack says, pointing to the fish locker at the rear of the boat. I hiss when my ass hits the cool surface, but I don't have long to suffer before Jack is on me. Kissing. Touching. When he finally takes me into his mouth, I groan, tipping my head back. He's hot and slick, and when he uses his tongue, it's clear he's a master at his craft.

"Jack. Oh Jesus."

He hums, and the vibration goes straight to my balls. I bury my fingers in his hair, and he sucks harder as I hold him down.

It's amazing. For the first time in weeks, I'm worried about nothing except that I might come too fast and ruin this for both of us.

"You're good," I say. "So good. Your mouth. Jesus Christ, your mouth. I want you, Jack. Wanna fuck you."

It's an empty stream of words, and as stocked as this boat is with everything from coffee to fresh clothes, there's no way they've packed lube or condoms. Hell, I don't even have any back in my room. That was the farthest thing from my mind when I threw a bunch of clothes into a suitcase and sulked all the way to the airstrip in LA.

Jack lifts up, and cold air hits my spit-covered dick, making me shout. Then, just as quickly, he slides down, swallowing me to the root. The sudden warmth and the pressure of the suction is enough that I lose control. I barely have time to give him a warning before I'm coming, the hot, wet rush unstoppable as I shake and shudder. Jack swallows it all as I pant through my orgasm.

The world is strangely quiet when he finally looks up. Water laps at the sides of the boat, but there isn't even a stray seagull to break the emptiness. My pants are around my ankles, and Jack kisses my thigh.

My opportunity is gone. If I tell him now, everything between us will be broken. I'll just be another rich, privileged asshole in his eyes—and maybe that's exactly what I am.

"What?" Jack asks.

"Nothing." I pull him up to kiss him properly. The tang on his lips makes me moan.

We make out for a bit until I start to shiver. Jack helps me to my feet, and I brace my hands on his shoulders as he pulls my pants up and does the zipper and button. His erection has gone down, but when I reach for him, he pulls me close, nosing against my neck.

"Later," he says.

Later. Yes, that's a great idea.

"Tonight," I say. "Come to my room." That big bed. The sofa. The balcony. So many possibilities. "Can you do that?"

He frowns for a minute, and I expect him to say no, which is more than fair.

"Yeah. It'll be late. After the rest of the staff has gone to bed, but I can do it."

My heart knocks against my ribs. All I can smell is Jack, and I want to drown in him.

Tonight. I may not survive until then.

20

JACK

By the time we get back to the lodge, I'm spun so tight everything makes me jump. A voice in the lobby. A light turning on. Water running in the kitchen as I make myself a coffee I definitely don't need.

"Are you okay?" Marci asks when my fork clatters to my plate. We're eating dinner with a couple of the staff—Ben who works in facilities and Iris who works in housekeeping—and I've been trying to keep up my end of the conversation, but every time I'm not speaking, my attention shifts back to the boat. To David. The fine hairs on his tanned thighs. The slight sting of pain as he held my head down.

"Jack?"

I jump again as Marci nudges me.

"Sorry," I say, giving everyone a tight smile. "Maybe I got too much sun on the water this afternoon."

They don't make any further comments on it and mostly talk among each other, which leaves me to my imaginings and plans and fantasies for tonight and—

Oh. That's a problem.

As we're leaving dinner, I tug at Marci's hand, holding her back as everyone else leaves.

"Something wrong? You've been weird all evening."

"I need a favor. A big one. I'd do it myself, but you know everyone, and I don't. But you have to swear you won't tell a soul about it. Ever."

Her eyes get big. She glances around us and whispers, "Is this about . . . your VIP?"

I need to vanish. Disappear entirely so all that's left of me is a heap of clothes on the floor.

"I think we need to take a plausible deniability approach here," I say, and she nods excitedly.

I might actually learn to like working with Marci this summer.

David and Mr. Morgan are in the dining room as I walk through the lobby. Okay, I pace through the lobby, after I'd paced down to the dock and upstairs to the lounge. I can't sit still. It gets worse when David catches my eye over his dinner, and I can only hold his gaze for a split second before I have to look away because otherwise I'll walk into something and hurt myself when I want to be at the top of my game.

I call Stef to kill time.

"Hello?" She sounds impatient. I deserve that.

"Hey, just wanted to see how it went with Graham?" The words are weak and I grimace.

She growls. "Don't even. I don't want to talk about the day I've had."

"What's wrong?" I have plans tonight, but if Stef needs me, I hope David understands. If Graham hurt her or upset her, all bets are off.

"Graham's not here."

Of course he isn't. "Where is he?"

"Well, he's not here *yet*. His flight from Dallas to Seattle was delayed, and he missed the connection to Anchorage. So we spent all day hanging around at the airport and now we're stuck in a hotel for another night waiting for him to show up."

My first instinct is to tell her to go home, but I don't want to start another fight with her.

"Is Robbie okay?" He's not great at sleeping in places he doesn't know.

"He is now. The drive yesterday was hairy. About forty-five minutes from home, he realized we'd forgotten his fish journal, and he absolutely melted down. I tried to help him recover, but in the end, we wound up going back for it because I couldn't—" Her voice wobbles, and my throat tightens.

"Stef, I'm sorry." She shouldn't be doing this alone.

"No, it's fine. We've got the journal."

"Not about the journal," I say. "About everything I said yesterday. You didn't deserve that."

"No." She laughs, looking at something off-screen. "You're right. I do this every time. He just lets me down over and over, but I can't stop hoping it'll work out in the end."

"You sure you don't want to go home?" I say.

"No. I'm exhausted. Even if he weren't coming at all, I don't think I could drive back tonight. I'll give him until tomorrow morning. If he's not here by lunch, I guess I have my answer."

I hope it doesn't come to that. Not that she doesn't deserve the happy ending with her son and her husband under one roof. I just don't trust Graham to give it to her. But at least if he shows up and blows it, she'll know for sure. If he keeps delaying the way he has, Stef will always have questions.

"I'm sorry too," she says.

"For what?"

"For everything. For showing up on your doorstep. For making you think you have to take care of us. For forcing you to take that stupid job. I know you hate it, but you did it anyway, because that's what you do."

"It's not that bad," I say. Not today, anyway. I glance at the clock. I still have hours to go before I can go to David's room, but just the idea of it makes everything seem better.

"I promise, regardless of what happens with Graham, whatever you want to do next, I won't give you a hard time. If you want to come home and work odd jobs until you can buy another boat, or if you want to be a digital nomad in Vietnam, I will support you."

"I don't even know what a digital nomad is," I say. Marci probably knows. I can ask her in the morning.

Stef grins. "You'd hate it. It involves a lot of computers."

We stare at each other silently through the screens.

"Maybe when I'm done here, I'll go to Europe for a little while. See the sights." With what money, I have no idea, but even just saying the words out loud is exciting.

"Oh, that's a great idea. You could go to Italy. We went to Florence on our honeymoon. Or France! Before Robbie was born, we—" Stef bites her lip. "Sorry. Getting ahead of myself. I'm sure you'll pick a destination that appeals to you."

"Do they fish in Europe?"

Her smile is relaxed now, and I'm relieved to see it. "I'm sure they do."

"Call me tomorrow after you see him?" I say.

"You bet."

It takes hours before the lodge gets quiet. The hall outside my door is like a freeway of people coming and going. Marci stops by, wordlessly handing me a small Wild Eagle gift bag and walking away without a backward glance. Finally, as the sun sets, the noise dies down. I let myself out of my room and everything is calm. Even the front desk is vacant. I make a quick trip from the staff door to the main stairs, keeping my steps quiet as I head up to the second floor, then down the hall to the stairway to the third and fourth floors.

I haven't been up here since the tour on my first day, and everything still smells like new paint. The fourth floor feels a mile away from everything else, and my knock on David's door echoes loudly. I glance around, expecting Harper to leap out from around a corner and demand to know what I'm doing.

When David opens the door, my breath stops. He's perfect and dressed in a white collared shirt with one extra button undone and pressed gray pants that fit him perfectly.

He looks like a model.

"Hi," I say, still trying to get my lungs to work properly again.

"Hey," he says. "I half expected you to come to your senses."

"Believe me, I tried." I was so determined to keep my head down this summer. Fly under the radar and help Stef get back on her feet. But maybe she doesn't need me anymore, and I can do something for me instead.

The door closes behind me, and David walks away when I expect him to grab me. The room is bigger than the ground floor of my house, and he walks down to the living area, where he's got a bottle of champagne in a bucket.

"Want something to drink?" He pours without waiting for an answer, and my hand shakes as I take the glass from him.

"You don't have to seduce me, you know," I say. "Pretty sure we've already got that covered."

He smiles, his perfect white teeth glinting in the low light. "I wanted to do something nice. You've taken such good care of me all week."

The champagne is light and fizzy, and I hiccup as I swallow, making the bubbles go up my nose. David's watching me as he sips his. It's like the first morning on the boat where we shared a mug of coffee. I felt connected to him despite all my resentment at being here and all the training that told me to keep my distance.

"How was your dinner?" I ask.

He slips a hand into mine, pulling me out toward the balcony.

"It was good," he says. "Everything here is good. Five stars. Will definitely recommend it to all my friends when I get home."

The stars are bright, dusting the sky in sparkling blue and white.

"Not everyone gets this experience," I say, putting an arm around his waist.

"I would never imply that they would. Even without it though, this place is pretty special. I was so down when I found out we were coming, but it's been better than I expected."

"Even with the fish guts?" I ask.

David laughs as he leans in to kiss me. "I'll leave that part out of my review."

He tastes like champagne. His glass has somehow disappeared, and he puts a hand on my hips, holding me close as he pulls me in. David takes my glass from me. He sets it down on a small table made from a tree stump, then comes back to kiss at my throat. His mouth is warm. So is my whole body. Even the cooling night air doesn't touch me as we explore. His shirt is untucked, so it's easy for me to find the smooth skin underneath. He murmurs appreciatively as he pulls my shirt from my waistband and glides his own hands along my belly and up my back.

"Mountain man," he says.

"I'm not much for heights."

He laughs and slides my shirt off over my head. Now I feel the chill, but it only serves to contrast with the warmth of his palms and his mouth as he touches all of me.

"What do you want to do?" he asks. "What do you like?"

It's been a while for me, and my interests have always been pretty vanilla. Hands, mouths, dicks.

"I've got a condom and lube in my pocket," I say. Marci said it was pretty easy to find what I'd asked for.

David kisses me, using his teeth to pull at my bottom lip while he slides one hand into my front pocket until he finds what he wants. He stays a moment longer, letting his fingers graze over the hardening outline of my dick. I groan, arching my hips, trying to give him the space to touch me fully, but even the thin fabric of the pocket is more of a barrier than I want. This would all be so much easier with no pants.

He must have the same idea, because he lets go of me and spins on his heel. "Come inside." He holds up the condom between two fingers like I needed any more enticement. I stumble after him, shivering without my shirt on, but by the time I've closed the door again, David has unbuttoned his own shirt and folded it gently over the back of the sofa. He unloops his belt and opens his fly. He's beautiful. He turns as he pulls his pants off, watching me as I watch the perfect curve of his ass when it appears from behind the gray fabric.

He smiles. "Like what you see?"

I've been staring, but the question drives me to act. I slip my jeans off and stumble toward him in my underwear. My dick is begging to be set free as I crash into him, taking us both to the bed. He laughs underneath me as he spreads his thighs, and I settle against him. I want to feel his long legs wrapped around me.

"Yes," he says, dragging his nails along my back. "You're so hot. Do you know that? I've wanted you since the first morning I saw you."

"I'm hot?" I slide a hand between us to grip him, and he drops his head back, arching underneath me. "I've never met anyone who looked like you. I think you could definitely try being a model. Not that I know anything about that, but look at you, David. I mean—"

"Jack." He stops moving against me. His whole body goes still.

"No, I'm serious." I kiss him, trying to get him to respond again. "You're the best-looking guy I've ever met. I—"

"Stop. This isn't right. Jack, I need to tell you something."

A knock is the only warning we get. It's followed immediately by the whir of the lock, before the door to the room is thrown open and Mr. Morgan storms in.

"You reckless, horny asshole!" he shouts.

"Jesus Christ, Vin." David's voice is even louder. "A little privacy would be good." He pushes against me, so I roll toward the big windows and away from his angry boss.

"You had one job!" Mr. Morgan is saying. Did David call him Vin? But Vin is David's best friend, not his boss. "One job. Lie low. We offered you alternatives. Roberta and Ivy and I have been busting our asses trying to figure this out, but all you had to do was keep your head down. And what do you do instead?"

"Get the fuck out." David points toward the door. His words and posture are full of authority. Even if Mr. Morgan is the twelfth wealthiest man in Boston or whatever, I would be so pissed about this violation of boundaries if I were David.

"Oh, sure." Mr. Morgan scoffs. "So you can get yourself into more trouble? You haven't even shut the curtains for fuck's sake." He strides over to the windows and pulls down the blackout curtains. He gives me an apologetic smile. I'm huddled up at the headboard, a pillow over my crotch, though at this point my erection is basically a thing of the past. He says, "Hi, Jack. Sorry about all this."

"All what?" I say.

His expression is sympathetic as he gives me a once-over, but it darkens again as his attention goes back to David.

"Roberta's calling in five minutes. Put some clothes on."

"I don't understand what's happening," he says, and that makes two of us.

Mr. Morgan pulls a cellphone out of his pocket and flips through a couple of screens before he shoves it in David's face.

"You thought Cannes was bad? That's nothing, honey. The chitchat with Anderson at the bar? Peanuts. Now the world knows what your O-face looks like."

The room is quiet. Slowly, David puts out a hand and gropes until he finds the mattress behind him.

"What's wrong?" I ask as he sags back down. I crawl over the bed. Never mind that I'm in my underwear in front of a guest. Something terrible has happened.

Mr. Morgan sighs as he holds the phone up for me to see. "It's only the back of your head, so you're probably okay."

But I'm not. I'm really not okay. Because I'm looking at a video of—as he said—the back of my head. I'm on the boat, the shot taken from overhead. My face is buried in David's lap, but the Wild Eagle logo on the back of my jacket is plainly visible, as is the ecstasy on David's face as he throws his head back.

"Jesus," I say. "What is that?"

"Congratulations," Mr. Morgan says. "You're now the supporting actor in a celebrity sex tape."

21

DAMIAN

B REAKING *EXTRAtainment News!*
    D AMIAN M ARSHALL'S A LASKAN S EX T APE

*After days of close calls and near misses, we finally caught up
with Damian Marshall, who has been taking a little R & R at a
remote Alaskan resort. The actor certainly seemed to be enjoying
himself in the arms of an unidentified man, lending further confirmation to the rumors swirling that the* Shadow League *star is gay and
that the altercation with director Anderson Lind at Cannes earlier this
month had to do with a relationship between the two of them,
whether past or ongoing.*

*Lind could not be reached for comment, and what he thinks about
the new man in Marshall's life—and his lap—remains to be seen.*

———

S HIT. Shit, shit, shit, and fucking goddammit.

A sex tape? I mean, honestly, what are the odds?

It was taken by a drone, from the looks of it. Must have been
up pretty high with a big ass lens, because neither of us heard
anything.

Then again, with the roar of blood in my ears and all my

other senses concentrated on Jack's mouth around my cock, I probably would have missed a fighter jet flyby.

And now it's on the internet. The video. Screen grabs. Edits with soundtracks. Memes. It's been barely twelve hours since we were recorded, and it's already taken on a life of its own.

Jack left at some point. I don't remember when. Roberta and Vin are on the laptop talking. There are four other people on the call. A lawyer, two crisis management PR types, and I don't even know who the fourth person is. I don't know any of their names. I can't even hear what they're saying. All I can see is the footage playing over and over in my brain. My fingers in Jack's hair, his head in my lap bobbing vigorously so there's no denying what's going on. No smoothing it over. The video has already circled the globe a dozen times.

"Leave in the morning," Roberta is saying. "We've got a plane set to go as soon as the sun is up."

I nod while she and Vin work out the logistics. An army of press will be here as soon as it's daylight. The sooner we get out, the sooner the lodge staff can go into damage control mode. They can protect their staff—protect Jack—without me creating a distraction.

The click of the laptop as Vin closes it brings me back to the present. The room is mostly dark. We're sitting side by side on the sofa. A standing lamp is on. Another light by the bed. I left that one on so I could see Jack's beautiful body, and in the end, I got to see the confusion and the betrayal on his face.

Shit. I fucked this up so badly, and I have no one to blame but myself. The sex tape would have been bad enough on its own, but it's a thousand times worse that it's how Jack found out I've been lying this whole time.

"You okay?" Vin says.

I nod. I'm not sure I've spoken since Vin got his call going. "Yup. Just staring down the consequences of my own actions."

He squeezes my hand. "We'll figure this out. We always do."

It's after two in the morning by the time Vin leaves. He tells me to get some sleep, and I honestly try, but every time I close my eyes, I'm tormented by the memories of Jack's mouth on mine. His hands on me. The trust he placed in me that I utterly destroyed all because I was too scared and self-absorbed to be honest.

After three, I find myself walking down the stairs to the ground floor. Marci is sitting at the desk, staring at her phone. I try to slink along the walls, but she must hear me, because her head snaps up. She opens her mouth, but I press a finger to my lips, and her jaw snaps shut again. Silently, I point to the Staff Only door, and she glances around us before she nods slowly. I can't tell if she knows or if she thinks I'm sneaking off for one more round with Jack. I hope it's the latter, but it probably isn't.

His door is the only one with a strip of light spilling out from underneath. My head spins as I tap on the wood so softly that I have to knock again. The sound of footsteps inside has my knees and guts going liquid, but I need to stay. He deserves to understand what happened.

Jack's in a worn T-shirt and faded sweats when he opens the door. He has to have known it was me, but he still looks me up and down like he doesn't know who I am, and in the end, he doesn't.

Wordlessly, he steps aside, and I let out a breath as I follow him into the room. He pulls out the chair from the desk and sits on it, so I have no option but to sit on the bed, which leaves me feeling unexpectedly vulnerable. *More* vulnerable.

"First off," I say. "I owe you an apology. Several, in fact. I might have apologized before, but I don't remember, so let me do it again. Jack, I'm so sorry."

He stays silent for so long it's like he's turned to stone. Finally, he folds his arms over his chest and says, "I need more than that, *Damian*."

Hearing him say that name makes me feel sick. "You've been online?"

"Didn't even have to go looking too far for it. The first news site I went to had pictures all over it. And your name."

I don't know which is worse. That he had to see us splashed everywhere for the world's amusement, or that he found my name before I had a chance to tell him. But I guess I had dozens of chances to tell him.

I was about to, right before Vin came in. Too little too late, but I was ready to accept the fallout. And Jack might have been pissed, but I had days left on this trip to make it up to him before I went back to California.

Now though, I'm leaving in a few hours, and I'll probably never get to make amends.

"David Morgan is the name on my birth certificate."

"Is that supposed to make me feel better? You've been lying every minute we were together."

"No. Not—" I fold my hands in my lap, choking back the protest because he's right, and I deserve every ounce of his anger. I try to ground myself in truth—the truth I should have given him from the minute we met. "When you get to where I am in my career, people feel like they have a right to you. Like they deserve answers to even the most personal questions. The thing at Cannes—everyone was watching me. I'm not out, not to the public anyway, and to clear the air on this I was going to have to come out, and I wasn't . . ." The words get caught in my throat, strangling me for a moment. Jack's expression is still excruciatingly blank, like he's happy to watch me dig my own grave.

I mentally flip through more words—more explanations— until I find more truth again. "The first morning . . . I couldn't sleep. Couldn't stop the second-guessing and the questions about whether I had to choose my sexuality over my career. And I found you on the boat, and you didn't know who I was. You didn't ask questions or want answers that weren't yours. And I . . . Jack . . ." I search his face, hoping he's looking back on that morning even a bit fondly. "I needed that. I'm sorry. It was selfish, but I needed space. A moment to not be Damian Marshall so I could breathe again. That was all it was supposed to be. You assumed I was someone else and let me be David. That's all I wanted."

I lapse into silence. I don't know what else to say. Somehow, everything I touch these days goes to shit.

He asks, "What happens now?"

A lump forms in my throat. "With us?"

But Jack shakes his head, and the tiny spark of hope that glowed to life inside me dies again. "There's no us. I don't know you."

"I'm still the same person."

He turns to the computer on his desk and the screen flares to life. I expect to see the pictures from the boat, blurry screen grabs that will haunt him forever. Instead, he's been looking at pictures of me. Promo stills. Red carpet shots. That fucking photo shoot on the yacht with the Scandinavian clone models. I've been primped and powdered and plucked until I look like a more polished version of myself. Like a wax figure in a museum.

"I don't know this person," Jack says. "I met a man named David. This guy . . ." He raps a knuckle against the screen. "He's a stranger."

"He doesn't have to be," I say in a rush. "What do you want to know?"

But Jack only shakes his head. My heart is in my throat. We're coming to an end. This whole week I've been so worried about protecting my career, and instead, here's something I'm suddenly far more worried about losing.

"I think it's better if you leave," he says. "I hope you've enjoyed your stay with us." Every one of his words is careful.

The syllables are so precise, it's like he's learning lines and terrified to forget any of them.

"You can't be this calm," I say. "After everything."

He laughs once. His whole body shudders with it. Then his eyes narrow, and there—I have just a second to brace before the storm hits.

"I'm calm," he says, "because this is my job. There are people —ones I have to speak to in the morning and every day after you're gone—on both sides of these walls, and they will hear every word I say if I speak even a little louder than this. And they're already going to see the pictures. When they wake up tomorrow, they'll check their emails or their social media, and they'll see me sucking your dick. Talk about answering uncomfortable questions. Look at the position you've left me in." As he speaks, my face goes uncomfortably hot, but I hold myself still because I deserve to hear everything he has to say. "My sister will see those pictures. Someday my nephew might see them."

"Your sister," I say, desperation rising. "She's on her way to work out things with her husband. Everyone deserves a second chance. If she can—"

"Don't." Spit flies from his lips. "You don't get to talk about them."

That was the wrong move. One of so many these last few weeks. "They'll disappear. The pictures. The video." One of those people on the call with Vin and Roberta said they were working on getting them taken down, right? But even I know that only goes so far. The internet is forever, after all.

"I had a plan this summer," he says. "It was simple. Keep my head down, do my job, make enough money to help Stef and Robbie. That was all I had to do. And then you showed up and *lied*. You selfish asshole. I trusted you, Davi—Damian. Whoever you are. I trusted that we were in this together. That you were here even though you didn't want to be, just like me, and we were doing what we could with our time together to make our jobs manageable, but you were playing from a completely different rule book from the beginning."

"Jack. I'm so sorry." I'll say it again and again until he believes me.

"And the worst part"—he stares down at his palms—"is that I've read the stuff they printed about you. Even while you've been here, they've still been talking about you. And when I look at your face, I can see how much it's eating you up. I want to forgive you. I can't imagine what it's like to feel like you have to come out to billions of people you will never meet but who can say whatever they want about you online. And I feel sorry for you. What does that say about me? That you can lie to me for days, have sex with me, put me in this situation, and I still feel sorry for you?" He pushes up to his feet, and for a second, I hope he's about to touch me, but instead he goes to the door, and my heart sinks. "I don't want to feel sorry for you, David. I don't owe you pity. Not after what you've done."

His hand on the doorknob is a declaration Roberta would approve of. We're finished here. He's got all the information, and nothing he's said is untrue.

I get up and walk through the door. The hall is silent. If anyone heard us, they're at least giving us the illusion of discretion.

The last glance I get of Jack is his back as he disappears into his room.

Surprising no one, I don't get much sleep. When Vin knocks on my door a while later, my eyes feel like sandpaper and my head is pounding worse than any hangover.

"Plane's ready to go," he says, not bothering to ask how my night was.

"Any press?"

"Not so far. Roberta and the PR people booked up all the charters in the area they could find. Paid them to fly around in circles for a few hours to give us a head start."

Unlike the day we arrived, the staff haven't assembled to see us off. No doubt they're inside circling the wagons. The kindest thing I can do is get out of their hair.

I step up into the plane first, then give Vin a hand up. It's only when I turn that I realize someone is already inside.

And he doesn't look happy to be there.

"Jack?"

His expression isn't a smile, more a grimace. That's the best he can manage.

"Guess we're traveling together," he says.

"What? Why?"

Jack smooths his hands over his thighs before he speaks, and when he looks up at me again, his eyes are dark like a thundercloud.

"Effective this morning, I'm no longer employed at the Wild Eagle Lodge."

22

JACK

I should have seen it coming, really, though I think I can be excused given that the list of ways I could embarrass myself never included being the second participant in a celebrity sex tape. My head's not on straight.

So in the morning, I get up, put on the pair of khakis Stef made me buy and my Wild Eagle polo shirt, and march straight to Harper's office. I ignore the stares and whispers from my coworkers as I go by.

"Jack—" Marci starts toward me as I walk through the staff kitchen, but I pretend I don't hear her and keep going.

I knock on the office door, and Harper's muffled "Yes?" is the only reply. I let myself into her office. She's on the phone, her back to the door, hunched against her desk, but when she turns and sees me, her eyes go big and she drops the pen she's been clicking restlessly with her thumb.

"Hang on," she says. "He just walked in. I'll call you back."

I sit gingerly. The chair feels like it's made of matchsticks, but the falling feeling might also be my whole life crumbling to pieces.

We sit in silence for a minute, aside from the occasional click of her pen.

Guess I'll be the one to start.

"I can only begin to imagine the hassle this is causing you and the rest of the company. And I know that giving guests blow jobs"—we both wince as I say it—"is pretty much a nonoption in any circumstance, but all I can say is that I legitimately didn't know who he was. I thought the other man"—what had David called him? Vin?—"was the VIP, and the man I was with was his bodyguard. He let me think that. And it doesn't excuse my behavior. But if I'd known who he really was, I might have reconsidered, or at least . . ." I grapple with how to phrase this. "Been a little more discreet. I'm sorry."

Harper blinks rapidly for a few seconds before she takes a slow inhale, then lets out an even slower exhale.

"I appreciate your apology," she says. "It was only brought to my attention recently that there might have been a misunderstanding about Mr. Morgan—by which I mean Mr. Marshall—and his real identity. You know the policies from corporate are very strict on what we're allowed to disclose about our guests, but Jack, I can honestly say I think those policies were written with the assumption that someone like Damian Marshall would be instantly recognizable to everyone, and we'd all agree not to discuss it."

"I don't watch a lot of movies," I say, then go cold when I realize Damian asked me the same question. I must have seemed so ridiculous to him. Some deep-woods hick who didn't know anything.

"Yes, I can see that," she says. "Jack, I'm so sorry. This whole situation is . . . unfortunate."

That's a very polite way to put it. "If you need me to pump bilges or prep bait for the rest of the summer, you won't hear a peep out of me."

She was on her way to a sympathetic smile, but as I speak, the smile makes a sharp U-turn and vanishes again.

"I . . ." Her voice is raspy, and her picture-perfect composure cracks. "You can't stay."

"Oh." My vision goes blotchy for a second as I take in her meaning. "Oh."

She straightens up in her seat. "It's not really even about the sex. You wouldn't be the first or last at a place like this with a guest of his status. But the optics here are . . ." She wrinkles her nose. "I'm sorry. But the logo is literally right there for everyone to see. We aren't even technically open yet, and—"

"No." I hold up a hand. "No, I get it." Should have expected it, if I'd been able to think straight at all.

"I'm sorry," she says, and she really does sound like she means it. "Maybe next season. There are other resorts in the family. No one can even see your face in the video, and—"

"Thanks," I say. "But I'm not sure I'm cut out for this job."

"There's a plane heading out this morning. If you could be on it . . ."

I should be humiliated, but mostly I'm relieved. That is, until I'm on that plane, and a tall dark frame appears in the door, and Damian's smile drops as he sees me.

Just great.

The first twenty minutes are silent except for the drone of the plane's engines. Damian is sitting behind me. His friend is sitting in the seat opposite mine with a pair of oversized headphones and his weird green-lensed sunglasses on. He keeps his face turned away, and that's fine by me. I try to give him the same courtesy.

But soon enough, Damian is in the narrow aisle between the two seats, speaking softly to Vin. Vin mutters something that sounds distinctly like "not a good idea," but it apparently can't be that bad, because the next thing I know, they're doing a complicated dance to swap seats, even though the space really isn't big enough for that. Finally, Damian is sitting next to me, and he is very close.

"Jack," he says.

I consider ignoring him, and I'd be within my rights to do so, but since I can practically feel his breath on the back of my neck, it's nearly impossible to do it convincingly. So I set my jaw and turn to glare. It must be effective because he swallows hard before he speaks again.

"I'm not expecting you to forgive me," he says.

"That's the first reasonable thing you've said."

He gnaws at his bottom lip, and the gesture is so at odds with the rest of his perfect, flawless face. Of course he's a movie star. How could I not have seen it before? Bodyguards don't have time for things like tanning and getting their eyebrows waxed.

"I want to help though," he says. "Things could get rough for you for the next little while."

I snort. "Pretty sure you've helped enough."

"They'll figure out who you are if they haven't already. They'll find your social media."

"I'm not on social media."

He sighs. "Of course you aren't. Please, Jack. I've made such a mess of this."

I'm done giving him space. Done trying to make either of us feel better about this. "You've cost me my job and a decent chunk of my self-respect. I think it's better if we forget this ever happened."

We don't speak again, but he also doesn't move back to his original seat. Once, I glance at him, but he's turned away from me, so I go back to looking out the window, staring down at the gray shield of the water and the black tips of spruce trees as we turn inward. It's uncomfortable, and my neck hurts from being stuck in one place. But I'll deal with that when we land because I can't look at him.

The trees are giving way to roads and houses when Vin speaks behind me. "Oh fuck."

"What?" Damian asks.

"Hey!" Vin gets louder. "Is that where we're supposed to land?"

He doesn't get a reply, and Damian shifts beside me, his elbow brushing my arm as he leans forward.

"Excuse me," he says to the pilot. "Are we heading down there?"

"Yes," the pilot says.

"Is there anywhere else we could go?" Vin asks, voice rising, not to be heard now, but with an edge of agitation I don't like.

"The flight plan says we're going there."

"But what if we . . . didn't?" Vin asks.

"What's going on?" I can't help the question as the tension rises in the small plane. No one seems to hear me. Vin and Damian are glued to their two small windows, and whatever they see can't be good, because Vin's punching at his phone furiously.

"How can we still have no service?" he asks.

"It's fine," Damian says.

"I need to call Ivy."

Damian glances over his shoulder at me, and his expression isn't the same apologetic one he's worn since last night. Nor is it the same relaxed one I'd seen so often from David. It's harder. Stronger.

"It'll be fine." But he's speaking to me now, and I still don't know what's going on.

"We'll have to run for the car. The security Ivy hired better be waiting." Vin's still scowling at his phone.

Finally, the plane wheels around so that our views are swapped, and I see what's got them so worked up as we come in for a landing.

There is a crowd of people.

No. A crowd doesn't really describe it properly. A . . . horde? An army. I'm not even sure what I'm looking at, but the people are so tightly packed together I can't even tell what they're standing on, whether it's grass or asphalt or gravel.

The plane comes splashing down and motors resolutely up to the dock. The pilot doesn't seem at all worried about the throng waiting for us. He kills the engines and turns to us.

"Just sit tight until I get that door open."

Then he's opening his own small door and stepping out as a roar of voices starts.

Before I left the Lodge, I had just enough time to pack up my stuff and call Stef from my laptop. I gave her the location of the marina and told her when to meet me. She had so many questions, but the plane was ready to go. I promised to tell her everything when I landed.

What I didn't realize was that I'd have to find her among all the fans and media who are here to see Damian, and now I don't know how I'll manage it. It's chaos outside. People are screaming. Cameras flash as the pilot walks along the float. A few pride flags are waving in the breeze, and one woman is holding up a sign that says *Damian, I Love Threesomes.*

Shit, are they here to see me too?

"Stay here."

I don't realize Damian is speaking to me until I feel his hand on my wrist. The gesture isn't aggressive, and my brain short-circuits again, pinging between leaning into him because I can't seem to help myself when he touches me and pulling away as a wave of hurt feelings threatens to choke me.

His voice is soft. "Vin and I are going to get off. I'll ask the pilot to close the door. Stay here until they all leave, okay?"

People can probably see me through the window. I shrink back, trying to pull the collar of my jacket up as high as it will go. Damian looks genuinely sad, and he brushes a thumb against the underside of my wrist. This is it. He's leaving. I should be relieved. That much closer to ending this pointless chapter of my life. But suddenly I feel like there are more things we should say.

The door at the rear of the plane opens, and the screaming gets louder.

"Damian! Who was the man you were recorded with?"

"Damian! Are you seeking treatment for sex addiction?"

"Damian! Are you gay?"

"Damian! What do you have to say to your fans?"

"Damian! When's the wedding?"

Vin mutters something, then slides his sunglasses into place and steps outside. The roar only grows as Damian appears in the doorway. He has to hunch to get through the door, and the questions get so frenzied I can't even understand them anymore.

He doesn't look back.

If anyone can still see me through the window, they don't care. They surge toward him. A number of muscly men in dark sunglasses form a human chain around him, giving him room to make his slow way forward. Actual bodyguards. They don't smile. They don't speak. They're all business, and it seems so naive to think Damian might have ever had that job. He keeps his head down as they go. All his easy friendliness is gone. He still stands a full head taller than everyone around him, and even as the crowd pushes inward and hurls their questions, somehow he looks very alone.

Soon enough, a car pulls away, and the reporters and photographers all rush to get into their own cars to chase after him. Fans linger in the chaos, but it starts to rain, and they move on pretty quickly.

Finally, when the marina is empty, I grab my bags and step down. A few fishermen on their boats lift their heads as I go by, but none of them give me a second look.

Stef is waiting in the parking lot. She's leaning against the car, wearing her rain jacket and rubber boots, looking every inch like nothing out of the ordinary has happened.

"How was your flight?"

"Bumpy," I say. "What are you doing here? Aren't you supposed to be meeting Graham?"

She flicks a hand. "Been there. Done that."

"And?"

"I'll tell you about it in the car. After you tell me about"—she gestures toward the main road where all the cars have disappeared over the next hill—"that."

I groan. "Good thing it's a long drive."

She reaches up and pulls me close for a hug. It feels good. Normal.

I'm back to my old life. No more hotels. No more movie stars.

Hopefully I never have to think about Damian Marshall again.

23

DAMIAN

E XTRAtainment UPDATE!
DAMIAN MARSHALL RETURNS TO HOLLYWOOD AMID SEX
TAPE SCANDAL

Actor Damian Marshall was photographed earlier today at a marina in Anchorage, Alaska, less than twelve hours after a video of him engaged in a sexual act with an unidentified man emerged on the internet. The movie star, recently involved in a bitter feud with director Anderson Lind, had been staying at the Wild Eagle Lodge, a luxury fishing resort in Alaska. According to the Lodge's website, they offer an exclusive and private wilderness experience for discerning travelers. No one at the lodge or its parent company, Wild Hospitality International, could be reached for comment.

Marshall is believed to be traveling back to Hollywood. What happens next is anyone's guess. His future with the blockbuster Shadow League *franchise was already in doubt after his fallout with Lind, and being the star of his own sex tape will make him a challenging property for a film franchise that markets itself to adults and teenagers alike.*

Is this the end of Damian Marshall?

———

CALIFORNIA IS SO LOUD. And hot. Was it always this hot?

We fly straight from Anchorage to a private airfield outside LA. Roberta's done a much better job of keeping the press away here than in Alaska, and we go straight from the jet to a black SUV with tinted windows.

"Ivy says your place is swarmed," Vin says, staring at his phone. He's been glued to it since we got in the car in Anchorage. "We're going to Roberta's instead."

Even with my social media accounts in Ivy's capable hands, I still have dozens of missed calls and texts from people I haven't heard from in months and voicemails I'm never going to listen to. Next comes the sinking realization that I never thought to ask for Jack's contact information—not that he would have given it to me, or that I have any right to call him—so he's well and truly out of my life forever.

Instead of listening to those voicemails, I make the terrible decision to check the entertainment news, and my name is plastered everywhere. Blurred-out screen grabs and pictures of the hotel. The headlines ask if I have a sex addiction, a drug addiction, or if I'm having a mental health crisis. There are insinuations and outright declarations that this plus the situation at Cannes means my career is over. That I've been out of control for years. People I've never spoken to for more than a minute are quoted saying they've been worried about me for ages. At least all the articles continue to refer to Jack as "an unidentified man."

"Stop." Vin's still typing hurried texts.

"What?"

"Stop self-flagellating over what those assholes write. They get paid by the click. No one cares if it's true."

But people take it as truth. And maybe some of it is. None of my behavior has been rational. I've been so busy protecting myself, I hadn't cared who I'd hurt in the process.

Roberta lives in a contemporary ranch in Studio City. I've been to visit a few times before, but today it feels like I'm arriving somewhere new. Were her front windows always that big? Didn't she used to have a gate at the end of the driveway?

But Vin doesn't seem to notice or be worried. He hands me a faded ball cap.

"Keep your head down."

I do as instructed, and we seem to have escaped notice for the time being. I don't hear so much as a bird call as I cross from the car to Roberta's front door, which Ivy throws open breathlessly the second we get close.

"Come in! Come in. Oh my God, how are you? Are you okay? How was the flight? Can I get you something to eat?" Ivy is everything Roberta is not. She's quick to smile and always looking out for everyone's immediate comfort. Her hair is a riot of blue curls, and she's wearing a pair of earrings Vin gave her last year that have "Highly Skilled" and "Hot Mess" woven into them with rose gold wire.

"Damian." Roberta cuts off Ivy's litany of questions, and my stomach twists at the hard edge to her voice. I move past Vin and Ivy, leaving them to whisper quietly to each other. Roberta is sitting on the patio, which is sheltered by a striped olive green awning. She strides up to me as I approach, and I stop when I'm only a few inches away, letting her look me up and down. She's as immaculate as always, but if I look closely, I can see the mascara under her eyes is slightly smudged like it was applied a long time ago, and the lipstick on her bottom lip is flaking. After Vin, she's been my staunchest ally for years, and I've made her life so much more complicated than it needs to be.

"I'm so sorry," I say.

She sighs, then gathers me in a long hug. I have to hunch my spine to get my head onto her shoulder, but it's worth it. She smells of jasmine, and the knobbly end of her collarbone pokes at my forehead, grounding me in something other than the guilt that's been eating at me. "It's okay. We'll figure this out."

"Thank you."

"I think you know everyone," she says when she lets me go, gesturing to the people gathered around the terrace. I assume they're the same group who were on the phone call last night. I still can't remember any of their names.

Ivy brings food, juice, and a pot of coffee I could drink all on my own. It's not as good as Jack's coffee, but I'm going for stimulation, not flavor. Everyone around me is in full-blown battle mode. The least I can do is stay awake.

And stop obsessing about Jack and his coffee. Or any other part of him. Not his hands as he competently went about setting up the lines to fish. Or the soft rumble of his laugh. The careful way he touched me when—

"Damian?"

I snap back to reality when Roberta says my name. She's got her back to the sun, and I have to shade my eyes to see her properly. Despite her gentle words before, she looks pissed now.

"Sorry, what?"

"We've had the video pulled from the major outlets," one of the lawyers says. "And the Wild Eagle Lodge has come out with a statement saying that they have no comment on your stay with them, and that the other man in the video is no longer employed there."

I should have done more for him.

"Can we send up some security?"

The lawyer frowns. "The lodge is more than capable of providing their own adequate security. They—"

"Not for the lodge," I say. "For Jack."

The space gets quiet. The lawyers and Roberta glance at each other. Vin and Ivy are sitting on a love seat looking at me sadly.

Roberta asks, "What exactly is the nature of your relationship with . . . Jack?"

"What do you mean?"

"We don't have time for you to be coy, Damian."

"I'm not!" The sound of my name on her lips rankles me. After being called David for so many days in a row, it's like I've already fallen out of the habit of answering to Damian.

She taps a perfect nail on the arm of her chair. It's a silent signal not to fuck with her. "Is he your boyfriend? Are you in love with him?"

We knew each other for less than a week. How do I explain to them what happened?

"No." I drop my head. "There's nothing like that between us."

"Then it would be better if we put as much distance as we can between the two of you."

She's right, I know she is, but the idea doesn't sit well with me. Letting him go feels like a loss, like I'm staring down the barrel of something I don't want to face alone.

Roberta proves my point when she says, "So *Beloved Cove* is still on the table."

"What is?" I ask.

"You know," Vin says, shooting me a meaningful glance. "The script Roberta sent. The one that you read."

The one I was supposed to read, except I chose to spend time with Jack instead.

"They're very excited about your interest," Roberta says, even though I haven't indicated anything of the sort. "It'll have a big summer rom-com push for next year. Filming starts next month. You'll be on set in North Carolina for ten weeks. Lots of time for you to rehab your image."

"Go back to being Damian, you mean," I say.

She pauses. "Well, we'll never be able to get this albatross off your neck entirely. But if we can spin it as you coming into your sexuality and learning to embrace your place in the LGBT community, I think in the long term, we can manage. A few years of films with a different appeal, then we can talk about getting back to the formula. A comeback tour."

The albatross she's talking about is Jack. We'll never brush him away entirely. Years from now, a fan with no tact will go, "What about that guy who sucked your dick in Alaska?" and they'll laugh like we shared a hilarious joke. I'll always be the guy who was forced out of the closet because he was caught with another man. Neither the first nor the last, but it will always be something shameful.

The people around me are still talking. Still making decisions on my behalf. Roberta and Ivy are brainstorming outlets we could set up an interview with. Should we go with something serious and remorseful? Or have a talk show host shout "What were you thinking?" at me before they get me to play Twister with a new it-girl in a tight skirt like we're all best friends?

"I need to lie down," I say. The last time I slept was the night Vin and I drowned my sorrows in champagne. It feels like a lifetime ago.

"Guest room is down the hall." Roberta waves me off. She's deep in her plans. Contracts to be negotiated, appearances to be made. She's talking about me like I'm not even there. No, she's talking about Damian like he's not even here, and maybe she's right.

I stagger to the spare room, kick off my shoes, and don't even bother with my clothes before I collapse onto the bed.

Damian isn't here. Because Damian's not a person. He's a creation. My face and someone else's name. My voice and someone else's sexuality. He is a persona. A brand, really. I don't manage my schedule, my social media, my life. I go where they tell me and smile when the cameras come on, and for a long time, that's been fine because it was exciting and was the means to the end I'd been dreaming about and didn't think I'd ever have when I first met Roberta. I have everything I want. Fame. Name recognition. I could get on a bus to North Dakota tomorrow, look my whole family in the eye, and tell them I got what I wanted.

But I've hurt people to get there. Jack. Even Anderson,

though he hurt me right back, so I still don't feel much remorse about that.

I told Roberta if she couldn't fix things, I'd quit, but we both know that threat was hollow. Making movies is the only thing I know how to do. But maybe it's the means that don't work for me anymore.

The door opens, and Vin slips in quietly. He settles next to me on the mattress, on top of the sheets.

"You okay?"

"Spiralling in an existential quagmire but otherwise peachy."

"They've decided on the late-night option. Roberta thinks the combination of humor and bravado will help soften the dude-bro fans who might be pissed otherwise."

I close my eyes. She means they'll be pissed I'm gay, like those are people I need to ingratiate myself to.

Vin sighs. "Yeah, I don't like it either."

"And then they're banishing me to rom-com purgatory."

"It's not the script I would pick for your first out role. But yeah. If you can't make it with the Memorial Day weekend blockbuster fans, then you get to try to buy goodwill with the summer date-night couples."

It's not enough. Maybe I'm burnt-out on *Shadow League*. I certainly don't want to cater to those toxic masculinity fans who say I can't be a real hero because of who I love. But there has to be something between that and playing the sidekick who's only defined by his sexuality. Something I'm excited to do.

"And this is how it's going to be?" I say.

"Unless you start your own production company so you can green-light pictures you want to be involved in, yeah. Roberta says jump, and we step off the cliff."

And hope the studios and moviegoers will be there to catch us when we land.

Unless we build our own net.

I sit up suddenly. Vin, who had curled onto his side, grumbles.

"What now?"

"When's the late-night interview?"

"Roberta's still working on it, but probably tomorrow afternoon."

Is that enough time?

"Where's the script?" I ask.

"Which one?"

"Any one. Find me something. Something queer. Something that won't get made unless it's got a big name attached to it."

"But *Beloved Cove*—"

"Not that one. That one's pandering. It says 'I'm gay, and I'm sorry.' I don't want to apologize." Well, there are a few things I'm sorry for, but I'm not using my art and influence to hide who I am anymore.

"You want a protest piece?"

"No. Nothing overtly political, no sad histories. I want something that's got raw potential. On a submarine. Set in space. I don't care. Something that will only work because it's got my name on it."

He cocks a hip, but he's smiling. "You want a gay space submarine movie that's basically a one-man Hamlet?"

"Vin! Find me a script before I have to go grovel to a guy in a tie with a monogrammed mug in front of a live studio audience."

"Okay." He pauses with his hand on the door. "What do I tell Roberta?"

"That I'm asleep. Otherwise, nothing." I'm about to blow up her formula, and I want to have all the pieces lined up before I tell her.

I'm done letting other people manage me. Done letting them pretend to be me or that there's only one way to play this game.

From now on, I'm only going to be myself.

Someone I can be proud of. Someone Jack can trust.

24

JACK

Graham's moving to Alaska. He and Stef are renting a house. Somehow they decided all of this over pancakes and coffee this morning.

I'm so confused. I'd be mad too because this is a terrible idea, but I'm out of anger. That part of me is numb.

"He's leaving the charity." She keeps her gaze fixed on the road ahead of us. We're barely out of Anchorage, and I already don't know how I'll make it home. I want to crawl out of my skin. Absolutely nothing makes sense anymore.

"And you're just going to forgive him?"

Stef grimaces. "We're going to try. He's giving up a lot, Jack. He's joining a family practice in Anchorage. He's moving up here. For us. For Robbie. He was never willing to make sacrifices before. If he's giving all that up, I have to give him a chance."

A grand gesture. If I were her, I'd make him grovel every day for a year before he could even move to the same town as me.

"Jack," she says, and her voice has a kind of sticky sympathy in it that makes me even more desperate to get out of the car. She'll want me to confide in her, and I don't know how. Can't make myself. She knows, of course. Because the more I think about it, the more my humiliation is turning into shame.

Because I fell for it. All of it. Yes, David lied, but there were so many gaps. How does a bodyguard even go on a trip with his boss and then spend all his time fishing? How did no one tell me who he was? Marci could have said something. Why didn't I ask more questions or dig a little deeper? Get on the goddamn internet because apparently there isn't a single website out there that doesn't have something to say about Damian Marshall?

"Uncle Jack?"

I've never been so grateful for a distraction in my life.

"Yeah, Robbie?" I twist in my seat. He's watching me seriously, earphones still on his head.

"You're living with us again." It's a statement, and he doesn't wait for a reply before he goes back to the iPad, which is just as well because I don't know what to tell him, and he doesn't like to be contradicted when he considers something a fact.

But if Stef's going back to Anchorage, if she and Graham will be all cozy, then there won't really be a place for me. And yeah, the plan had always been for her to move to the city, but I was supposed to spend the whole summer showing tourists around the coast, and then after that I'd figure out what happens next for me. Instead, it's been less than a month, and I'm back with nothing to show for it.

"What was he like?" Stef asks after she's let me brood in silence for a few more minutes.

"Who?"

She gives me a hard stare. Of course she knows. She's on social media. She's sworn she hasn't watched the video, but she knows what happens.

I sigh. "He was a selfish asshole who lied about who he was."

"You may have mentioned that part already."

"Well, it's still true."

"But—"

"But what? I should give him another chance because he's really sorry? He's not Graham. He's not my husband." Not even a boyfriend or a friend. A stranger looking to blow off some steam, who didn't care who got hurt in the process.

Stef puts on her perky mom voice. The one she uses when the teachers want to have another "chat" about Robbie. "Do you want a coffee? I should have stopped for coffee."

I stare out the window. "I want to go home."

But when we get home, it's not the same there. The swarm of reporters hasn't materialized, but the house feels emptier somehow. Stef took my absence as an excuse to do a deep clean, and now nothing's where it's supposed to be. The change just makes me feel unsettled all over again. Once I bring in my stuff, I tell her I'm going out to buy groceries for dinner.

"You should go see Mom and Dad," she says.

But how can I? They'd have no idea who Damian Marshall is either, but even if I skip over the sex tape part, I still have to explain why I'm back so soon.

"Maybe tomorrow," I say.

Outside, I still have an itchy feeling along the back of my neck, like I'm being watched. I keep looking for someone lurking in the bushes with a big camera, but they're either really well-hidden or I'm being paranoid.

The market is the way it always is. It's a small family-owned store, and I say hi to four people before I've even grabbed a cart. They're faces I've known for years, and if anyone is surprised to see me back in town so soon, no one comments on it. I grab lettuce and tomatoes for me and Stef and a bag of baby carrots for Robbie. He doesn't like most vegetables, but he'll eat carrots if you let him drown them in ranch dressing.

A couple of teenagers are hanging out by the fruit. They're huddled together over a carton of strawberries, which at this time of year will probably set them back half a year's college tuition. As I approach, one of the girls looks up at me and her eyes widen, then she and her friends bunch closer together, whispering even faster.

I'm nearly past them with my cart when one of them, a boy with green in his hair and a ring in his nose, says, "Um. Hi."

"Hi," I say.

"How are you?"

Are they trying to steal the strawberries? Prank me? "Fine. Yourself?"

His nostrils flare, making the ring flash, but instead of answering, he spins back to his friends. There's more whispering, but they don't say anything else to me, so I keep going. Whatever they're up to, it's not my business.

I make my way down the next aisle. Someone must have gotten a new shipment of toilet paper, because it's on sale. I grab two packs, then put one back because Stef and Robbie are leaving for Anchorage soon, and I won't need so much when I'm back to living by myself again.

The thought makes me uneasy. I liked having them close. I didn't like that Stef was struggling, but I liked being able to help. And now what would I do? I was supposed to be at the lodge all summer. My boat's gone, and the licenses for the season will have been sold and distributed. If Damian hadn't—

A crash brings me back to reality, and I turn to find a man and a woman staring at me where they've run their shopping carts into each other.

"Oh, I'm so sorry," the woman says to me. "I didn't mean to bother you."

I don't know why she's talking to me when she should be apologizing to the other guy. I give them both a smile and carry on my way.

At the end of the aisle, the kids with the strawberries are waiting. They push the green-haired boy toward me again.

"Hi." He's breathing so hard he must be dizzy.

"Look, whatever you're doing, I'm not interested. Buy what you came for, or I'll call the store manager."

The girls behind him giggle, and he seems to take a little

courage from that, but only a little, because the next words out of his mouth are so fast I can't even understand them.

"I'm sorry, what?"

"You could call the manager," he says, more clearly this time, "or you could let me call you Daddy."

The girls all laugh hysterically. One of them lifts her phone to take a picture.

Oh God.

"Is this about . . ." I can't finish the question. I glance over my shoulder, and the two people who ran into each other before have come down the aisle and are hovering behind me. There's more than enough room for them to go around, but they stand there, gaping. Over my other shoulder, another group of shoppers is standing together, watching me and whispering.

David was wrong then. No reporters, but that doesn't mean I've escaped.

"Excuse me." I push past the teenagers. They watch after me with awestruck faces, but they don't say anything else. The same with the other people. As I approach, they scurry to get out of my way, but no one says anything, at least not to my face. But once I'm past, I hear someone whisper, "My daughter said it was on the internet. I haven't watched it, of course."

No, of course not. Why would anyone watch what was meant to be a private thing between two consenting adults?

Ridiculously, I suddenly wish David—or Damian, or whatever he wants to be called—was here. It's his fault any of this is happening. And he probably knows how to deal with things like this better than I do. Hell, he practically offered to help. All I can manage is to push my cart to the cash register. Since everyone's watching me, there's no line, and I throw the vegetables and toilet paper on the belt without glancing back.

The cashier is Sandra. She and her husband, Al, own the store. They're older than my parents, and I've known them forever.

"Is that everything?" Sandra asks as she puts my things in a bag.

"Yeah," I say. "That's all." Stef doesn't know it yet, but until she moves to Anchorage, she's in charge of all the shopping.

I pay, and Sandra smiles blandly at me as she hands me the bag. "Have a great day."

"I will. Tell Al I said hi." I turn to go, relieved that at least she isn't eyeing me like I'm a sideshow freak, then pause. "Sandra?"

"Yes, dear," she says.

"Have you ever heard of Damian Marshall?"

The change is startling. Her lips slam shut, and she goes so pale she's almost gray. For a second, I think she's having a heart attack.

"Sandra? Are you okay?"

Her eyelashes flutter, and she looks me up and down before nodding vigorously. Her cheeks turn bright pink, and the color spreads down beneath the collar of her shirt.

Behind me, the people are still watching and whispering.

"My grandson said he's a famous actor," Sandra says. "When I asked . . . When I . . . about . . ." She makes a squeaking noise as she claps a desperate hand over her mouth.

Great. Just fantastic.

I get home and leave the vegetables on the kitchen counter, then go to the living room where I slump on the couch and pull out my laptop.

"Did we become vegetarians when I wasn't paying attention?" Stef calls from the kitchen.

"We'll order pizza," I say, pulling up one of the celebrity news sites I've discovered over the last couple of days. It shows a bunch of pictures of Damian. A screenshot from the video, except now I've been blurred out so I'm a dark shape in his lap. A picture of him trying to get through the crowd of people at the marina in Anchorage. It still refers to me as "an unknown male employee of the Wild Eagle Lodge," and I guess I'm supposed to be relieved about that because it means they don't care enough to find out my name. I'm not the story. Damian is.

But the thing they're all forgetting is that here, in my home-town, with people I've known forever, I'm the most interesting thing that's ever happened. One step away from someone they idolize. Someone they think they know.

Someone I thought I knew.

"Stop torturing yourself with that asshat," Stef says as she comes to sit next to me.

"Language," I say. "There are children present."

Robbie's been drawing at the kitchen table. He's got his headphones on, but despite them, he laughs softly to himself and mutters something that sounds distinctly like "Yeah. That asshat."

I try to keep myself busy, but with my house already scrubbed to the baseboards and dinner coming in a box, there's not much to do. Normally this is the part where I'd go down to the wharf and work on the boat, but I don't even have that option. Dinner's awkward because the obvious topics of conversation are Damian—who I don't want to talk about—and Graham—who I do want to talk about, but I will almost immediately say the wrong thing. So we let Robbie talk about salmon spawning while Stef and I avoid making eye contact.

Once Robbie's in bed though, I quickly run out of places to hide.

"So," Stef says. "When you headed off to that job fair in Anchorage, I bet you didn't see this coming."

"Can we not?"

"Okay. Then do you want to talk about what you plan to do when I move and you're up here all by yourself?"

"I was by myself before you arrived."

"And you were lonely. I saw. The state of this place was—"

"Hey!"

She puts an arm around me, and it's an uncomfortable feeling to have my little sister dispensing life advice.

"You've given up a lot for this family," she says. "For Dad when he got sick. For me. I want to make sure you'll be okay."

"I'll be fine."

"By living on salad and take-out pizza while you hide from the rest of the town?"

"That's not my fault. I'm sorry a moment of poor judgement has turned me into the subject of local gossip."

Stef sighs, dropping her head on my shoulder. "You could come with us."

"What am I going to do in Anchorage? I can't be in the way while you try and figure things out with Graham."

"What will you do here?"

"I'm going to bed, that's what." I try to move slow enough that I don't dump Stef onto the floor, but she clings to me as I stand.

"Bed? Jack, it's not even nine o'clock. Come on."

But I'm done. Done with people who want things from me. Done with making hard decisions.

"No. I already let David go. I did the right thing and left my job when they told me to leave, even though what happened wasn't my fault. I'm standing by while you try to patch things up with a man you've been fighting with for over a year."

She pinches her lips. I should probably apologize for that last part, but I'm so tired and frustrated, I don't even know what's right anymore.

"Why do you still call him David?"

"What?" I'm still standing, and I don't want to sit next to her again, but I can't make myself leave the room.

"Damian Marshall. Why do you still call him David?"

I can't get it right in my head. I don't know Damian. None of it makes sense.

"Because that's what he said his name was. That's the name

of the man I knew. That I spent time with. That I—" It was too soon to paint fairy tales of a life together after he left the lodge, but David was a man I would have liked to see again. Damian? Damian is the kind of person who isn't even supposed to know people like me exist. He's not supposed to be real.

Stef says, "It's okay to be angry with him and still miss him. Trust me. I'm very familiar with that emotion."

But it's not okay. What happened was unforgivable.

"He lied," I say.

She shrugs. "Maybe you weren't the only one he was lying to. I've told myself a lot of things this year. Reasons why I was right to move Robbie up here and try and do it all on my own."

"If you needed more help, I—"

But Stef holds up a hand. "I was hurt. Graham wasn't there, and I needed him and didn't know how else to tell him. Before Robbie was born, before Graham was traveling so much, we promised we'd be there for each other. And things didn't work out that way. I told myself the only solution was divorce. That I didn't love him anymore, even though I've missed him every day since we've been here. Sometimes we lie to protect ourselves. Maybe Damian needed to be David for a while."

"I thought he was an asshat," I say. "And why would he want to be David? He literally has everything anyone could want. Who would want to be nobody?"

She scrolls through her phone to show me the picture of him trying not to get crushed in the crowd at the marina. "If you had a choice between pretending to be someone else so you could kiss a hot guy on a fishing boat and this, which would you pick?"

David's head is down, his shoulders slumped. Even under the shadow of his ball cap I can see the unhappy set of his mouth. It reminds me of the day he stepped off the plane. He'd walked like he was doing his best to be invisible. It hadn't looked like much of a life.

"Am I the hot guy in this equation?"

Stef blows me a kiss. "You're my brother, and I've already spent way too much time thinking about your sexual habits in the last twenty-four hours, so I'm only willing to go so far down this conversational detour. But yes, you're the hot guy I was thinking of."

I sit back down. "I don't know what I'm supposed to be feeling here."

"And that's okay. If you decide later we're going back to full-blown asshattery, forget I said any of this. I want you to be happy." She turns on the TV. "Let's watch a movie. Your choice."

She scrolls through Netflix. I don't recognize anything. But she stops at something called *Shadow League* and throws me a meaningful glance.

There he is. Well . . . sort of. It's David but not. Maybe that's the difference between David and Damian. His face looks like him, but at the same time, the shape is different. His smile as he grips his gun is artificial. His neck is oddly angled.

But his eyes are the same. The dip under his nose. It's David in a Damian costume, then dressed up to be someone else entirely.

"Not that," I say, and Stef doesn't push it. Maybe she's ready to forgive Graham, but Damian and I have a long way to go.

25

DAMIAN

E XTRAtainment UPDATE!
 DAMIAN MARSHALL TO BREAK HIS SILENCE

After weeks of silence following his outburst at Cannes, and with his career hanging in the balance, Damian Marshall will make his first public appearance tonight on The After Hours Show. In the interview with host Topher Brown, Marshall is expected to discuss his future with the Shadow League franchise, his relationship with director Anderson Lind, and the sex tape that has now been viewed almost 50 million times since it was first posted two days ago. Marshall will have to do some fancy footwork, as it's rumored Shadow League executive producer and New Film Cinema studio head Cedric Oberman is more than a little unhappy with his star. With the next Shadow League film not set to begin filming until the fall, a course change for the franchise is still a possibility.

————

SO IT TURNS out executing my master plan is not the overnight thing I was hoping for. Roberta makes it look so easy, but by the time I'm scheduled to record my interview, I still have a lot of balls in the air.

"Damian, what were you thinking?" Topher Brown leans against the edge of his desk while his audience laughs at his antics delightedly. I give them all my best aw-shucks-you-caught-me smile because it's what's expected. Secretly though, when before I tolerated this as part of the business—a necessary evil—now I hate them all for thinking they get to be part of this story.

But I have to get through this because I owe it to Jack to make amends publicly. If what we did in private was tossed out for the world to see, then my apology needs to be too.

"It was a lapse in judgement," I say, dropping my chin enough to look repentant.

"I'll say." Topher mugs for the camera. We met once, last year at an Oscars after-party. He was wasted and dumped his drink down the front of my shirt, though somehow the cameras missed it. But either he was too drunk to remember it or his people have decided it's better for appearances if we all pretend the incident never took place.

"I will say, and it's all I'll say"—it's not actually all I'm going to say, but Topher and the audience have to feel like they've won something here—"that what happened was between two consenting adults, and we had no idea anyone was filming."

"You looked like you were doing more than consenting." The crowd roars its approval, but since there wasn't a question in there, I give them a what-can-you-do? shrug and let them laugh at my expense.

"So, Damian." The host leans in for the kill. Even though I know the question is inevitable, my heart races. "I think what all these nice people and all those watching at home want to know is, are you gay?"

My mouth is dry. Technically, this show doesn't go to air for another six hours, but every single person in the audience has a phone, and the moment the words are out of my mouth, I have to assume the confirmation will be beamed around the world in seconds.

This is exactly what I didn't want. When Anderson grabbed me at Cannes and Roberta said I could either go to Alaska or tell the world the truth, this is exactly what I was hoping to avoid, and now here I am, mostly willingly. I didn't owe Anderson anything, but I owe Jack everything.

"Yes," I say, already envisioning the headlines. "I'm gay."

The ripple of shocked gasps, even though everyone here knows what I look like with my cock in someone's mouth, is audible through the whole studio.

Topher's expression softens sympathetically. "And is this something you've only realized about yourself recently?"

I don't have to answer this. All I had to admit was I'm attracted to men. From here, I can be as coy as I choose.

But I don't want them thinking what happened with Jack was some weird experimentation.

"No," I say. "No. I've known I was gay since I was fourteen. But it was something I was taught to hate. That I should be ashamed of who I am. Even after I told the people who care about me, it's taken me a long time to be comfortable with it But I didn't feel it was something I needed to talk about publicly before, with people who . . . " I trail off. I nearly say people who think they're owed answers for their entertainment. But I'm trying to win support, not alienate the audience. "With people who only know me through my movies."

"Speaking of movies"—Topher leans in with a grin, and where my heart was doing a tap dance routine before, now it ratchets up to a whole new tempo—"what about the other man in the video? Is he someone we'll be seeing more of in the future?"

This is a fine line. If I say too much, I violate Jack's trust again. If I hold too much back, their interest will be piqued, and while Jack has so far remained anonymous, that can change on a dime if anyone thinks there's money to be made in finding out who he is.

"No," I say. "As I'm sure you can imagine, he's not too happy with me." The audience gives me a sympathetic chuckle, which I appreciate. "I suspect he's had more than enough of his brush with fame."

"There's some speculation out there that what happened in Alaska is related to what happened with Anderson Lind at the Cannes Film Festival last month. Are you able to comment on that?"

Step two. Here we go. They're all expecting me to say I won't talk about Anderson. Roberta didn't put it on the list of approved questions because I asked her to leave it off to see what they'd do.

"Anderson and I had a relationship while we were filming *Shadow League 4*. It ended, but I didn't handle things as well as I should have."

Topher is bug-eyed. He stammers, "And have you spoken to him since then?"

"I haven't."

Topher eyes me, working something out, then his gaze slides over my shoulder toward the big game show–style wheel that was brought out right before I came on set. It's brightly colored and covered in glitter, and it has words on it like "Pig Saliva" and "Shirtless Polka" and whatever song and dance routine they think I'm about to do for them, beyond the one I'm already performing. I'd like to put it off for as long as possible.

"If I can say . . ." I put my hand on his arm.

"Well, sure, but we've got commercial break in forty-five—"

"For a long time, I thought I didn't need to own my sexuality publicly. That it was between me and whoever I might be involved with. That I didn't need to be a role model for anyone. Fans aspired to be like the characters I played on screen. But in my personal life, I never tried to be. Didn't think I needed to be, as long as I kept my head down."

"That's very interesting, but—" He glances nervously at the camera, then cocks his head in a way that means he's got a producer screaming in his ear to fuck the advertisers, they'll stay on me for as long as I keep speaking because whatever I say will have a zillion views online by morning.

"And I think in protecting myself, I hurt a lot of people. And I want to apologize to anyone who has been hurt by my actions."

"Okay, Damian. That's—"

"Going forward"—I push on because this is the part I came here to say, the groundwork I'm trying to lay for what happens next—"I want to make sure the roles I'm involved in bringing to the screen are the kind I wish I'd seen growing up."

He wants to ask a question; I can see it on his lips. Topher fumbles over the words. Will I only be playing gay characters from now on? What does that mean for *Shadow League*?

But a twitch of his neck muscles says there's more chatter from the producer, and he straightens in his chair.

"Damian Marshall, everybody!"

The audience applauds as the structured feel of the set relaxes and PAs move things into place. I stare at the camera long after the red light has gone off. It's impossible to hope Jack will see this. If he didn't follow my work before, he'll be steering as far away from it as he can now. But maybe, somehow, he'll hear about a part of it. This interview or what comes next. Maybe he'll know that I'm trying.

We leave the studio. Vin's got a car waiting. We told Roberta I was taking the rest of the night off. Instead, he drives me to Beverly Hills where he's booked a private table at La Niña, a new Chilean restaurant that's been written up everywhere and is almost impossible to get into. But Vin made one call, and suddenly a table opened up for us. I'm using my powers for good now.

We go through the front, but the clientele is all highbrow enough that there isn't much fuss. One man asks for a selfie for his daughter, which I give him, but otherwise we're escorted quietly to a small table in the back, where our guest is already waiting.

Tino Del Ray is taller than I expected. They're decked out in a studded and distressed leather jacket and round wire-framed glasses that make them appear twelve years old, but Vin assures me they are exactly the person I'm looking for.

Tino looks flustered and starstruck as I shake their hand. When Vin set up the dinner, he left my name out of it, because even if I'm trying to take control of my narrative, I'm still a hot topic in LA, and the fewer people who know where I am at any given moment, the better.

"You. You're—" Tino stammers.

"Damian. Nice to meet you. I love your work."

They turn white and have to grip the back of the chair. "You've read my work?"

"Well, sort of." I take a seat so poor Tino can do the same before they pass out. "I read a script recently called *Beloved Cove*."

Tino's budding excitement falls. "Oh." They pull the big white napkin off the table in front of them and let it drop deject-edly into their lap.

"But Vin here tells me there's an earlier version that you worked on."

"It won the—" Vin pulls out a sheet of paper from a brief-case I didn't even know he was carrying and pretends to scan it, even though he's got all the facts and figures memorized. "The Goldman Prize for unproduced new works a few years ago, right?"

"Yeah." Tino smiles proudly at us before it droops again. "But it wasn't called *Beloved Cove* then. The studio changed it when they bought the option. They said it was too queer to be produced the way it was, and I really wanted to sell a script, you know?"

I hurt for them. I know the pain that comes from dividing up parts of yourself and hoping you can put them all back together one day. I'm hoping I can help Tino do it sooner than I did. And others too.

"I want to read it," I say. "Your version."

Their head pops back up. "What?"

"My agent sent me a copy from the studio, but it didn't sit right with me, you know?"

"I—" Their mouth is open, and apparently that's the only word that's coming out.

"But then Vin said he heard a reading of the original version at a showcase."

"I did." Vin nods eagerly. "It was hilarious and so authentic. I loved it."

"I want to make it," I say before I lose my nerve. "Your version."

"My—" Poor Tino's back to looking like they're about to hyperventilate. "But you can't. The option. It doesn't expire for—"

"I'm going to buy the option out. And then you'll rewrite it. Your way."

A waiter comes to take our drink orders. Tino's so speechless I order a bottle of Syrah and hope they like red wine.

"Look," Tino says when the waiter is gone. Their voice is steadier. "Is this a joke? Did someone put you up to this?"

Yes and no, but not in the way they think. We all know my back is up against a wall, but the point is, I'm choosing to do good things instead of continuing to run and hurt people in my wake. I could have been doing an interview with Anderson tonight about how it was all one big misunderstanding so I can continue to enjoy the career I've built, but instead I'm choosing to be here.

"I genuinely want to read your script," I say. "Assuming it's as good as Vin says, I want to make it into a movie and ideally find more scripts from more queer writers like you."

"But why?" They sound so baffled, and it hurts that they're already so mistrustful. They can't be more than twenty-five or twenty-six. They should be dreaming up new stories and preparing acceptance speeches they're never going to deliver. It's too early for them to feel so beaten down.

"Because I'm tired of letting the machine control me. It's made me a lot of money, but now I want to use that money to do something new. I'm starting my own production company, and with my name attached to a project, you'd be amazed at how many doors will open for you and how many fewer script notes you'll get from the studios."

It's a risk. They could all laugh in my face. But I'm still a name, and once I've got my plan solidified, Roberta can help me pitch it in a way that makes it clear it's a redemption arc and not me trying to cover my ass. I was terrified that coming out would pigeonhole me into the gay best friend onscreen until I retired. The solution is to make the movies I want to be in.

Jack said I could make my own future.

I hope someday he sees that I did.

26

JACK

Two months later.

"When does it start snowing?"

I stare down at the boy sitting on the bench. He stares right back at me, all seriousness. I point to the mountains in the distance. "You see up there? The snow never melts. It stays cold all year round."

He looks amazed, and I guess for a kid from Texas, the very idea is probably amazing. The little boy—his name is Jayden—was feeling a little seasick as we bobbed on Kachemak Bay, and if I can make him think of anything but the rolling waves and the movement of the boat, then I've done my job. Jayden and his family are on summer vacation, and all I have to do is make sure they get back to the wharf at the end of the day with a few fish in the cooler and some fun pictures on their phones. Compared to Harper's checklist of expectations and procedures, this job is a breeze.

A voice calls out behind us, rising in panic. "I got one! Oh my God, I think I got one!"

Jayden's Aunt Gloria is gripping her fishing rod like it might explode at any second and staring at me with a frightened expression.

"It's fine," I say. "You've got time. Let him have some line."

A job wasn't easy to come by. The seafood plants are always hiring, but my body can't handle standing for that many hours in a row. I need movement. Fresh air. Stef encouraged me to travel, but that required having money to spend, and all I had was a few weeks of pay from the lodge. But my dad knew someone who knew someone who ran fishing charters out of Homer. Just day trips for tourists, nothing fancy. The pay sucks, but people tip surprisingly well, and the captain—an old man with no teeth and fewer people skills named Hank—splits the proceeds with me when he sells whatever fish the tourists don't want to take home.

It's not how I thought I'd be spending my summer, but at least I'm still on the water. The people are nice, and they ask the same questions over and over. When does it snow? What's the biggest fish you've ever caught? Have you ever seen a moose?

No one asks about the movie stars I might have met.

"What do you do, Jack, when the fishing season is over? Do you have a different job in the winter?" someone asks later as we motor back into the harbor.

That is an excellent question. I've got a job here for sure until the end of August and then however long the tourists keep coming after that. Once they've all gone home though, I don't know. Stef wants me to move up to Anchorage. She's been there for a month and already found a job as a receptionist at a shipping company. She says they're always looking for people to work in their warehouse, and she could get me set up no problem. It would be easy, but I don't know. She's doing pretty well with Graham. He ran into some kind of licensing holdup about practicing medicine in a new state, but instead of backing out like I expected him to, he said he'd take the summer to spend time with Robbie before school starts, and he's held true to his word. He's trying, and I have to give him credit for that.

So moving to Anchorage feels like getting in the way of a good thing that's only starting to gain momentum.

But my guests don't need to hear any of that.

"I'm thinking of moving south," I say. "Maybe California. The fishing seasons run longer there."

That's the only reason. It has nothing to do with California also being where Damian might be. Honestly, I have no idea where he is. The sex tape story disappeared off the main news sites within a week or two, and I haven't seen his name online since. Not that I check much. But there's a coffee shop with free Wi-Fi in town that I go to sometimes, and even if I spend more time looking at the entertainment news now than I did three months ago, it still hasn't given me any more information on the mystery that is Damian Marshall.

It's a warm, blue-sky day, and the family thanks me as they disembark. Jayden gives me a high five. His dad shakes my hand and slips me a hundred-dollar bill.

"For looking after Jayden when he wasn't feeling good," he says with a wink.

With the tourists gone, I take what's left of the fish off to the shed to clean. Hank will put it in a cooler and sell it from the back of his truck on the road out of town. It's not fancy, but it works.

"Excuse me," a voice says behind me as I'm filleting the second halibut. "I'm looking for a fishing guide."

"You'll want to talk to Hank about that," I say, using the tip of my knife to point toward where Hank is spraying down the decks.

"I'm sure he's very good, but I'd like to talk to you."

It's only as he finishes speaking that recognition finally hits. I nearly put the knife through my hand as my grip slips.

I turn, and David's standing there dressed in a pale blue Henley and dark blue jeans that still fit him too well.

"Where's your parka?" Not the first thing I meant to say, but it's what comes out.

He smiles and something inside me quivers. "Apparently Alaska's nice in the summer."

The wind blows against my back, reminding me I smell like salt and fish slime. I take an involuntary step back trying to keep some space between us, but he follows.

"So you're looking for a guide?" I ask. It can't be me. He can't expect that.

"Not really. Just seemed like a safe opening line," he says, grinning crookedly. He looks good. Healthier. There was always something tired about him before. Drawn. Most likely it was the lies eating at his soul.

"Oh." Then we don't have anything else to say to each other. I get back to work. Halibut don't clean themselves, and even though the sun will be up for hours still, it's getting late, and I'm hungry.

"Can we . . ." He runs a hand over the back of his neck. "Can we start over?"

"So you *are* looking for a fishing guide?"

"No. Jack, Jesus." He scuffs a toe in the gravel.

"What are you doing here, Damian?" I ask.

"My name's David." He half shouts it, and his voice cracks at the end like a nervous teenager asking his crush to prom. He takes a step back, brushing his palms down his thighs. I've touched those thighs. It's unfair of him to remind me of the sensation of warm hard muscle and soft curly hair beneath the denim.

The second time, he speaks with greater control. "My name is David Morgan. I'm an actor who goes by the name Damian Marshall in Hollywood."

"I don't watch a lot of movies."

"Yeah." He laughs sadly. "Yeah, I know."

Hank wanders up, puffing on a cigarette. "You looking to fish?"

"No, that's okay," Damian says. "I was hoping to speak to Jack. We met a few months ago and I thought I'd look him up while I was in town."

So smooth. So vaguely accurate without disclosing any of the important details. It's like he's used to lying. Or used to getting paid to pretend he's someone he's not.

If I'd been hoping Hank would be my backup, I would be disappointed. He glances between us, spits once on the ground, and says, "I'll be in my truck," then wanders away.

Just great. Damian's watching me nervously, and I really don't understand why he's here, and I can't see that we have anything to say to each other that'll be worth the time.

"Look," he says, obviously sensing my waning goodwill, "I know I'm not in any position to ask you for anything."

"Uh-huh." I stab at the fish with more vigor than needed and go right through to the other side. Damn. Nothing like a mangled halibut filet to spoil your night.

"But can I take you out for dinner?"

The harbor is silent except for a gull that squawks the song of its people on a piling in the distance. I spin back to David— why can't I decide what his name is?—and stare at him. That he has the balls to come up here and ask me on a date is ridiculous. That I still want him hurts more.

"How did you even know where to find me?" I ask.

"Marci," he says. "I called the lodge. Well . . . I called a few times. She really gave me the runaround."

Marci's the only person I've kept in touch with, mostly at her insistence. She started by emailing, but we talk once a week or so. At no point did she mention that Damian had reached out to her.

I sigh. I'm tired. A little sunburned. My plans for tonight included some reheated spaghetti and early to bed.

I could invite him back to my place. It's close by. In fact, it's a trailer at the far side of the parking lot. I could take him there, fuck him—he wouldn't say no. I'm sure he wouldn't. Maybe that's all he's here for. And then I can send him on his way. Get him out of my system and never think about him again.

But the thing that has haunted me all these months is the conversation I had with Stef that night I came home. What if he wasn't only lying to me? What if he was lying to himself too? I've considered that question and hated it because so many of the answers give me the one thing I couldn't have: hope. Maybe not everything was a lie.

This is a bad idea.

"Pamela's Fish House. Seven o'clock. It's up that way." I point along the road that runs from along the spit to town. "Green roof, orange fish on the sign. You can't miss it."

"I'm staying at a cabin near Bluff Point. I was thinking—"

"No." I keep my hands busy working on the next fish because otherwise I'll point the knife at him so he understands how serious I am, and that'll come back to bite me. Surely there's someone with a long-range camera waiting for the perfect picture. "Damian Marshall Threatened with Knife in Lover's Quarrel." Exactly what I need. "Pamela's. You don't get to ask me for anything, and you don't get to set any of the terms. Or say goodbye now. It's up to you."

He nods. "Got it. No problem. I'll see you there."

I don't breathe easily until his car—a sleek black sedan that looks out of place among the aging pickup trucks in the lot—is halfway up the road.

This is a terrible idea.

I finish up and leave the cooler with Hank. He doesn't ask about my visitor. I head back home to wash off the day and regret my choices.

My hands shake as I dial Stef's number.

"Hey! How's it going?"

"He was here," I say as I sit on the lumpy sofa. The trailer is Hank's and has all the comforts he deemed worthy, which is to say not much at all. He lives in a cabin just outside town, but when I asked him about a place to live, he said I could use the trailer.

"What? Who?"

"David. Damian. He showed up."

"Like in a movie?"

"No, this is not a movie, Stef. This is my life and he's here."

"What did he say?"

"He wants to have dinner."

"And you told him to take a long walk off a short pier?"

"I told him I'd meet him at the fish house at seven."

"On a date?" she whisper shouts.

"No, not a date. It's a—" I wish I'd clarified. I wish I'd said no. I could still stand him up. Hopefully he'd take the hint.

"Okay. Okay. It's okay. We can do this. What are you going to wear?"

"Nothing."

She snorts. "Well, that'll make an impression."

"Stef!" I don't know why I'm panicking. This should mean nothing. We'll clear the air. He can say whatever it is he still needs to say, and then we're done.

She talks me down. Really, there's nothing particular for me to wear. Everything I brought is for working on the boat. Nothing to have dinner with a movie star.

But the whole point of having dinner at the fish house is because I want him to understand who he is to me, and it's not the movie star. If he can't function at a place like that—if he thinks everywhere needs Michelin stars and a tasting menu—then we really do have nothing to say to each other.

I take a shower, find a pair of pants and a shirt that are clean enough, and at seven, I walk up the road to the fish house. He's waiting outside, but he has his back to me. There's still time to turn around and go home. Duck in behind a couple of the trucks and SUVs parked in front of the restaurant and wait for him to realize he's been stood up and go.

But then I'll never get answers to those questions that hope keeps asking.

So it's time for my dinner with Damian Marshall.

27

DAMIAN

E XTRAtainment Update!
       Where Is Damian Marshall?

After a tumultuous few months, Damian Marshall has been keeping a low profile. While he's still listed among the cast for the upcoming Shadow League *film, news of any other upcoming projects for the actor has been scarce.*

He was spotted yesterday at LAX catching a flight to Seattle. Whether he's on his way to a shoot, looking for a little privacy, or carrying on to more exotic destinations remains to be seen. But we have to say he's never looked finer, dressed in ultracasual Bermuda shorts and a stylish chambray button-down.

———

We're deep into summer and the sun never quite sets in Alaska, even more than when I was at the lodge. The endless daylight does weird things to time, giving the illusion that days don't end. Like today and the day I left Jack on that plane are the same.

The hurt look in his eyes is definitely the same.

I shouldn't have turned up like I did, but I wasn't sure what else to do. Marci told me—after I swore up and down a million times and then complied when she said to wait a week and call back if I still really wanted to know—he was in Homer, but she wouldn't give me any more details than that. And Homer isn't huge, but I still wasn't comfortable with the idea of driving aimlessly through town asking people if they knew a man fitting Jack's description.

I should have known he was down by the water.

And now he's walking toward me, dressed in a denim jacket, faded hoodie, and dark sweatpants cuffed at the ankles. Something inside me settles, even though we could be minutes away from him telling me to eat shit in front of a room full of diners. It's the same way I felt the first morning when I found him on his boat, like he'd been waiting for me to arrive so he could pour me a cup of coffee and tell me I would be safe here.

I want him to feel the same way. He can be safe with me.

"Thank you," I say when he's close enough.

"For what?"

"For coming. I wasn't sure you would."

He shakes his head. "Seems like I still don't have much common sense when it comes to you."

Likewise. The last few months had been a whirlwind. Tino's original script is as amazing as Vin said it was. Turns out the *Beloved Cove* project was essentially dead in the water. Oscar Kane had already backed out for some beach bingo musical thing, and if I wasn't going to take the part they'd offered me, then they were more than happy to take my money and get the option off their plate. But now's the part where we're supposed to be convincing other studio heads that Tino's version, the one where the gay best friend becomes the love interest, is worth producing.

No matter how busy I was though, no matter how many meetings I went to or scripts I read, I couldn't stop thinking about Jack.

We walk into the restaurant, and a young woman who can't

be more than twenty years old takes one look at my face and goes completely white. She does her best to be cool about it as she walks us toward an open table in the middle of the room, but we don't get very far before the whispers start.

"Oh my God."

"It's him."

"Damian Marshall."

Shortly after, the first person comes up and asks for a selfie. Then another. Then a few more. Autographs, handshakes. There have to be sixty people in the restaurant and once the avalanche starts, they all want a minute of my time. One teenager cries so hard he has to be helped outside. One mom seems to think I'm going to record personalized messages for each of her five children, who she and her husband left at home with their grandparents while they took a vacation for their fifteenth wedding anniversary. I know all of this because she tells me before I politely remind her that I'm here having dinner with a friend.

Though that friend has been completely swallowed up by the crush of people. Even the staff from the kitchen have come out to say hi. Their enthusiasm is gratifying. There was some backlash at first, especially online, after I came out. Sometimes people ask questions they shouldn't and that I don't want to answer. But most of the time, they still only want a smile and a selfie so they can tell their friends at home.

I catch sight of the top of Jack's head at the back of the crowd. But he makes no move to get closer. No one seems to notice him either, which makes me feel a bit better. They haven't put the two of us and the sex tape together, which hopefully means Jack's been able to live a relatively normal life these past few months.

Finally, the people go back to their meals and their jobs. The hostess reappears and apologizes like she'd have been able to stop the tide of fans. She offers to find us a table that's a little less exposed.

"This one is fine," Jack says, reappearing at my shoulder. Without any further ado, he pulls back one of the chairs and sits down.

"Sorry about that," I say as I sit across from him.

"I wanted to see what it was like."

"What what was like?"

"Being somewhere with a movie star."

The waitress who comes to our table is so nervous she slops water over the sides of the glasses as she pours from a pitcher. She can't quite look at me, so she takes Jack's order first.

"Fish cakes and a beer," he says.

She can only get her gaze to reach as far as somewhere around the middle of my chest, so I smile and say, "The same, please," and she actually does something that looks like a curtsy before she blushes and rushes away.

When I turn back to Jack, he's watching me. More like studying.

"Go on," I say.

"Go on what?"

Now he's playing coy?

"Ask whatever you're thinking. Whatever you want."

"Do you enjoy it? The fans?"

People are listening. The tables around us are hardly speaking to each other, but I have zero room to ask Jack for anything, even if it's that we talk about this somewhere else, so I go for honesty. Maybe the eavesdroppers around us will learn a thing or two, though so far they've all been pretty well-behaved.

"The fans are why the movies I make exist. If it weren't for them, I wouldn't have a career. So yeah, it's always great to meet people who like what I do."

Jack waits, expression flat. He can tell that's the canned response.

"Things like this, where everyone wants a few seconds of my time, maybe a picture or an autograph, and then they let me get on with my night, that's pretty easy. It's when they don't take no for an answer that it can get tricky. I've had fans follow me for blocks when I'm stopping somewhere for a coffee, or others that try to sneak into my hotel. That's not okay."

Jack's eyelashes flutter like he's thinking, but all he says is, "No, I wouldn't think so."

I drop my voice so the people around us would really have to lean in to hear. "Or when they think they deserve parts of me that are private. The people who are important to me. I don't owe them that."

After the late-night interview, Roberta booked me a bunch more appearances so I could repeat my story. All high profile, all with sympathetic hosts who asked preapproved questions. It still doesn't sit easily with me that I had to share that part of myself. Within the first week, Roberta got calls about a dozen different projects that all needed a gay lead. We turned them all down. The people who wanted to cast me were looking to ride my coming out coattails, and those aren't the projects I want to be working on right now.

I want to tell Jack about what I *am* working on, but I also want to give him the space to figure out what he needs to. He hasn't stalked off yet, so that's promising, but this is my one and only chance to make amends.

"How's your ex?" he asks.

Anderson is not what I want to talk about here. *Shadow League* is still happening, and my contract commits me to two more movies. Roberta and I talked about it and agreed I'd be in a good position if I wrapped them up while the production company gets up and running. She's happy to support the new plan but doesn't want to burn all the bridges from her formula until we know what the future holds. We've scaled way back on the amount of promotional work I'll need to do with each release, which will give me time to work on new projects in between shoots.

And also . . .

"My ex is gone." It hasn't officially been announced yet, but Anderson has been notified he won't be needed for *Shadow League 5*. Of course, they'll say it has something to do with scheduling conflicts, but once the truth was out to Cedric and the rest of the *Shadow League* team, there was no question about the studio keeping him on.

"Sounds like everything is going great then," he says as the waitress comes back with our beers.

It is, but it's not the way I want things.

"Jack," I say.

"Why didn't you tell me?" he asks like he can't hold it back.

"I'm sorry," I say. "If I'd known someone was filming, I would have—"

"It's not about that." He drums his fingers on the side of his beer bottle. "Not all of it anyway. You lied. Even if no one else had been there, you let me think you were someone else. I kissed you. All while thinking you were someone else named David."

"I know. It seemed like the right choice at the time, and when I knew it was the wrong one, it was already too late, because . . ." God, there are people everywhere. Phones. Every second of this could be online before the night is out. It's like the air is being sucked out of the room and dragging the words out of my lungs with it.

"David?" he says, and some of the hardness has left his voice, but the way he uses my name makes a wave of cold wash over me. I have so many regrets, and hearing him call me David brings them all to the surface again. I lift the water glass to my lips and manage to swallow some of it, focusing on the cool slide of it down my throat. The buzzing in my ears gets louder. "David?"

I set the glass down and look around me again. The woman to my left smiles before she drops her gaze back to her meal, but otherwise everyone is eating and talking like nothing weird is going on.

"I'm sorry," Jack says. "We shouldn't have come here."

"Because I liked you," I say, surprised at the emotions that clog my throat. "I liked who you let me be. I liked myself—being David when I was with you—more than I've liked myself in a long time, in spite of everything I have. But mostly I liked you and you didn't seem very impressed with people like me, so it seemed easier to be the person you thought I was. It was selfish, but I didn't want to lose the time with you. And then I ruined it all anyway, so I guess I got what I deserved."

Wow. I haven't had to spell it out so clearly before. When I do, it leaves me feeling ridiculous. What did I think would happen by coming back up here? Was I satisfying my own guilt? Looking for absolution? Because I have nothing to offer someone like Jack. I can't even take him out for dinner.

So I play the only card I have. "I'm starting a project. A production company aimed at getting more queer movies made by mainstream studios. I've been following a plan for so many years, and it gave me what I thought I wanted, but I didn't like the person I became. I failed utterly at being a role model for gay kids who might watch my movies. Failed at being a decent human being, really. I figure if I can help make movies that show more queer experiences, maybe I will have helped in some small way."

He nods. "I never saw anyone like me in movies when I was growing up."

"Yeah, well, you never saw straight people in movies either because we've already covered that you don't watch them," I grumble.

His lips twitch, and he glances down at the table. "Yeah, okay. That's fair."

Is this . . . Are we having a conversation? Cracking jokes? Honestly, it's probably the best I can hope for, but I press my luck.

"I hope you'll watch our movies when they're released."

"I might."

For a second, I wish someone really was recording this, because Jack just said he'd watch my movies. It feels like an achievement when it could be an empty promise. If I never see him again, how will I know?

"I'm thinking about setting up a screenwriters' retreat. We're working on an amazing project right now from this kid who wrote something they were really passionate about, but then had to change it before they could sell it because the studios didn't want it. There are writers like them all over LA. Ones who have the talent, but keep having to water down their work because the studios don't think the mainstream is ready for truly queer characters, and especially queer leads. I want to find a few of them, get them together, and write some incredible movies."

"That sounds like a great plan."

The server brings our fish cakes. They smell heavenly. Jack dives into his immediately, but I won't let myself get distracted.

"I was thinking we might set the retreat up in Alaska. Somewhere we can get away and focus on the writing without the distraction and the games in Hollywood."

He blinks up at me, fork halfway to his mouth, but he sets it down again, sitting up straight. He knows what I'm saying, even if I haven't put the words to it yet.

But I will, so we're perfectly clear.

"Jack. I was so selfish. I've been so focused on myself and doing what I needed to build a career and then stay on top of the game. I'll apologize to you forever for that, but I'll mean it every time." I can't help but look around me. The woman on my left is definitely listening, but when our eyes meet, she drops her hand to her lap so Jack can't see it, and she gives me a tiny thumbs up that almost has me laughing out loud. "If we come up here, could I see you? Here. In the city. Wherever. We'll take a train to Denali. I'll get a jet to fly us anywhere you want to go."

The woman beside me gasps. Jack flicks her a quick glance before he picks up his fork again. My heart sinks when he doesn't reply. In fact, he doesn't say anything at all. He eats, working his way through his fish cakes methodically and silently. I pick at mine, and I'm sure they're delicious, but every time I put a bite in my mouth, it feels like it swells and turns into the consistency of day-old scrambled eggs.

The waitress looks disappointed when Jack declines dessert. My heart races, but he's very clearly decided our evening is over.

At least I can say I gave it my best shot. There never was much hope to begin with.

We head outside. It's still disconcertingly bright, but I use it to memorize every line of Jack's face.

"Well," I say.

"Let's go for a walk."

The simple request shocks me into silence. Does that mean we're not done? But he doesn't say anything else. He stuffs his hands in his pockets and starts walking down the hill, leaving me to follow after him.

28

JACK

To say this night has not gone the way I expected implies that I had expectations at all. Taking Damian to the fish house seemed safest. I could see what it was really like to be out in public with him, and we'd both have to be on our best behavior.

What I didn't expect was for his behavior to be so sincere and heartfelt that I could barely look at him.

We walk down to the harbor. It's quiet except for a few local kids riding their bikes in circles through the gravel and gulls calling to nothing from the tops of the boats bobbing quietly between their pilings.

It's still a few hours before the sun dips below the horizon. We're past twenty-four hours of daylight, but even now, the shadows are only starting to lengthen.

"What do your friends call you?" I ask.

"Damian."

"Does anyone call you David?"

His face glows in the light. He's close-shaved now, instead of his careless stubble from the spring. Jaws like his don't exist in nature.

"My agent," he says, "when she's pissed at me. My family would if I still spoke to them. My accountant because that's the name she has to put on my tax returns, and she says she can't keep it straight if she calls me Damian."

"Is it weird? Using different names?"

He shrugs. "It was at first. I used to practice by telling the baristas at Starbucks my name was Damian. But now it's as much my name as David."

"So should I call you Damian?"

That draws his attention away from the horizon. "I'd really like it if you called me David."

That's good enough for me. I don't know what our future looks like, but I want to find out. Starting right now.

I reach for him and bring his mouth down to mine to kiss him. He doesn't resist, not for a second.

Instead, David sighs. "Jack."

Do I forgive him? It'll always be a thing between us, that rocky beginning. Am I willing to see what happens next? It might be that he leaves again, and eventually, after a few months of plans and last-minute cancellations as he flies off somewhere exotic while I'm left ferrying tourists around, we both realize it was never going to work out. But at least then we'll know we tried. That we finally started from a place of understanding, and it turned out our lives really were too different after all.

He slides his hands underneath my jacket. The layers beneath keep me from feeling the heat of his palms. I step between his feet, nipping at his bottom lip and making David groan.

"How long are you here for?" I ask.

"I have to fly back to LA tomorrow."

"What time?"

He laughs, pressing his hands against my cheeks long enough to still me. "Not until late."

I kiss him again, and behind us, someone whistles. I glance over my shoulder, and the kids on the bikes have all stopped to gawk. They laugh when they realize we heard them, but then one of them drops his mouth open.

"You're . . . you're . . ." he says, pointing with a shaking hand.

Two pull phones from their pockets, and David stiffens next to me.

"Is there somewhere we can go? How far is your place?"

"Uh . . ." I glance over my shoulder. "It's right there." And it's not the place I want to take him. The inside may be even more crowded than the cabin on the *Hawk*. "It's pretty small."

"My car's at the restaurant," he says.

"Can you . . . entertain them for a minute?" I nod in the direction of the boys. "I need to go grab something."

I rush into the trailer and pack a small bag. Before I open the door again, I send a short text to Stef.

I'm okay. DO NOT call me until I text again.

She replies with a bunch of emojis that might be a shopping list or a weather report, and I don't understand any of it. Then there's a string of hearts. That, at least, I get.

Outside, David is on his knees while the boys take turns standing in the middle of the group taking selfies. They're all grinning from ear to ear, even David.

"Okay," I say. "All set."

"Guys, I gotta go."

"Is he your boyfriend?" the tallest of the boys asks.

David glances at me, and my heart quivers, but he gives the boys a sneaky grin and simply says, "No comment."

They howl in protest, but they don't follow us as we walk back up the hill.

The car glides smoothly out of town. David tells me about the movie he's working on. I tell him about Stef and Graham and that I'm still not sure she's making the right choice.

He smiles at me. "The heart wants what it wants."

As he turns off the highway and onto a dirt road that leads into the forest, we get quiet. A lot of the rentals in this area are built up on top of the hills farther inland, usually in clearings so visitors still get a view of the water. But David drives us to a sprawling A-frame cabin deep in the woods, surrounded by trees. The whole property is densely shaded.

He takes my hand as we go inside, but when I go to press him against the door, he slides away.

"Not here," he says, glancing at the tall windows stretching over two stories at the front of the house. "Someone might see."

The trees make sense now.

"I'm sorry," I say. "For not being careful before. Down at the wharf. Those boys . . ."

He shakes his head, pressing his lips softly to mine. "You didn't know. That one's all on me. I've learned my lesson. So many lessons."

The bedroom is at the back of the house. It also has long floor-to-ceiling windows, but David pulls the blackout curtains over them. He's left the door open, so light from the front of the house filters in, which is good because I want to see him. But no one else can see anything, and that's the important part.

When he pulls me to him, we fit together as well as we did before. Hands, mouths, hips, legs. He smells different though. The mint and leather scent is gone, and maybe that's for the best. We're starting fresh.

"Touch me," I say, trying to get closer even when there's almost no space left between us.

He slides his hands under my shirt, running strong fingers along my spine. He's hard in his pants and so am I, and when he dips into my jeans to squeeze my ass, I groan.

"What do you want?" he asks as he grinds our dicks together. "Anything you say. I want to do it for you."

He wants penance. I can hear it in his rushed breaths and

feel it in the way his hands move restlessly over me. So I take his wrists and slowly suck two of his fingers between my lips, one at a time. He shudders as I swirl my tongue over his knuckles.

"Jack."

"Shh." What I want is for him to let go. To stop worrying. It has to be exhausting, constantly checking curtains and wondering what people are thinking. I want to take that from him, even for a bit.

I push his shoulders and he falls back willingly, knees against the mattress so he sinks down. His erection presses against the front of his pants and he grips it, his eyes never leaving me. His mouth falls open when I pull my shirt off, and he reaches for me.

"I'm sorry," he says.

"Stop." I frame his face with my hands and kiss him. "Not now."

He sighs as his lips slide over my body before he rests his forehead against my chest. I bury my fingers in his hair but don't pull. He can stay there as long as he needs. His breath is warm on my skin, and my erection strains for freedom.

"I'm going to love you," he says. "I might already be in love with you, but I'm going to love you even more, Jack. So much.

"Sweet words like that, you should be a movie star," I say. He stares up at me, eyes shining, and yeah, that's enough. The fear is gone. I sink down next to him so we're face-to-face. Equal. He lets me unbutton his shirt while he mouths against my neck and shoulder. The skin beneath is as perfect as I remembered. Tanned and trim. He doesn't protest when I push him onto his back, then move between his legs to undo his pants and tug them off. David's erection bobs in greeting, the head flushed, the shaft straining.

I draw a gentle line with a fingernail along the vein that runs under his dick, then continue over the seam between his balls. He gasps when I take him in my hand and lick the tip.

"I want you to remember this," I say. "Not the last time. This is our first time. You and me."

He nods jerkily before I put him in my mouth and suck him down.

"Oh. God. Jack." The syllables are short and strangled. I squeeze the base of him, asking for patience. No one is watching. We can take our time.

David lifts his feet, planting them on the edge of the mattress so I have all the space I need. So much better here than in the tiny trailer where we'd have been banging everything instead of each other.

David pushes back so he can spread out on the mattress, and I follow after him, climbing the length of his body. I've barely settled against him before he's sliding a knee between my thighs, and who am I to complain? I throw a leg over his hip and moan when he grips the two of us together, stroking until I'm leaking.

"Jack," he says. "Can I fuck you? I want to feel what it's like to be inside you."

"Yes." I've wanted that since the beginning.

Suddenly, he goes very still beside me. I pull back enough to see him clearly. His eyes are closed, and he's frowning deeply.

"You thought I'd say no?" I ask, pushing up on my elbows.

"What? No. Maybe." He shoves me back down. "I don't know what to think when it comes to you."

"No common sense whatsoever."

He finds the lube and condoms I stashed in my bag, then settles between my knees.

"Go slow," I say. "Been a while."

David kisses the inside of my knee. "As long as I make my flight tomorrow." He follows with a trail of kisses down my calf before he lifts my foot and kisses the arch. I hiss, and he grins at me. "I remembered that. Been waiting for months to try that again."

He's so careful. He kisses my ankles, runs his hands along

the backs of my legs. He swirls a fingertip over my hole, then follows it with his tongue. By the time he gets even one slicked finger inside me, I'm begging.

"David. David, please."

He brushes his knuckles over my cock; the noise that comes out of me is ninety percent howl, and I'm so grateful there's no one around for miles.

By the time he's opened me up and is sliding on the condom, I'm so aroused I can't stay still. My muscles jump sporadically, and random streaks of precome are smeared on my stomach. David's breathing hard and grinning wildly as he strokes on lube before he leans down to kiss me. He hums against my lips, and he's practically vibrating with excitement. I bump my hips against him, urging him on, and he laughs before he rights himself and lines his cock up against my ass.

The first inch of pressure squeezes all the air out of my lungs, and I gasp, arching back, trying to find room to breathe.

"Okay?" he asks.

"Just a second." I clench and unclench my fists. Curl and uncurl my toes. I focus on relaxing and tilt my hips so another fraction of an inch slips inside me.

"Jack." David pulls back, giving me a second to catch my breath before he presses forward again, and it's easier now. He takes his time, gaining entrance agonizingly slowly. The burn makes me grunt, but I grip his biceps to let him know whenever it's too much, and he waits.

Finally, his pelvis settles against my ass, and we both groan. He comes forward again, planting his palms on either side of my head.

"You're amazing," he says. "You feel amazing."

"Kiss me," I whisper. The sensation of him deep inside me is almost too much. I need him to move. He tugs at my lips with his teeth, biting down hard enough to sting. The sensation pulls my focus long enough that when he slides halfway out of me, I gasp, pushing up and trying to hold onto him.

"It's okay." He wraps his arms under my shoulders so our chests are pressed together. On reflex, I lift my feet so I can lock my ankles behind his back and squeeze his ribs with my thighs. "Uh-huh. You've got this."

Finally, he moves, picking up a steady rhythm that sets my body on fire. With each thrust, I relax a little more. Just the two of us like this, we really do fit together like we always have. Jack and David. The *real* David. Mine. Imperfect. Wildly famous. But the rest of the world hasn't seen the David I know.

I'm pulled out of the thought as he changes his angle and drags against my prostate.

"That." I gasp. "Do that again."

"I've got you," he says, mouth at my throat. "Hang on."

It's fast and hard now. He hits my prostate like he can see it. Every time he does, I shout, and soon he's growling as he pounds into me over and over. The bed rattles, and the headboard bumps against the wall in a steady rhythm.

Finally, like a storm front breaking, I arch, and the sound dies as I throw my head back. I don't even have time to warn David before I'm thrashing and shuddering from the orgasm pulsing through me. He moans against my neck, thrusts twice, and then he's shaking and gasping as he pumps his own orgasm into the condom.

We stay like that, sweaty and trembling, for what feels like a long time. Eventually he pulls out of me, and my ass throbs. I hope he's feeling half as shaky as I am as he crawls from the bed to deal with the condom.

I'm half asleep when he returns from the bathroom, but his concerned "Hmm" has me opening my eyes. He's staring above me, and I strain my head back to find what he's looking at.

We've made a sizeable dent in the wall where the headboard had been banging against it.

"Oops," I say, but in truth I don't really care. The wall is a problem to be dealt with in the morning when more of my brain cells are firing again. Besides, who knows? We might knock a couple more holes in there before the night is over.

I roll until I can pull the blankets loose and slide under them. David crawls in next to me. I'm sticky and sweaty, but he curls around me like I'm precious.

"Guess I'll have to buy the place," he says.

"I'm sorry, what?" I roll so I can face him, and his expression is perfectly serious.

"Well, I'll need a place to stay if I'm going to be up here every weekend."

"Every weekend?" I ask, suddenly feeling way more awake.

He frowns. "Is that too much? I want you to know I'm committed to this. I didn't fly up here for a one-night stand. I thought—"

I put a finger to his lips. "Buying a house is a lot for some broken drywall. I figured we'd grab some filler in the morning and fix it."

He grins under my touch. "But the rest? I'm serious about this between us, but if it's too much, then you can—"

"It's fine." I kiss him.

"I'll be in the Czech Republic in October and November to shoot *Shadow League 5*. It's intense. I may not be able to see you as often. But if you . . . " He keeps talking, but I lose track of his words as the realization settles in that he may be David when he's with me, but in public, he's Damian and still a movie star.

"I don't know where I'll be in October," I say. "I'm only guaranteed a job here until the end of the tourist season."

"Well, wherever you are, Jack, I'll come see you as often as I can. Or if you want, you can come to Prague with me."

I snort. "What would I do in Prague?"

David tangles his feet with mine and presses his lips to mine.

"Whatever you want," he says as he winds his arms around my neck.

I'm not sure he means it or if he's really thought it through. But now I'm thinking about it, and while there are a lot of unknowns, maybe that's the point.

Stef did say I needed to live more. Find new adventures.

With David, I think everything will be an adventure.

EPILOGUE

DAMIAN

One year later.

The plane is late. Rough weather kept it in Anchorage for two hours, so we don't touch down in the cove until late in the evening.

Fortunately, the sun only sets for a few hours here, and it isn't down yet, so even if we're late, it's easy to get the full effect.

"Wow." April presses her nose against the window.

"It's special, isn't it?" I ask.

She glances over her shoulder at me with a wide grin that makes her blue eyes twinkle under her slate gray hair. Since the first time we met, April's been a cool customer, interested in collaborating without ever fully committing.

Alaska wins everyone over.

April was Tino's teacher. She published a couple of novels twenty years ago, then turned her hand to screenwriting but never had much success. A few TV movies after the content had been "sanitized" for network tastes, options that never went anywhere. She started teaching creative writing at a community college, and that was how she met Tino.

When filming wrapped on *The More the Merrier*—formerly

known as *Beloved Cove*—this spring, Tino said we needed to meet her too.

The plane, still essentially a tin can, motors up to the dock.

"And everyone else is here?" April asks.

"The others flew in this morning," I say, drumming my fingers against the arm of my seat, trying to hide my impatience as she continues to block the window. This trip is about April and the three other screenwriters who have come up north. She deserves to see every minute of it.

But I want one second to peek outside and make sure he's there too.

Although she's supposed to be here for a month, April has apparently packed everything she'll need in a single backpack, so getting off the plane takes a matter of seconds. I follow, squinting into the late day sun. A couple others have come out to watch us arrive.

When I told Jack I'd buy that cabin last year, I was kidding. But then we started talking about places we could use to house the screenwriters, and Jack said the oddest thing.

"Too bad we can't take them to the lodge. It's got lots of room."

And it did. More than they probably wanted, because it turns out when accommodating your first guest leads to an international sex scandal, there's a lot of interest, but no one feels a hundred percent comfortable staying there, and marketing gets complicated.

Frankly, buying the Wild Eagle Lodge was probably the fairest thing I could do. Though when we looked into it, turns out the lodge and the property are two separate things, so basically we lease the cove, and then we can take the lodge to any other destination if the next crop of screenwriters needs new inspiration. Have tugboat, will travel. We're thinking about going down the coast to Baja California before the weather turns too cold.

Jack's in charge of the logistics. He's good at it.

"Hi! Welcome!" Marci skips down the dock. She's our guest services coordinator, which means I've essentially given her an unlimited budget to make sure the writers can have whatever they want while they're here. Fortunately, with the first group we had in the spring, most of what they wanted was coffee, scotch, weed, and scented candles, so Marci hasn't bankrupted me yet.

April follows Marci up to the lodge and joins the others, which leaves me alone with the person I most wanted to see.

"Hi."

Jack's standing on the dock, lit from behind by the sun, making his edges glow. His beard is thicker than it was before I flew to New York last week. Or maybe it's the shadows playing along his cheeks.

"How was your flight?" he asks.

"Bumpy."

He grins as he folds me into him for a kiss. Even though it's only been eight days since we saw each other last and we've spoken every night, it feels like forever.

"Roberta called," he says, making me groan. "No, it's fine. She said something about Vin being lost on a road trip somewhere in Middle America and wanted to know if we had any other way to get hold of him."

"Vin's a big boy," I say. "Whatever he's up to, I'm sure he'll figure it out."

"What time are we leaving in the morning?" he asks.

"Seven." I'm here just long enough to make sure everyone gets settled for their retreat. Then I'm off to LA for three days for a quick check-in with Roberta, then sixteen weeks in England and Scotland to shoot a King James biopic. I was skeptical about it at first, but Roberta argued it was the perfect mix of action for my old fans and updating straight-washed history for my new ones.

Jack's coming with me.

It'll be his first time on set. First time in Europe. I'm looking forward to this movie and showing Jack all my favorite places in London and the Highlands.

"David," Jack says, tilting my chin down to kiss me.

"Yeah?"

"Let's take the boat out."

"Now?"

"They don't need us in there. Marci's on top of everything, and she already packed us a picnic."

I smile against his mouth, centering myself more firmly along his solid body.

"Oh yeah?" I ask, already starting to heat up. "You made plans."

"Yeah." His kisses turn hungry. "I know a place."

We know a few places. Quiet, out-of-the-way places where we can tie the boat off and disappear into the woods for a little privacy. We learned our lesson well, though it turns out we're not nearly as interesting now that I have nothing to hide.

"Let me change," I say. With the time difference, my flight from New York, and the delay in Anchorage, I've been in the same clothes for close to twenty-four hours.

"Already got some clothes onboard." Jack tugs me down the dock to where the *Winter Hawk* is tied up. He said he didn't need anything so fancy, but I know how much he likes that boat, and we need some way to get around, after all.

"You think of everything," I say, stepping over the side and onto the shining aluminum deck.

"Got tired of waiting."

So impatient.

Turns out, Jack manages our relationship the same way he manages everything else—with quiet competence that means he's always one step ahead of me, even if it's just making sure there are dry clothes on the boat for after our woodland shenanigans. Life with Jack is never boring, but sometimes it gets downright messy. I once found a twig in my hair in the middle of an interview. It had to have been there for at least two days.

This afternoon's storm is long gone as he turns on the engine and guides us out toward the ocean.

"You excited?" I ask.

He glances at me. "You know I always want you."

If he keeps looking at me like that, we won't make it to the trees.

"I meant about England," I say.

Jack laughs. "That too."

And that's just how he is. I could give him so much. Fly him around the world and back. Buy us a castle in the Alps. But all he wants is a boat ride and some quality time in the woods.

And to call me David. That's who I am to him, even now. The world will always want Damian, but for the first time in years, I feel most like myself, and my name is David.

"Well, let's get going." I bump his shoulder. "Daylight's wasting."

He snorts. "No, it's not."

With Jack, no time is wasted. And everywhere is home.

But I hope we never stop coming up north.

ABOUT THE AUTHOR

Whether she knew it then or not, Allison has been a writer since the second grade, when she wrote a short story about a girl and her horse. Her grandmother typed it out for her and said she'd never seen so many quotation marks from a seven-year-old before. Allison took that as a challenge and has tried to break that record in all the stories she's taken on since then.

Allison lives in Toronto with her very patient husband and the world's cutest team of rescue pets. She tries to split her time between writing, exploring Toronto's parks, and traveling anywhere that has good wine. Tragically, this leaves no time to clean the house.

CONTEMPORARY ROMANCES BY ALLISON TEMPLE

Out & About

Work-Love Balance

Honeymoon Sweet

The Seacroft Series

Top Shelf

Cold Pressed

Hot Potato

Standalone

Up North

Puppuccino

Boyfriend With Benefits

The Pick Up

LGBTQ+ FANTASY BY ALLI TEMPLE

Uncharted

Unbroken

Unleashed